# ArtScroll Series®

Rabbi Nosson Scherman / Rabbi Meir Zlotowitz

*General Editors*

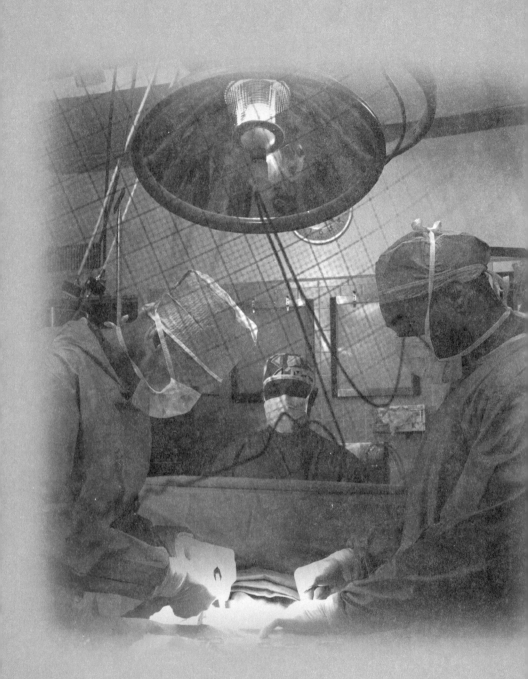

Published by
Mesorah Publications, ltd

# ENCORE

## A YOUNG COUPLE TRIUMPHS
## OVER A DREADED ILLNESS

### MIRIAM DANSKY

FIRST EDITION
*First Impression ... October 2001*

Published and Distributed by
**MESORAH PUBLICATIONS, LTD.**
4401 Second Avenue / Brooklyn, N.Y 11232

*Distributed in Europe by*
**LEHMANNS**
Unit E, Viking Industrial Park
Rolling Mill Road
Jarrow, Tyne & Wear, NE32 3DP
England

*Distributed in Australia and New Zealand by*
**GOLDS WORLDS OF JUDAICA**
3-13 William Street
Balaclava, Melbourne 3183
Victoria, Australia

*Distributed in Israel by*
**SIFRIATI / A. GITLER — BOOKS**
6 Hayarkon Street
Bnei Brak 51127

*Distributed in South Africa by*
**KOLLEL BOOKSHOP**
Shop 8A Norwood Hypermarket
Norwood 2196, Johannesburg, South Africa

**ARTSCROLL SERIES®**
**ENCORE**
*© Copyright 2001, by* MESORAH PUBLICATIONS, Ltd.
*4401 Second Avenue / Brooklyn, N.Y. 11232 / (718) 921-9000 / www.artscroll.com*

The names and identifying features in this true story
have been changed to maintain the privacy of the protagonists.
People in similar circumstances who would like guidance or moral support
may feel free to call them, in Israel, at (02) 500 2177, fax : (02) 537 1544.

Typography by CompuScribe at ArtScroll Studios, Ltd.

Printed in the United States of America by Noble Book Press Corp.
Bound by Sefercraft, Quality Bookbinders, Ltd., Brooklyn N.Y. 11232

*Although I dedicated this book*

*firsthand foremost to my Creator,*

*I would like to make another dedication.*


*This is to my husband,*

*who stood by me*

*during the darkest hours of my nisayon,*

*with patience, forbearance, courage, ingenuity*

*and above all, love.*


*May we together continue*

*to derive much nachas*

*from our children.*


*Ruchi*

# ACKNOWLEDGMENTS

We would like to take this opportunity to express our deepest gratitude and thanks to...

Our dear parents for their tireless support;

Our wonderful *kinderlach*, for bringing so much joy into our lives and for the abundant *nachas* they give us, *baruch Hashem*;

Our beloved siblings, for always being there and for their constant assistance;

Our cherished aunts, uncles, and cousins who opened their hearts and homes to us and whose cheerful visits brightened the darkest days;

Our community of friends from all over the world who went the extra mile;

"The Tuesday Club" for being with us at some of the most difficult of times;

To Chumie B, for whom caring and sharing are a way of life. She was always ready to help, and more importantly, she was always there. This book was her idea, and it was she who introduced us – dragged us, actually – to ArtScroll;

To Mrs. S. who has always been, and continues to be, a role model for us. She encouraged us to tell our story so that others might be helped;

Bikur Cholim of Rockland County – and Rabbi Shimshon Lauber – who outdid themselves in their dedication, care, and concern;

Professor Binzwanger and Nurse Julia, a wonderful medical team whose devotion and professionalism continue to help me to this day;

Dr. Butt and his dedicated transplant team. In addition to being a physician who is outstanding in his field, Dr. Butt is also a great human being with a big heart;

All members of the medical, operating room, and hospital staff. There are too many of you to list, but you all mean so very much to me, and you all did so much to help me achieve a speedy recovery;

To the wonderful staff at ArtScroll/Mesorah, who shepherded this work from original idea to final book. In particular, we would like to thank Rabbi Avrohom Biderman, Eli Kroen, Hershy Feuerwerker, Mrs. Judi Dick, Mrs. Rivka Hamaoui, Mrs. Zissel Keller, Mrs. Tova Ovits, Mrs. Mindy Schwartz, and Tzini Hanover. Their forbearance, understanding and sensitivity is rivaled only by their expertise. This beautiful book bears testimony to their dedication to this project and to everything they do;

*Acharon, acharon chaviv* – Mrs. Miriam Dansky. Her wonderful personality and her acute sensitivity to another person's pain beautifully complement her ability to convey the most heartfelt emotion through the written word. She sensed the very feelings that we had been unable to express; she crystallized the thoughts we were unable to articulate. Working with her was both a pleasure and a privilege. May she and her husband share many years of good health, *nachas* from their children, and success in all of their endeavors.

Above all, our thanks goes to *Hakadosh Baruch Hu*, Healer of all, for the boundless kindness He continues to shower upon us always.

With deep appreciation,
"Yanki and Ruchi"

# AUTHOR'S INTRODUCTION

THE COMPLETION OF THIS PARTICULAR BOOK REPRESENTS A SPECIAL journey for me, too, as it does for the subject of the book. There is "writing" and "writing." There is "understanding" and "understanding." When I was first approached by ArtScroll about writing a book about a very special couple who had overcome a "modern-day *nisayon*" I hesitated, for this was uncharted territory. I had scant knowledge of the workings of the human body or the process of transplantation and the issues involved. And did I really want to delve into someone else's *nisayon*? I would have to be intrusive, even a little aggressive, to uncover the story. But when I first flew out to Europe to meet this Chassidishe couple and discuss the project, my doubts were dispelled — but only a little. My husband and I spent two days in their home, recipients of their hospitality. We visited hospitals, dialysis units and the lake where the husband, Yanky, had so often meditated in his lowest moments.

So far I had received mainly Yanky's remarkable story on tape — here was a couple, who far from being torn apart by their terrible *nisayon,* had obviously grown closer. They think and feel together and finish one another's sentences. This was the first thing that struck me about them. Also, that they had so obviously grown from their *nisayon.* I remember Yanky saying, 'I wouldn't have had it any other way." How could he make such a statement? I wondered then. But I could see that as a couple they have become nothing less than a center of advice and practical help to all those who suffer adversity, and also experts in the area of kidney problems, dialysis and transplants.

But Ruchi, the wife, was more reticent. I felt how hard it was for her to actually relive the past. It must have been like opening up a can of worms. It took many months for her to find the courage to do this, but when she did so, it was with determination and fortitude to tell the world her story. And their motive in all this? To give *chizuk* to others enduring days of darkness, in whatever form; to show that a young couple tested to the utmost limits can draw together and grow together in a quite remarkable way. So that by the end of the project, I felt it had been a privilege that these two unique individuals had crossed my path.

Now about "writing"' and "writing". Unfortunately since I began this project I have undergone my own *nisayon* and felt many days of darkness following the death of my beloved father, Rav Mordechai Singer *zt"l* 10 Adar 5758. When I finally returned to the book, it was with a different understanding of the words I had actually written almost four years earlier. Did I write those words? Yes, with my head, but not with my heart. And now these very words had a special message for me.

The ways of Hashem are indeed mysterious and beyond the understanding of our limited, mortal comprehension. "Our little lights have their day and cease to be," but as Ruchi says, there is a master plan and a Master Planner.

I would like to thank all those who helped me in the completion of this project.

Rabbi Shaul Wagschal *shlita,* who remains in many ways my mentor, who took time to read the manuscript and made useful halachic and practical suggestions.

Mrs. Rochel Greenbaum of Topic Publications, who typed and made many insightful comments about the original manuscript.

Mrs. Chani Zahn, who with speed and efficiency helped me to complete the task. (Chani has recently published her own book *My Father, My Rebbe*, which is a fascinating tribute to a remarkable man, Rabbi Benzion Rakow *zt"l*. She too has now been initiated into the joys of authorship!)

Dr. Rutenberg, our family doctor, who not only took the time to proof-read the manuscript, but who has written a medical foreword.

In the Rosh Hashana and Yom Kippur liturgy we say, "How many will live and how many will die:" Dr. Rutenberg more than any other individual 'lived' through these 'words' with us, and excelled both in the exercise of his medical skills and of his humanity.

Mrs. Judy Oppenheimer and Miss Perla Schleider for their proofreading of the original manuscript

To my mother, Rebbetzen Aliza Singer, who for forty-eight years was a loyal *Eishes Chayil* to my father, Rav Mordechai Singer *zt"l*. It was to her wise counsel and perception that he turned again and again — but as she once said to me: "I was always happy to walk in Daddy's shadow." She has borne his tragic loss with courage, fortitude and dignity. During these dark months she supported me in every conceivable way towards the completion of this project, which also represented "regaining the light".

My mother-in-law, Mrs. Henna Dansky, whose loyal support, encouragement and understanding has helped our whole family through a difficult time. In Gateshead, her cheerfulness, generosity of spirit and *bitachon* are a byword, despite having endured many lonely years herself. Having attended no seminary but the seminary of life, the *Shem Hashem* is never far from her lips, nor a *siddur* far from her hands!

May both grandmothers derive much pleasure from all their children and grandchildren.

I would like to pay a personal tribute:

To our Gateshead family, Geoffrey and Yocheved, Harvey and Jennifer — my thanks as always for unfailingly loyal support!

To my sisters, Mrs. Shulamis Kuperman and Dr. Rifkah Goldberg, with whom I sat *shivah* in Adar — my thanks for their loyalty.

Shulamis has endured her own *nisyonos* and emerged whole — with a wit and a charm all her own! May her husband, Avrohom Leib, be granted a speedy and complete recovery. To Rifkah goes my thanks for her words of **timely** advice. May she enjoy *nachas* from her sons, Eli and Avi.

To my husband, Chaim, who always delights in my achievements. To my children, Yehoshua, Moishe, Beilah, Rochel, Rifki and most especially to our baby Mordechai. He has lit up our lives after our terrible loss in a very special way. And here I must thank each of my children for the wonderful way they have taken our new baby to their hearts. May he grow to emulate the ways of his grandfather, whom he never knew and whose name he bears.

To the staff at ArtScroll, Rabbi Nosson Scherman, whom I always try so hard to impress with my writing, and Rabbi Avrohom Biderman for his humanity, warmth and general good advice.

The words of the *Asher Yatzar* blessing, so often recited as though mundane, come to mind with new force after having completed this book:

*Blessed are You Hashem our G-d, King of the universe who fashioned man with wisdom and created within him many openings and many cavities. It is obvious and known before your Thorns of Glory that if but one of them were to be ruptured or but one of them to be blocked it would be impossible to survive and to stand before You. Blessed are You, Hashem, who heals all flesh and acts wondrously."*

Finally, in the Grace After Meals we ask that we not be brought to be dependent on the gifts of *bassar vadam* — people. Someone pointed out to me that the words *bassar vadam* literally mean "flesh and blood." Unfortunately, the subject of this book necessitated gifts of both flesh and blood — a transplant and transfusions. That she and her husband have emerged not only as whole but inspirational human beings is a source of never ceasing wonderment to me.

The subjects of the book also wish to impart a piece of *mussar to* us all. If you know people undergoing a *nisayon*, don't cross the street to avoid them! Ask them how they are coping. Don't be afraid of being intrusive, for just a few well chosen words of sincere inquiry can ease the heart of the sufferer, and make him feel that we are all together. Each of us has the capacity to offer this wonderful gift of empathy — even though we may sometimes doubt our ability to do so.

It was a great honor to have worked with this special couple and to have grown along the way in the completion of this book.

Miriam Dansky
Gateshead
Rosh Chodesh Cheshvan 5762
October 2001

# PROLOGUE

"LISTEN DOCTOR," I BEGAN, "MY WIFE IS A VERY YOUNG WOMAN. I know that possibly for just this reason you are afraid to tell us the true situation. But in reality, I would prefer to know the extent of what we are dealing with. Let me tell you now that I am handling everything on my wife's behalf."

This doctor was quite young, and I could see now, nervous. In a way, at that moment, I pitied him. He was in possession of certain facts and he did not, for the life of him, know how to transmit them to this strange looking Jewish couple.

He gulped once or twice as if to prepare for his revelation,

"Sir, let me tell you at once — your wife has a sickness which is incurable. There is absolutely **no way** to naturally reverse the change."

*Does he understand the depth of hurt he has just had to inflict on me? Never, never again normality!*

"Perhaps I will travel abroad? Perhaps get a second opinion."

"Travel, go round the world, but you will come face to face with the eventuality. It will sit there waiting for you, like some grinning toad, when you come back."

These words are some of those that return to haunt me most frequently, for they have come to exemplify — more forcefully then most — the nature of our extended *nisayon*. "The grinning toad" which awaited us at every intricate turn, epitomized all that we most came to fear — and it was against this symbol of black hopelessness that we pitched our prolonged battle. This battle, then, is the substance of our story.

# ENCORE

ALLOW ME TO TELL YOU OUR STORY. WHEN WE THINK OF A STORY, we visualize a straight line that takes us from the past to the present, sometimes even pointing a finger towards the future. But let me point out at once that this story, although possessing a beginning, a middle and an ending of sorts, is primarily one of shadings and textures. It comprises neither the complete blackness of night, nor the total brightness of day — but a sort of shifting canvas of clouds, chasing one another in quick succession. And somewhere from within the alternates of hope and apparent despair, resentment and humor is the meaning of the story. Can you walk through an unimaginable *nisayon* or test of moral mettle — and come through — we would dare not say unscathed — but changed and strengthened in unimagined ways — like a man walking on a bed of nails? Our story might just affirm that one can. And if this is so, then perhaps this is the point both of our story — and of our *nisayon* — that sways high above our heads like a banner in the breeze. And let me both finish and begin by saying too, that our *nisayon* does not belong locked away behind the windowpane of years, to some other era — of deportations and lagers. No, it is a story of here and now, of the 1990's, of a young couple so ordinary you would pass them by on the street, wholly undistinguished in lineage or status. This, too, is what motivates me to set this story down in black and white. You might ask, why would anyone want to relive the pain, to disturb freshly settled memories, lying like summerhouse furniture covered by dust sheets in winter? Leave well alone, isn't it enough that you have lived through and endured these things of which you are about to speak? The answer is yes and no. To have survived — to have survived intact in spirit — is truly *dayeinu*, this is enough. But then there is the undeniable fact that this experience, although thrusting us to the depths of despair, has also, in some mysterious way, lifted us up, elevated us above the norm of human experience. And it is this sense of elevation, of closeness to the Master of the Universe in our troubles, which we wish to impart. So let no one say, "I am not wise enough or old enough or learned enough to undergo a supreme *nisayon* and pass the test." For our story attests to quite the reverse. And if, in recounting again all the details of our many years of trial, just one individual or one family undergoing this or any other of the innumerable tests that cross one's path in life, will turn the last page and feel in some way strengthened — then the story has surely been worth the telling.

**Beginnings**

AS I SIT HERE, ON THE PORCH OF OUR SUMMERHOUSE IN THE mountains, I place the tape recorder firmly on the table in front of me, determined to speak, to tell the story simply and honestly, as it transpired and from the beginning. But immediately, I find myself hemming and hawing. How to begin? I remember then all those times during the past seven years that I have wished to speak and simply been unable to express what lay in my heart, and other times, when words flowed endlessly, like a silvery stream trickling down an Alpine mountainside. So forgive me, dear reader, if things sometimes appear confused or contradictory. It is not that I am exaggerating or falsifying the facts, G-d forbid, but rather that all these facets were somehow present, side by side and at different times. And where is the real beginning of our tale?

The beginning is utter normality and it would have been ever so simple, I suppose, for things to continue in this easy fashion. But the fact remains that that was not the path designated for us, was not part of the all-encompassing "masterplan."

My name is Yanky and I married Ruchi Freedman in 1983, in the United States of America. I had studied for several years in a Chassidishe yeshivah in New York, and, through a mutual cousin, was introduced to my wife. After our marriage we settled in a small European country. Here I must add that the type of country is important, in that it represents not only a picturesque backdrop of mountains and lakes to our later troubles, but provides an essential human element to our story. We are speaking here of a small, self-contained country, and so one can deduce an ever-smaller Jewish community. The town in which we live, although a largish one, numbers perhaps one thousand religious Jewish families. Thus, although Orthodox Jews are present in various neighborhoods, there is no real concentration or ghetto resembling orthodox Jewish strongholds in other parts of the world. Consequently one feels, how shall I best describe it, a little alien, a little isolated. The general atmosphere, too, is one of cleanliness and a certain aloofness or coolness which permeates every aspect of life. I tell you these facts not in the way of criticism, but merely in order to provide a necessary ambience to the events of later years.

Early marriage, as I have said, was complete normality. Following the arrival of two cherished boys, my wife was expecting our third child. At this point, Ruchi and I mutually concluded, the apartment was becoming too small for our needs, and we must look for another roomier one to suit the growing family.

We decided this one day, as the severe winter was just beginning to turn a corner into spring. We scoured the newspaper advertisements, until our eye fell upon an apartment to rent in a house owned by Jews. We travelled to the other side of town to look it over.

As soon as we opened the heavy door, we experienced an inexplicable feeling of homecoming. We immediately visualized our furniture and rugs and other paraphernalia transforming the six-room apartment into a home — our home.

As I look back on that time, I realize primarily how young we were, young and inexperienced, if I might use that word to describe adults. For to us, life was still something meant to fit into a preconceived mold. Yes, we could envision things stretching on and on into the future, developing in the way we had imagined. A succession of healthy children, please G-d, a home strewn with toys and toddlers' laughter. It was with these feelings that we moved into the new apartment that February, just a few weeks before Purim. (The apartment itself was part of a building renovated by a wealthy businessman for his daughter and her family. The floor beneath hers he had laid identically — to house a Jewish neighbor. He provided for all religious requirements, such as a succah and kosher kitchen).

Imagine a soldier standing in front of a minefield. He is just one step away from oblivion. But he is unaware, supremely and blithely unaware. This is a last moment of sorts — a moment of innocence, made all the more poignant by what is to come. That is how I think of us now just at that very moment — as if from the other side of a perilous mountain pass traversed, one inch at a time, and fighting for dear life.

## Night of Bedikas Chometz 1987

WEEKS PASSED IN A FLURRY OF PRE-PESACH PREPARATIONS. Finally, it is *bedikas chometz* night. All the tensions of the past few weeks are almost resolved. I am in our front room attending to last minute preparations. Suddenly, a cry from the bedroom — Ruchi's voice. Entering the room I see her surrounded by a sea of old clothing and shoes.

"Ruchi, what are you doing?" I ask.

"I've been trying on shoes, to see if I can get rid of any old ones. And you know what, Yanky?" she says, turning towards me, and suddenly I notice her face is pinched and white, "I simply can't get my foot into any of these! Look!"

Looking down, I notice, for the first time, that her feet are swollen to nearly double their normal size. Actually, now that I **really** look at her, I see something that I never saw before — she is visibly swollen throughout. We are both concerned — but not unduly so. We feel that it will turn out to be a minor matter. It needs investigating so that we can set our minds at rest, and then continue with our lives on their pre-oiled tracks.

I phone the hospital where my two sons were born. I speak to a nurse. The doctor was on vacation and this particular nurse was in fact a midwife, who was familiar with my wife from the previous two births. She suggests we come in and have my wife checked.

"Of course, there is no reason for alarm," she adds reassuringly, "just a check-up, to make sure everything is fine."

It is nearly midnight. I look in on the boys; the older one is asleep in a characteristic pose, pacifier in mouth. The younger one lies more tidily in his cot. I arrange for a young neighbor to come downstairs and keep an eye on them. We get into our car and speed through the midnight streets. All is quiet and deserted. The shapes of the mountains behind the houses are visible only as indistinct outlines against a starless sky, like felt tip shadings in a child's picture. Soon, the familiar facade of the hospital looms ahead. Up the stairs, through the swing doors which come to rest behind us — past admissions, down familiar corridors. We describe the problem again. Various routine tests are carried out. We sit in the hospital's waiting chairs and await the results.

Time is passing slowly, so achingly slowly. And we are tired. We both long to get this over and return to our apartment and our sleeping children. Tomorrow is *erev Pesach*. How can we afford to tire ourselves out like this and face the long day of preparations ahead? The hospital clock, with its clear demarcations, ticks on. Finally, the nurse who met us at the desk returns. Something is wrong. I know that before she opens her mouth to speak. Her expression has changed from the mask of efficiency it was an hour ago to something a little more human.

"Our preliminary tests show that something is not quite satisfactory. There is too much protein in the urine," she enunciates crisply.

"Not **quite** satisfactory" — these words do not **quite** spell doom, but we had expected to be allowed to go home, to be reprieved with an admonition to arrange an appointment perhaps next week or the week after. These words leave us teetering on the edge of a cliff, between things being all right as expected and a vast unknown. We had not then the experience to imagine what that "unknown" could be, for our sights up to that point were well defined. Everything must be all right, for that is the way things always are. She directs us to a university hospital across the road.

"We do not have the facilities here," she says as she walks us back down the corridors.

❧

I hate hospitals. All my life, I could never stand the sight of blood, injections, drips, white-clothed nurses and doctors — all the paraphernalia of sickness. Hospitals represent a sort of microcosm, an enclosed world, wholly unconnected to the world outside. This world has its own hierarchies and politics, its own statutes and ordinances. You cannot measure anything outside to anything inside. And once you are inside, you sink immediately into the system. No status, marital or professional, exists here — you are Patient So and So, defined only by your sickness and its daily needs. If you want to go to sleep a little earlier, or wake a little later in the morning, you are in breach of regulations. But these barely suppressed feelings of unease, surely these were present, the next day or the next week but not at that precise moment, crossing the street, from one hospital on our way to another? Perhaps not. But then this is part of the strangeness of this story, that you cannot pinpoint one particular moment and say: "This is what I was feeling there or then..." or "Maybe that emotion came later or earlier." No, all compounds of all emotions were present at different moments. So that it might well be true to say that I felt a sense of foreboding or premonition even at that exact point, when things were between "not **quite** satisfactory" and all that was to follow crashing over our heads, like giant white-tipped waves in a stormy sea.

❧

## Ruchi:

FOR MY HUSBAND, YANKY, SPEAKING ABOUT ALL THIS IS RELATIVELY easy. He places the tape-recorder in front of him on the kitchen table, he shifts a little in his chair and then he begins. Out it all spills — dates, places, medical appointments. But for me, oh, how to describe it — it is like uncovering an old wound. It is more than pain — it is a sort of "gut wrenching" process. Why, why go back — that is the question I ask myself again and again — why take a needle and stick it into your own skin and bone, as I did over and over again on dialysis? For that is exactly what this **feels** like. But in the spring of 1995, when we had finally reached the mutual decision to set all this down on paper for posterity (at the request of many acquaintances familiar with our story who had asked us to set it down as a *chizuk* to others in adverse situations), to record the entire experience from beginning to end — the weeks, the months began to tick by. Yanky recorded tape after tape. It seemed an almost effortless process for him. But what about me? What would happen to my side of the story?

"Nu, Ruchi," he would urge me gently when he returned home from work each evening. "Have you spoken into the tape recorder today? Have you made a start?"

"Give me time, just a little longer, Yanky," I would answer him, pleading for time, in just the same ways as I would answer him when he had urged me to stick the needle, and begin dialysis.

But I know that if we are to make this record of our experiences, for it to be an honest account, it must be as nearly complete as possible. It must contain my story from my point of view. That is now I suppose, one night lying awake, long after everyone else is asleep in the quiet, now-orderly apartment, the thought comes to me — and it is so simple and overwhelming that I wonder why it has never occurred to me before — that I must literally "go back." I must revisit those places — which my husband describes in such precise detail, where these events mostly took place, reinvoking all the old sights, sounds and smells. I must somehow find the courage to retrace the winding tributary of what is after all MY STORY until I reach the source itself. And then, only then, finally will the story have reached what we might call a kind of ending.

⚜

It is a brisk, slightly coldish spring day in May. The children have left the apartment some time ago, knapsacks on their backs, their feet clattering excitedly out of the building and down the street. Suddenly silence reigns. I put on my coat, take the elevator downstairs, then cross the open square where the flowers and potted plants are already on display outside the shop on the corner. Along the main road, trams, cars and bicycles pass each other. Someone waves from a bicycle — I recognize her as a woman who lives two streets away. Outwardly, I suppose I look calm and collected, on this day so much like any other. I am doing everything mechanically now, inserting the money for my tram ticket and then, when the tram finally arrives, finding a seat by the window. The streets are already beginning to fill, with people going to work. In the famous main street, shoppers are starting to filter in and out of fashionable department stores. But the tram winds its way slowly out of town and begins to mount a little. We are moving steadily upwards now, into a suburban, tree-lined area. We pass detached residences and villas set back from the roadside. Finally, we pass larger official-looking buildings. We are entering the university campus, with its stained glass windows and libraries. The atmosphere here is more rarefied, students stride leisurely along the pavements, books under arms. Occasionally, we pass a cluster of nurses in uniform. The tram-driver announces the stop. I have arrived.

Up the winding path, past potted geraniums and hydrangeas. The building really does not look too forbidding. So why is my heart lurching, over and over, as if it will never stop? Sliding doors open noiselessly. Now, I imagine that there is a companion at my side, someone who is a stranger, yet an interested party, who is seeing all this for the first time, to whom I have the task of explaining the significance of everything that we see.

"This is the reception area," I hear myself saying, "where we entered on that fateful *bedikas chometz* night, my husband and I. We came through these doors and up into the emergency room." This is a university hospital, so you will see many student doctors here. This is really a rather oldish building, as evidenced by the well-worn grayish tiles on the floor. Everything is grey and rather worn. Now, here as we ascend this slight incline — can you begin to smell it? It is a kind of sticky-sweet, antiseptic smell — and this, I suppose was the first time in my life that I really encountered it. It knocked me sideways, so to speak; I felt nauseous, almost faint. This smell was with me always, afterwards in hospitals and dialysis units. And it came to somehow symbolize the entire experience for me.

Anyway, we were brought up here that night and I was placed on a bed. Yes, perhaps it was that very bed nearest the swinging doors. This is a busy emergency room, and there is usually a lot of activity here, you understand. On that night, it was nearly midnight — but the room was still half-full. I remember noticing one youth in the corner. His eyes had the glazed look of a drug addict. He was rocking himself ever so gently backwards and forwards and moaning.

An official voice had interjected: "Please, Mrs. Guttfreund take off your shoes and lie on the bed. "The doctors will be with you as soon as possible."

The nurse had glanced at my husband cursorily, taking in his Chassidic grab and black hat. Her eyes grew slightly colder, I fancied. So, there I lay. It was my first encounter with this microcosmic world. Hospitals for me, up to that point, bore no real significance — they were places which you visited briefly, perhaps to have a baby, and then go home again. Certainly, they were not places in which to linger.

Oh, how easily it all comes back now, standing in this emergency room. I imagined that going back would be like prying the lid off a can of worms — but until this moment, I never had the courage to confront this inevitability. The entire experience oddly enough, is symbolized for me by the smell. The impersonal, sickly-sweet antiseptic smell which makes your stomach lurch and then lurch again. It grabs hold of all your senses, and suddenly you are floating on a different planet — far away from all the homey, kitchen odors, the familiar smell of polish in the dining room, the scent of flowers in the hall. This smell penetrates your very bones and sets you outside the realm of daily experience, with a terrible certainty. And along with the smell are linked a thousand tiny sounds, the swishing of carts, up and down endless corridors, the sound of the nurses' rubber heels squeaking on tiled floors, the strange ringing of bells, which stop and start, and which one never ever discovers the significance of. Even voices here sound more muted — not the voices of ordinary human conversations which take place freely on the spring pavements outside.

Well, we are still inside this emergency-room. Now I am lying on the bed. Something is happening to me but I cannot quite say what.

Doctors assemble around my bed and then leave suddenly, like flurries of swallows. But at that point, I was not really suffering. And I will tell you why — it is quite simple really. It was because I was not really there! Three quarters of me or more was back at home in our comfortable apartment, sorting out cupboards for Pesach. Well, isn't that after all where I left off? This is merely some kind of unpleasant interlude — but soon the lights will darken, the curtain will rise and the play, the "real business" of our lives will continue. This was a blip, an untoward interruption in the pleasantness and well-ordered nature of our lives. What we did not sense then was the "uniqueness" of this event, how it would come to change our lives, molding both of us in quite new and unexpected ways.

⁂

In this emergency-room, something else comes to mind. My husband and I disagree on the response to the following question:"When did your world fall apart?" His answer to this question is: "Just here, in this emergency room." Doctors clustered around my bed — Pesach preparations left off as hastily as the enactment of *Yetzias Mitzrayim* itself. For him this was nothing short of an all-encompassing nightmare. For me, however, I was so sure this would all pass soon enough. (No, for me the real feeling of blackness, of "caving in" came much, much later, when I finally understood that there was no way out but dialysis — when I first looked at the machine with all its knobs, dials and pipes in the square hospital room, and knew that my earlier erroneous concept of having had control of my life now lay inert and lifeless.) And we differed too, in our ways of dealing with this confusing "in between time." He became, as it were, my secretary. He had to deal with the myriad of arrangements, paperwork, interviews, discussions, timings, which my illness created. And after all, he still had to face the real world — to mediate between hospital and normality. I, on the other hand, was very busy simply being ill, which left no time or energy at all for thinking. Everything was simply happening to me and in spite of me. I have an abiding memory of those days — of lying almost flat on a hard hospital bed, six or seven bespectacled doctors standing around, peering down at me. I was no longer "me," no longer a person in charge of her own household, her own children, her own destiny, just an interesting specimen, to be peered at and examined. For the most part, that is how I progressed through that endless waiting time.

**Yanky:**

WE ENTERED THE HOSPITAL ACROSS THE ROAD AND THEN THINGS began to move more swiftly in their inevitable direction — and as if with a momentum of their own. Further tests revealed something was definitely wrong. My wife would have to be kept in at least overnight. In the morning, the professor would examine her — and come to some decision. All this transpired in the emergency room — in a small cubicle, partitioned off by curtains, of a faded flowery print. Into this confined space our world had shrunk within the space of a few hours. Everything extraneous to this, or the sight of my wife crying on the hard bed, as I turned to leave, ceased to have any functional reality. Emerging from the hospital, I saw that the sky had already begun to lighten and streak — in preparation for dawn for a good portion of the night had gone by. There was no tiredness now as I climbed into my car and switched on the engine — just an indescribable fear — like a weight, crushing me from above. Was it just hours before that the future had seemed bright and beckoning in its certainty? Now, I had left behind a young wife, crying in a white washed emergency room — to return home alone. In addition, there was no one to whom I could turn — my wife's parents were overseas and my own parents were aging and could not be burdened with this extra worry.

SOMEHOW THE FEW HOURS LEFT OF THE NIGHT PASSED, AND THE next morning dawned. I retraced my steps along the same streets of the night. Now, everything was washed in clear sunlight — houses, trees, cobblestones all became imprinted on my mind with astonishing clarity. Up hospital stairways, along grey corridors, my steps echoing the uncomfortable pounding of my heart. When I reach my wife, seven doctors are around her bed. She looks like a minuscule doll, surrounded by these gravely nodding, observing faces. From the gravity of their demeanor I feel in my bones that something is profoundly amiss. My wife is confused. She does not clearly understand what the doctors have been telling her, for her mother tongue is English. She has stopped crying now, but looks bewildered, as if lost in a strange city where the signposts are all in a foreign language.

"What do they say?" Ruchi asks me as soon as I enter on the scene. "Tell me at once."

One doctor draws me aside — he maneuvers me into some waiting chairs. Then in his native language he tells me:

"The child your wife is carrying is not healthy. The fact is sir, this baby is missing one chromosome. If it is born, it will be little more than a vegetable. You have no choice therefore, but to abort the baby."[1]

Is this then the news I had waited the whole achingly long night to receive? I was literally transfixed, stunned into immobility, afraid to utter a word or signal in response. I put my head in my hands and uttered some words of prayer. But I was like a man who speaks his plea quietly, for his own ears alone. This is what I said: "*Ribbono shel Olam*, Master of the Universe — why? Why this *mabul*, this drowning out of normal circumstances which has come upon me and my family? We are so young — so naive and inexperienced. Up till this moment everything has gone our way. Marriage, children — everything delightful and neat. Please let us retain that quiet normality."

And, in that split second, I see my wife and I like two children riding on freshly painted, gaudy carousel horses. The ride is thrilling, houses and fields flash by in a whirl of color, but in the deepest

Erev Pesach - 1987

1. *Medical note: It would seem, according to all medical opinions impossible to diagnose any chromosomal abnormality in less than about five days. Here it seems to have been accomplished in eight hours!*

*Encore* ❖ 27

recesses of our hearts, did we have, even then some 'child-like' notion that at one point the ride and its gay music would have to end? And even then, at that very instant, in the cold, forbidding hospital, as I divined that something was about to go terribly wrong, to veer off the path which had seemed so straight and narrow, I questioned whether the Jewish outlook on suffering, inbred from years of Torah study, and imbibed from childhood as naturally as mother's milk, was already in place — ready to support me, like a sturdy parachute? Is it possible that I could have remembered in a flash a story from long ago — from my yeshivah days? Perhaps it is not only possible, but probable, for I believe now that at moments of supreme crisis, all one's former experiences and knowledge rush to support one.

A certain Jew was once undergoing very severe suffering. He went to visit his Rebbe and said to him quite simply, "Rebbe, I cannot bear this suffering any longer. You are a *tzaddik*. Take these *yisurim* from me."

The Rebbe thought for a long moment. He knew that he had to convey to this poor *chassid* the significance which these particular *yisurim* had for him and him alone. Finally with a deep sigh, he turned to the waiting disciple and told him the following parable: "G-d," he said, in his slow sonorous way, "is a trainer, and you, my dear son, are the trainee. Just imagine that someone is training another fellow to play a game such as tennis. He holds the racket and the trainer stands and throws balls to him. To begin with, these balls are aimed to the center of the racket. So, back and forth balls fly in a pleasant, comfortable fashion. But now the trainer wants the trainee to progress to a higher stage. He begins to shoot to the sides of the court. Now the trainee has to jump and make daring lunges to reach the ball. Perspiring and exhausted he lets out a bitter protest, 'Look at my friend on the next court. I returned the balls much better than him, and now I have to jump. He doesn't do it at all that well, and still the ball goes exactly to the center of his racket. Why is this?'

" 'My dear friend,' explains the coach, 'you are past that stage and have reached the next level of difficulty, that of jumping. You are making progress while that poor fellow is still stuck at his stage, so he receives the ball easily.' "

The Rebbe concluded his parable, and directed his dark eyes at the troubled *chassid*: "Everything, my child, is dependent on purpose. If the purpose is training and not just ease and comfort, then the situation is totally transformed. Likewise, if the trainee misunderstands the purpose, and refuses to jump, eventually, he will have to redo that test anyway. So, why repeat it twice? If I take your *yisurim* from you, you will not gain what you should have from them, G-d will have to give you the suffering again, in another form. So why not benefit from them the first time?"

❧

So, there I sat on the hospital chair, listening and not listening to the professor's grave words, and this story flashed to mind, to support me on what I intuitively knew was the long road ahead. As I asked before, is this true? Was it then or was it perhaps later — on one of my long walks around the lake, where I retreated both for solitude and inspiration in some of the bitterest, most challenging moments — that this story flashed into my mind? Or perhaps it matters not in the least, for chronology is not all that important here — whether one event or feeling happened before or after another. What matters is texture, depths, changing feelings and responses...

❧

I returned to Ruchi's bedside. Now she was crying real tears as I apprised her of the situation. Somehow she didn't believe that this was all the doctors had said. Terrible as it was, she felt — as time would later prove, as if with some kind of chilling foresight, that this was only a piece of the menacing jigsaw. Since this news had been conveyed in a language not her own, her doubts and suspicions were all the stronger. I uttered the words, prophetic as they were to be: "Whatever shall come, we will fight it through together."

Later, after I had managed to reassure her, I waylaid one of the doctors whom I recognized as having been at her bedside.

"Doctor," I said a little breathlessly, for I had hurried down the long corridor quickly to reach him. "Doctor, tonight our festival of Passover begins. In fact, in just a few hours. You must let my wife out to join the family, and in two days time, I promise you, we will bring her back in."

He shook his head and continued to shake it from side to side rapidly, as I spoke. "I am sorry sir, but we absolutely cannot allow it. She must remain in the hospital, under close supervision."

I saw then that all my pleadings would be utterly useless. I saw then too, the measure of this tragedy that was sucking us in. For she no longer belonged completely to me or our boys. She was now incorporated into this vast, impersonal system of beds and corridors, ringing bells, operating theatres, drips, transfusions. Our reality, the homey apartment, Pesach, the starched cloth awaiting the seder participants, could no longer pull her away or claim her. Everything broke down rapidly at that point. I took leave of her, promising to be back as soon as I could. This time, I had to turn away quickly from her eyes, still bright with tears. I ran to my parents' home, made arrangements to leave our two infant sons with them, depositing too their little sailor suits, so carefully chosen by my wife in honor of Yom Tov. I would have to join my wife's lonely seder in the hospital. I gathered the requisite articles, in haste but without any joy. For what sort of seder could it be in a hospital ward? Surely it would be an empty rite?

# Ruchi:

LYING ALONE IN THE HOSPITAL, I KNEW IT TO BE EREV PESACH. APART from the strangeness of the situation in which I now found myself, another urgent need gnawed at my spirit. I knew that as it was *erev Yom Tov* my parents miles away overseas would be expecting their customary phone call from me.

They knew next to nothing of my situation for I had only told them that I was a little more swollen than was usual, at this still early stage of pregnancy. I knew that realistically there was little they could do for me, should they be made aware of the true situation at this point — for Yom Tov would soon be in. Yet, I feared picking up the telephone and, on hearing their voices being reduced to tears and allowing the whole story to gush forth. It took all of my will power to pick up the phone and wish them a cheerful "Good Yom Tov" — and I still remember replacing the receiver and feeling a sense of desolation, more powerful than I had ever experienced, sweep over me in relentless waves.

# Yanky:

THE SPRING DAY WAS ALREADY BEGINNING TO DECLINE AS I REACHED the hospital once more, and rode the elevator to the twentieth floor. This was one of the tallest buildings in our historic city, for in keeping with its special atmosphere, city planners had forbidden buildings to exceed twenty stories. Here I *davened Ma'ariv* alone, completely alone in spirit. In reality, the view from the massive, darkening window was beautiful. The whole city was laid out before me, as lights came on one by one. I could not see but could merely imagine the narrow steep alleyways, which I knew to be there, rising from a cluster of historic buildings. Immediately below us was the inky shape of the edge of the lake and majestically erect behind it, turn of the century mansions. Further beyond, and dwarfing them, was the faint outline of mountains which I knew to be snow-clad on their peaks. I saw all this, seeing but not seeing. For I would have preferred to be anywhere but here, and in any but these circumstances. But somehow, the quiet beauty of this panorama must have entered my psyche and soothed my soul. For as I turned towards Ruchi, I had stopped crying and saw that she had too. I laid out the seder-plate, the matzos and other requirements as well as I was able, and I began to recite *kiddush*. From that second, it was as if something was released in me, a secret spring, for I began to conduct a seder which was uniquely fitted to this, the strangest of circumstances. Exactly what I said I can no longer recall but it was a mixture of *chizuk* to my wife and of startlingly original words of Torah — things I had never said before or since. It was such a seder as I can only think of as a gratuitous gift from the One Above. Now too, I knew the truth about all those sedarim or other religious rites I had read about which had taken place in ghettos and concentration camps, without even the necessary components except for salt-water and bitter herbs in plenitude. When I had read those accounts I had often wondered, what kind of sedarim or other ceremonies could these be? What spiritual uplift could they provide? And in a flash, I realized a truth so simple that it had passed by unawares all these years. If the *Ribbono shel Olam* so wishes He can grant one a spirit of closeness to Him and, in its wake, elevation and well-being. And He can do so in the worst imaginable of human scenarios. This is truly a *matnas Elokim*, and is not contingent on external circumstances. For here we were, a young couple (I was just twenty-three, my wife but twenty-one) in an unfolding tragedy or *nisayon*, so it would be no exaggeration to say that we hardly knew or recognized what world we were in. We were like two moon walkers emerging from their spacecrafts, moving clumsily on the surface of a new planet. And yet, paradoxically, I can truly say that, that that year we experienced, on that first night in the hospital, a seder of astonishing beauty and depth.

CHOL HAMOED THAT YEAR PRODUCED IN ME A MIXTURE OF feelings. As I strolled in the park with our two young boys, I reflected that we were a "torn" family. My young man's dreams of family-life, as epitomized by images of families strolling in the park on *Chol HaMoed*, now lay shattered like so much broken glass. For here I was alone, watching the world of "whole" families go by, and wondering when we would ever enter that category again. Here was one of the few occasions in the year when Orthodox Jews were a fairly prominent presence in parks and other leisure spots. On such a day, as this too — a quickening spring day — a gentile festival was celebrated with the burning of straw snowmen the symbolic burning of the winter. Despite all this, it was still midwinter in my heart.

❧

Ten days later found us still in the midst of turmoil. Ruchi was still hospitalized. I had consulted a Rav about our predicament, and he called me back with his decision: "The child cannot be aborted." Several days later a biopsy revealed that the baby was most certainly a completely normal child. By now, we were totally disorientated. My wife had spent three weeks in the hospital, seemingly for no purpose. But something was deeply wrong — we knew this by the several troubling signs of my wife's condition. She continued to swell, as though she were a rising dam that would one day burst. There seemed to be something else underlying this whole episode, like a monster below the smooth surface of a Scottish Highland lake. The doctors too were astonished at her physical state, claiming they had never seen an individual retaining so much fluid. All her limbs were unbearably swollen and remained as solid and immovable as rocks. The slightest movement was painful. She needed help just to raise her legs onto a chair. All that summer untold doubts and fears burned through our minds, like a slowly smoldering autumn fire.

Another image too, of that time. An arctic hut — a trapper secure inside with an oil lamp and log fire, and everything warm and dry inside. Outside a blizzard rages and snow is piling up silently at the door. A great weight is forming against the timber, the bolt straining in its socket. Minute by minute, the white heap grows until suddenly, as the sun comes out, the thaw moves, slides, tumbles; the whole hillside is falling. The little lighted place is torn asunder, rolling into the path of the avalanche, and suddenly it is no more, as if it has never been. All is whiteness and silence.

I WALK BACK DOWN THE ENDLESS CORRIDORS, THROUGH SWING DOORS, down steps and all at once I am outside in the thin sunlight again. From here it is only a short walk to the clinic — the next port of call on today's strange pilgrimage. The path winds and climbs quite steeply. I have soon left behind the main suburban road, where the trams' pathways intersect. Here, on this side street the pavement is being broken up, bulldozers move in cumbersome fashion like warrior elephants, workmen in hard hats call to each other. Nobody is sure why the pavements are being rebuilt or what will ultimately be achieved, but all over the city this kind of work is taking place. Now a modern multi-storied building looms ahead.

"This is the hospital to which I was transferred from the emergency room of the university-hospital," I tell my imaginary friend. "Let's take the elevator — and ride upwards to the twentieth floor. Do you see how suddenly everything becomes remarkably quiet up here? The atmosphere is subdued, rarefied and slightly detached from reality. Let me show you why. This is the day-room — but look out of the sliding windows that span the length of the room, and what do you see? The entire city lies in front of you like some child's jigsaw puzzle — industrialized zones, lakes, houses, suburban districts, bus lines, train stations. But the noises of the city are blocked out, both by the double-glazing and by the height."

So here I lay, totally disoriented. The days passed in a sort of hazy grayness — long periods of time spent lying on the hospital bed —

punctuated only by the intermittent "blood-pricking". (Blood tests were taken three times a day for three weeks.) Oh, the endless blood and urine tests — and never a word of explanation, or real human sympathy! All at once, some sort of decision seemed to have been reached. I heard the words "child" "abnormality" "abortion." I remember the cold Germanic features of the doctor who first uttered these words. I was nothing short of petrified. That something may be wrong with my unborn child — this seemed a fate worse then anything I could have imagined.

We often sat in this very day-room and tried to puzzle out what was happening to our lives. And when we tired of talking or think-ing, we turned to face this spectacular view. In a way, this con-tributed to our sense of detachment from reality — we were so far above the city, in a literal sense, floating between what might, or could or should be. And every day that passed I thought: "*Ribbono shel Olam*, let this be all — the tests, the waiting. I have overcome the *nisayon* that today has brought. Tomorrow, G-d willing, I will go home and pick up the threads of my life where I left off."

⚜

And it was here too, in one of these rooms on the twentieth floor, that Yanky conducted a seder for me. We felt as though we were per-haps the first people in the world to celebrate a seder, or such a seder, in such unprecedented, perplexing circumstances. But with the seder, a kind of calm descended on us both, as if in the very act of following the ceremonial "order" we had succeeded in ordering, for a while, our own chaotic emotions and fears.

⚜

Let me tell you about these weeks after my discharge from the "hospital of the twentieth floor." Incidentally, I well remember the way we left that hospital, in dramatic fashion. The doctors had finally, as it were, acceded defeat: "You were right, we were wrong" — that is what their grudging expressions seemed to imply.

"The child you are carrying is normal — we don't know where the problem lies."

They had carried out amniocentesis — at our insistence. This was recommended to us by our Rav who advised us not to have an abortion, but to insist on this test being carried out instead.

So when a tall, thin doctor approached us one morning saying:

"So, Mrs. Guttfreund, you can go home whenever you like. Of course, if you would like to stay longer, it might be advantageous to you."

My husband, who was standing at the sidelines, suddenly interposed with, "Sir, I will tell you when we would like to go home. We would like to go home NOW!"

The last word was almost thundered with uncharacteristic loudness. It seemed to echo around the reception area, into the day-room, possibly out through the windows, and float high above the city. The doctor seemed transfixed into immobility. Suddenly, everything sprang into motion. I remember thinking how easy it was just to get up and leave — a matter of emptying a locker, negotiating a suitcase into a lift. In fact, I could not understand why I had stayed transfixed for so many weeks, cut off from my own reality?

So I arrived home one spring day. Everything seemed unchanged, the busy city streets around our house, the glass entrance hall to our building and then the apartment itself. The children seemed a little shy, a little wary as I stepped over my own threshold, for they had grown accustomed to associating me with the hospital environment. But if we had hoped everything would now become crystal clear, and we could lapse back easily and quietly into the old life, we were mistaken. For if my baffling condition was simply a complication of pregnancy, it was something so rare that the doctors with whom I maintained constant contact remained deeply baffled.

It was now that the words "nephrotic syndrome" hung in the air, but in a vague, cloud-like way, not in any concrete fashion.

Have you ever seen a human being retain so much water that there is simply nowhere in the body for it to go — it just seeps and seeps out through tiny pores in your skin? This was me, in those remaining weeks of pregnancy. I seemed now to be composed of water, an organism of water. Every time I touched my legs — I would look down and my hands would be wet. My legs swelled to such a degree that they were literally as hard and immutable as a rock. One could strike them and hear an echo, just as on striking wood. The fluid in other parts of my body seemed to be of a static amount. If I pushed on it in one direction, it simply moved along — like pushing on a fully-inflated balloon. Every movement became arduous. I spent most of the next few weeks rooted in one spot on our balcony. But if this was a nightmare, it seemed to me to be something that would ultimately pass with the end of the pregnancy.

We were shielded from the truth — like two children sheltering from the storm under a cliff. It is said that a human being cannot be shown too much of the emess — otherwise, his free choice (*bechirah*) would be eradicated. Perhaps also, he would just collapse under the sheer weight of what he sees, the seeming impossibility of it all. If we had known then, if the 'end' had been revealed, in those months ripening into spring and summer, when my body grew swollen to be grossly misshapen, it simply could not have been borne. But we did NOT know, so we paddled onward with our little oars through each day and each new challenge.

One day, nearing summer, I remember walking into Dr. Meyer's office, near the point of collapse, both physically and emotionally.

"Dr. Meyer," I said. "I am at my wits' end. I can't go on. I can hardly walk or move. You must help me."

His tired eyes behind his spectacles revealed a sense of bewilderment, but also of pity. I must have looked a strange object to him, a young pregnant Jewish woman, close to tears.

"My dear Mrs. Guttfreund," he began, "I vow that I will help you. I have something in mind — a contraption which may help to contain the fluid a little. It will take me a few days to perfect the design, and see if it can be made to my specifications."

A fortnight or so later, the contraption arrived in a box. It was all straps and buckles, and we immediately, jokingly, called it "the parachute," But in truth, it helped very little to alleviate my physical discomfort. Yet in another way, it represented something of significance for me, for it was the first shred of human sympathy that I had yet encountered in my worsening situation.

Dr. Meyer's sympathy and support was crucial to me in those difficult months. One Shabbos afternoon during these weeks — a ring on the doorbell. We both looked out to see Dr. Meyer outside our apartment building, wearing his motorcycle helmet. Knowing that we would not pick up the phone on Shabbos, he had decided to drop by after surgery hours to see how I was faring.

BY THE END OF AUGUST, MY WIFE'S DOCTORS WERE BECOMING increasingly nervous. My wife was in her eighth month, yet her problems had not been resolved. She spent three days in the hospital (a private Red Cross hospital, which housed a maternity unit). A nephrologist was called in to offer his opinion as to her baffling condition. This was Professor Bindzwanger, a colleague of Dr. Meyer, whom Dr. Meyer had consulted. On examination, he pronounced the words "kidney problem." However, he hoped that after the birth the problem would resolve itself. This, incidentally, was the first time the words "kidney problem" had been uttered. Later, they would become engraved on our hearts and on our minds, so that they would become as inseparable to us as our own skin. But for now, we listened to the words and they passed over us ever so lightly, leaving us essentially untouched. For our minds were focused elsewhere, on the upcoming birth of our child. After that, we believed or so we had been led to believe, normality would return, filling in all the gaps and rents made by this difficult time.

**Ruchi:**

SOME OF THE PLACES I HAVE TO REVISIT MENTALLY ARE AT A DISTANCE, somewhere at the end of a tram-line, in a far-off tree-lined suburb of the city. But some places are closer to me than my own bones.

They are here, in this very apartment. A balcony, a chair, the view from our bedroom window. Don't they look innocuous on this sharp spring day, as if they have never been anything other than just what they purport to be? But there you are mistaken. That chair on the balcony became a virtual prison for the last few months of my pregnancy. It was as effectively a prison as if iron bars were in place. For there I sat while helping the children to dress, my dreadfully swollen legs supported by a small stool; there I lay and dozed, when the house grew quiet, except for the sound of the cleaning-lady passing methodically from room to room. The shape of the building facing me, the balconies, awnings, potted plants trailing over balcony railings, the square plot of grass behind, became as familiar to me as my own features. Sometimes I just sat, without the strength to raise myself from the chair, to drag my body around to do daily chores. Yet despair was never there, because quite simply, we always saw an end in sight, like the beckoning lights of the shore after a long sea voyage. The end would surely come with the end of my pregnancy, and a return to something of normality. Thankfully, we never fully understood that these weeks signalled the last of one order, and the first of quite another.

❧

What I must mention too with regard to this trying "in between" time was the unbelievable kindness of my aunt and uncle and their two daughters. They decided that a change of scenery would benefit us all immensely at this point, so they took me and my husband on an extended long weekend — leaving our children behind with their grandparents. I remember their cheerfulness finally penetrating the blackness of our moods, so that we eventually forgot ourselves and our troubles. Another image from that time is that of my two cousins helping me to physically "pick up" my legs every time I would climb the stairs — for it was impossible for me to bend my knees. My legs were literally like two swollen logs — utterly lifeless and inert.

**Yanky:**


AT THE BEGINNING OF HER NINTH MONTH MY WIFE GAVE BIRTH TO A BABY girl. The birth proceeded quickly and normally and the child was completely normal. Our joy was boundless. (It was well expressed in a *Remez,* which my father-in-law discovered, in the words: "*Az tismach besulah*" — indicating that אז [Gematria 8], or eight days before תשמ״ח [as representing the year תשמ״ח - 5748] there would be a *besulah*, a girl.) After the birth too, my wife's condition appeared to stabilize, as the excess fluid appeared literally to pour from her body, and she seemed to return to normal.

Our lives, too, briefly seemed to return to normal. Was the menacing shadow which had loomed over the last few months suddenly to be dissipated, like so much chimney smoke? Was the nightmare of the past, with its freshly spun memories of baffling anxiety, the seder spent in the hospital, to retreat as mysteriously as it had come, in the clear atmosphere of daylight?

In those few weeks we dared to hope, with a new and timid hope.

22nd Elul 1987

Hope & Endurance

THROUGH OUR *NISAYON* I HAVE LEARNED SOMETHING VERY strange about the human condition: a time of trial can be a time of hope. There is a popular saying: "Hope dies hard" — and in truth, within even the most desperate of situations, there is hope. For hope is endemic to life itself, and just when one would think, according to all human logic, that "hope against hope" all hope is hopeless, look, there it emerges like tiny cracks in the frost on a windowpane, after a long winter's snows have thawed. And that surely is the secret of how we actually live through the most dire of situations, a moment at a time, with hope still lodging in our hearts, still standing its unlikely ground. This is in line with the well-known Talmudic teaching which exhorts a person never to despair of mercy, even though a sharp sword rests upon his neck.

⚜

A story is told concerning the Skulener Rebbe[2], Reb Eliezer Zusya Portugal (1896-1992). He was incarcerated in prison in Romania on the charge of instructing Jewish youths how to avoid being drafted into the army. He found himself thrown into solitary confinement, in a damp dirty cellar. Totally bereft of contact with the outside world, he pondered, even more profoundly than was his usual custom, on the meaning of every word of those prayers which he knew by heart. When he came to the *Baruch She'amar* prayer (*Shacharis*), he was deeply troubled by one particular aspect. The blessing: "*Baruch gozer umekayem*" "Blessed is He who decrees and fulfills his decrees..." seemed out of context with the tenor of this prayer, which describes the positive aspects of G-d's inter-relationship with the world. For example, "Blessed is He who has mercy on the earth," "Blessed is He who gives good reward to those who fear Him." Here, however, we have the word *gozer*, which usually refers to edicts of a harsh nature, and we say that not only does the Almighty make such decrees but He fulfills them. The Rebbe delved over and over again into the apparent mystery while simultaneously feeling a certain annoyance with himself that he had never before noticed this contradiction despite reciting these words daily. He intoned the words again and again, hoping for inspiration. And then, as though a sudden shaft of light had inexplicably been admitted to his cheerless cell, the answer struck him — indeed, it seemed so obvious, that he became ashamed that he had not thought of it earlier. The word *mekayem* apart from

---

2. *Around the Maggid's Table: Rabbi Peysach Krohn*

meaning to fulfill, also means to endure or prevail. The Almighty must sometimes issue harsh decrees with regard to individuals or nations, but at the same time, he endows man with the ability to **withstand** or endure those decrees.

This ability to "endure" is the source of this deep, almost insane optimism implanted within the heart of man. It is the hope of "better things to come" which we might imagine lived in the heart of a Jew in some or other desolate ghetto or concentration camp. Can hope still breed in such places and under such circumstances, we wonder? A real, sincere hope in the future, and for the future? The answer must be a resounding "Yes." Hope survives against all odds, a solitary blooming flower in the slow moving mud.

## Ruchi:

THE BIRTH, WHEN IT CAME, PROCEEDED REMARKABLY QUICKLY AND easily. Although the baby was tiny, she was completely healthy. My first question to the doctors and nurses was, "Is she all right?" forgetting for a moment the precariousness of my own situation. With the birth, much of the fluid that had plagued me for months, was released, but by no means all of it. When I asked the doctors if they were satisfied with the outcome, they seemed to nod absentmindedly,

"Has the fluid passed out?"

"As much as was necessary."

"It will right itself," they seemed to say in a vague, generalizing way. Looking back, I think it was probably true that they knew more than they were telling us at this point. At that time, we were so young and naive, we suspected little, took everything at face value, or perhaps we simply had no desire to probe too deeply. If "they" had said it would be all right, invested as they were with knowledge and experience, so it would be.

So my story continues with what I suppose is the first stage in an ongoing series of unpleasant tests and medical examinations, with a biopsy[3] on the kidney. This occurred a period of time after the birth of my baby, which I tend to think of in the following way. If someone would ask me now to describe that time, I would only be able to say: "It's as though I don't have all the words in my possession to describe it. Some of the words are missing." I felt unwell of course, but could not put a name to what I was feeling. And without a name, you feel almost as if you're not entitled to feel the way you do. Once a diagnosis has been made, there is momentarily a deep sense of relief. You feel like a child whose parents vaguely infer that he or she is staging an illness in order to stay home from school. However, when the doctor calls and says in his slow ponderous way "tonsillitis" or "chicken-pox," the child's condition has been named. The doubts swept away. The child now has a "right" to feel the way that he has been. He is vindicated.

***

## Yanky:

BETWEEN YOM KIPPUR AND SUKKOS, MY WIFE HAD A FURTHER SERIES of tests, the results of which were apparently far from satisfactory. Doctors advised her to undergo a biopsy of the kidney. This was carried out after Sukkos and a few days later, a diagnosis was made — nephritis. Nephritis is a persistent inflammation of the nephrons of the kidney and, as such, is one of the commonest causes of kidney failure. If the inflammation is widespread many nephrons are lost and the kidneys become unable to fil-

Sukkos

---

3. The biopsy was more of an intrusion in the body much more dangerous than the scan, so they did it more carefully. Lots of doctors around more, like a surgery, with their green coveralls, everyone discussing, joking here and there with me sweating on the operating table. This intrusion was more on the surface instead of right into the kidney so it was less painful. There has always been the risk that they may damage to the kidney because to do the biopsy they had to insert a needle to bring out a *speck* of the actual kidney. After all this, the kidney had to rest under a special pillow put in my system. Everything was more uncomfortable than painful, but of course the *fear* was always there.

ter sufficient water and waste products. These waste products begin to build up in the system and cause other symptoms, such as lethargy, weakness and discoloration of the skin.

The kidneys perform the life-sustaining job of filtering and returning to the blood-stream about two hundred quarts of fluid every twenty-four hours. Approximately two quarts are eliminated from the body in the form of urine and about one hundred and ninety-eight quarts are retained in the body. The inflammation is not due to bacteria but is caused in a very complex manner by the body's immune process. Nephritis is a painless disease. Once it exists in the body, it is often not possible to halt the disease process.

The doctors suggested a course of medication with which to fight the disease. However, after several weeks, it became clear that the situation was not improving. This was apparent from the measurement of the amount of creatinine in the blood, which provides a quick and fairly accurate guide to the filtration efficiency of the kidneys. This creatinine level now rose alarmingly, attaining a level of two or three times the normal amount.

My recording of that time now inevitably becomes bogged down in medical explanations and data, as things began to point irrefutably in one direction — the poor condition of my Ruchi's kidneys. Sometimes you work late at night in a room lit by an electric bulb. You become aware of tiny flashes blurring your field of vision. You look up from your desk, you think of possible explanations — a migraine threatening, perhaps — until suddenly your eye is drawn upwards. You notice a slight characteristic buzzing whir of moths around the neon brightness. At once everything slides into place and becomes explained. There is no migraine, nor other disturbance, simply the physical presence of moths drawn to a light. This is how I tend to think of those months before the diagnosis was made, of the false starts and wrong turns, the hoping and the subsequent dashing of hope. As soon as the fateful words "kidney disease" had been uttered, everything fell into place. In fact, armed with our new knowledge, we even wondered how we could have remained blind and innocent as it were, for so long. I suppose this is a normal enough reaction to a definite diagnosis following months of uncertainty and speculation. When I said earlier that we had come to a momentous watershed — the uttering of these two words — I meant just that, that life never would be the same, before it or after it, and that now everything "before" would necessarily be rigorously re-evaluated in this new and unrelenting light. The words "kidney disease" would literally become engraved on our hearts and on our minds, "when we sat in our house, when we walked by the way, when we lay down to sleep and we arose." Never in any waking or possibly even sleeping moment would we become rid of them. This, although my wife often would jokingly turn to me and say, "You know that up to now, I vaguely knew where they were situated and the importance of all their functions."[4]

And did the question occur to us — why this particular *nisayon*? Of course it did, and with an unremitting logic. Sometimes I would look out of our darkened window, and I would think there are so many forms of *yisurim* in this world, so many forms of instructions in the ultimate master plan. Why this form? But to this, of course, there was no answer, for surely this was simply the type of suffering we had been chosen to know over and over again.

---

4. *The kidneys have been described as the master chemists of the body. It has been said: "Bones can break, muscles can atrophy, glands can loaf, even the brain go to sleep without immediate danger to survival. But should kidneys fail, neither bones, muscles, nor glands brain could carry on." (Dr. Homer W. Smith: From Fish to Philosophies.)*

*Kidneys perform crucial and complex functions which indeed affect all parts of the body, keeping everything else in balance. Conversely, when the kidneys become damaged by disease, the other organs are affected as well. The kidneys are located behind the other abdominal organs.*

**Ruchi:**

DURING THIS DIFFICULT, AND AS IT WAS TO TURN OUT, TRANSITIONAL period, we met the doctors frequently to discuss our situation. I felt one of the doctors was being evasive. Seated in his leather chair in his office, he would never directly meet my eye. He would look at a point somewhere either to the right or left of my head when he made his deliberations. Instinctively, I felt that he was hiding something — there was some basic truth he was skirting around, like a seagull circling a wide expanse of white-tipped waves but never landing. I could see that my husband was getting edgy, and I had the feeling that he felt as I did. We would like to extract the truth from this doctor. Yanky addressed him boldly.

"Listen, doctor," he said. "My wife is a very young woman. I know that possibly for just this reason you are afraid to tell us the true situation. But in reality, I would prefer to know the extent of what we are dealing with. Let me tell you now that I am handling everything on my wife's behalf."

I could now see that this doctor was nervous. In a way, at that moment I pitied him. He was in possession of certain facts and he did not, for the life of him, know how to transmit them to this strange looking Jewish couple.

I had read somewhere that when they have to deliver dire prognoses, all doctors undergo a process of "distancing" from their patients. The less they conceive of the patient as a complete and vulnerable human being, as they are themselves, the easier to dispense the necessary words and formulae. He shifts in his chair slightly, he adjusts his glasses ever so slightly. He is waiting for my next move. He is waiting, so that I will enable him to go forward on this slippery slope. He is perhaps as dependent on my next move as I am on his, like two climbers yoked together on a rock face. If I slip, he falls; if he slips, I fall. Something in my mind starts to coalesce — why are my thoughts focused on this doctor on the other side of the desk?

He gulped once or twice, as if to prepare for his revelation. Then he clasped and unclasped his hands, which lay on the desk in front of him, a couple of times. Finally he cleared his throat, met Yanky's eye and began.

"Sir, let me tell you at once — your wife has an illness for which there is no cure. There is absolutely **no way**," and he stressed these last two words, "to reverse the damage. The only way forward is dialysis and eventually a kidney transplant. I'm sorry." With that he lowered his eyes once again.

I heard his words, and although the formula was entirely new, as I had never in my entire life, to my knowledge, heard these particular words placed in this particular order before. Oddly enough, it seemed as if they were not new at all. It seemed as if they had been waiting there all this time, and now I had turned a corner and these precise words were waiting for me just as I knew they would be. How can this be? Is this some form of premonition that prepares us to accept the worst in life?

⁂

So I am still, to all intents and purposes, sitting in this middle-aged doctor's office — still here in this very spot, have not moved so much as an inch or made so much as the tiniest gesture to betray the fact that I have heard what he has just said, nor allowed it to enter into my consciousness. He sits on; apparently, he is observing me. And suddenly, quite unpredictably, my thoughts leap to his side of the desk. Who is he? Is he married? Does he have young children perhaps? Does he understand the depth of hurt he has just had to inflict on me? Never, never again normality? But then perhaps he does not think of us as real people; a caricature to caricature, Yanky in his black hat and garb, the archetypal Jew, and with my modest attire only found in story books. Certainly not neat and clean and efficient, as his other countrymen typically are.

"Tell me, sir," I hear Yanky ask at last, and it is a shock to hear his voice, sounding as if it has travelled a great distance and seen strange sights. "Tell me, what are our options? Please, no more, no less."

"Dialysis is a process," he began gravely, "which clears out the blood artificially. Somewhat like a washing machine, in fact." Here, he gave a slight cough. "You insert two needles in two different places. One draws the blood from your body, which is then passed through the machine and cleansed, and eventually returned to your body — through the second needle. Of course this is a gross simplification, but in broad terms, this is what actually occurs. This process is called hemodialysis. There is a great deal more involved than I can explain in a few minutes, but I hope you get the overall picture. Unfortunately, dialysis is a restrictive process. Generally speaking, it must be carried out in a hospital, in a special unit, about three times a week. Alternatively, there is a relatively new development called peritoneal dialysis. This process is simpler than hemodialysis but takes more time. Also, every four hours the water must be changed, not in a hospital, but in a completely sterile place. This cannot be overstressed, because should infection ensue from lack of sterile care, the patient will end up in the hospital. There are four treatments needed every twenty-four hours, and this process does not require hospital attendance, providing proper care is taken. Once your wife is on dialysis, she will eventually be placed on a transplant list. With a transplant she can hopefully return to a normal life, without the need for constant dialysis." He coughed again to indicate that he had finished for the moment.

I listened patiently to his flow of words. He said all this in kindly, measured tones, as if explaining to a child how to cross roads, or how to deal with his first day at school. It was as if he was saying: "I am explaining all these details to you now. Later on, they will become totally familiar and known to you, and you will be expected to handle these circumstances on your own. I am holding your hand now, but soon I will let it go, and you must go forward alone."

As soon as he stopped, Yanky bursts out almost impatiently "Is that it? Is that all?"

"More or less," the doctor nodded in assent.

"No other options?"

Yanky pressed him, because he felt deep down that there must be another way for us, something the doctor was, if not exactly holding back, not putting forward as forcefully as he might.

"Well," he said, dropping his voice a little, "in rare cases, hemodialysis can be carried out at home."

"Rare cases?" Yanky queried.

"Yes, where the partner is properly trained. But this, you must understand, requires extensive and proper training..." his voiced trailed off.

"Yes?"

"Well, surely you see that this is not really a viable option in your case. You are religious Jews. You have three babies at home. Let me tell you now that I think this is less than a good idea. No, no, let me assure you, hospital dialysis is your safest and most convenient option at this point."

I didn't have time to formulate a reply. I heard Yanky say "Sir, I must disagree."

He looked at me, and then looked at Yanky as much as to say, in your position and with your lack of proper understanding, just be a good child and do as you are told. I imagined the doctor coming over to Yanky's side of the desk, patting his head and saying: "There there, run along now, don't be troublesome, and we can conclude this interview happily for everyone."

Now he glanced at his watch, as if to indicate that time had somehow run out, like sand in an egg timer, and we were now detaining him from more pressing commitments.

"I will carry out hemodialysis at home," I heard Yanky say loudly, the quiet room suddenly filling with the sound of his voice.

## Yanky:

AND IN TRUTH, WHEN I LOOK BACK, THIS WAS REALLY AN ACTION IN THE category of *Na'aseh Venishmah*. Did I know the full depth of what I was so loudly and boldly committing myself to? Of course not. I knew next to nothing — I had just listened to some medical terminologies, a few phrases, a few descriptions. But something had clicked in my head. This is the course of action I will take. I will find out later, what it involves, like a kitten unravelling a ball of wool, all the time not knowing what it will find at the end. And all the time, a strange or peculiar thought pursued me right to the very end of this whole period of trial and *nisayon*: How would it be if I were sick and my wife healthy? What would I most prefer her to do for me? Would I not wish her to help me to retain as **normal** a lifestyle as possible, spending as much time as possible in the comforting presence of my own home, with my own family, surrounded by my own furnishings and possessions? And then I imagined what would otherwise face my young wife, who had developed an inherent fear of hospitals. Endless hours spent in a cheerless surroundings, tended to by strangers, separated from family and friends, wondering through the long, lonely hours, "What are they doing at home now? What are they doing without me? Are the boys home from school? Is the baby awake?" Then the chair she sat in would come to be a dreadful prison, not only of the mind but of the spirit. How could I, in all conscience, abandon her to such a fate, if there was anything at all which lay within my power to avert it? And here I must repeat again. I am not a *tzaddik*, nor truly a great *ba'al middos*, just an ordinary young married man, young and also self-centered. But I can only say that something came upon me at that moment and lifted me up so that I rose to a new and quite uncharacteristic level of altruism. After calming Ruchi down a bit and dropping her off at home, and with the excuse that I had to take care of something, I drove to one of my favorite spots in my beautiful city. The lake was very clear on this mid-November afternoon. Its surface rippled a little, in the slight breeze as I sat, head in hands. Far away, towards its farthest slopes, two pleasure boats crossed one another, voices and hands were raised in comradely greeting as this occurred. I saw all this, but it was outside my realm of experience.

I had come to this particular spot, as I had done several times since "the beginning," to reflect a little alone, even, in an unorthodox sense,to pray. The truth was also that I could not yet face my wife. I knew it now and had accepted it with every fiber of my being. But I needed a little time, alone. Frankly, although I had had some idea of what the doctor's prognosis might be, I was actually shocked to have heard it clearly stated. Well, I said to myself, now that I have heard the *emess* (truth), I will proceed with the *emess*. I was totally alone in making such a profound decision, for my upbringing had conditioned me not to speak of illness or misfortune: "*Al tiftach peh lesoton* — Don't mention it, don't speak of it, don't try to understand or face facts — it will solve itself, or it will never happen; it will go away all by itself." This was the ever-assertive voice of my childhood, and now here I was, and I had not only to face the most difficult of facts head on, but to take this monumental decision alone — all alone. At this moment, I reflected about the way I had recited *Shemonei Esrei* since my wife's illness. Which *berachah* spoke to me, in our particular *nisayon*, the most eloquently? *Refoeinu?* Of course I said this *berachah* slowly and deliberately, inserting my wife's name. But that was not it. The one *berachah* at which I felt my whole self being drawn, in concentration and desire, was not *Refoeinu* but that which begins: "*Atah chonen l'odom da'as* — You Almighty Who grants man wisdom." Yes, I asked for wisdom, understanding, insight, perception **beyond myself** to deal with these circumstances which tested us beyond the normal run of events. Wisdom is that quality which sets man apart from the animal kingdom. With proper insight we can draw the right conclusions in every situation which we encounter, thereby achieving intellectual discernment. And since that time too, at the risk of sounding naive, I felt that Something, a Divine Presence, was there guiding me continually at my elbow, propelling me, leading me, granting me an understanding of strange and never before dreamt of situations. Truly, I did not act or make vital decisions, during those years **alone**, and of my own volition. Ideas, plans, resolutions all fell into my head inexplicably, like inspiration does to a writer or composer. I was a man inspired. Perhaps this is the literal meaning of *Siyata diShmaya*. Now this inspiration spoke to me again. It said to me in clear, no-nonsense tones: "Go home and deal with the stark facts. Discuss everything with her. Prepare her for the worst, for if you try to spare her the worst, she will lack the mental preparedness for the eventual and inevitable outcome." So I left the lake that day and wound my way upwards and homewards. I sat my wife down. She was a little pale, but nonetheless composed. She knew that this was one of those moments of decision in a crisis for which one waits and waits with a terrible longing to know the truth.

I said to her, "My dear Ruchi, this is the story. The need for dialysis may come tomorrow, it may come in a few months, but come it will, as surely as night follows day."

She nodded. But then, demonstrating that she had not really accepted the enormity of what we had heard earlier, she said in a clear, almost childlike tone, "But perhaps after all, there is a way for me to become healthy again?"

I shook my head. Only the Almighty Himself knows how much it cost me in pain and tears to shake my head and dash her timid hopes, like waves dashed relentlessly against a cliff wall. But this was just the same way in which my hopes had been dashed a few hours earlier in the doctor's office.

"Listen," he had said to me, his voice dropping a little, almost confidentially. "If your wife should become healthy again, it would be acclaimed as an unprecedented miracle in the world of medicine. This infection, this nephritis," and he had emphasised every syllable, as if taking part in some elocution class, "literally burns out the kidney. Believe me, there is no way out in the whole wide world, except dialysis and transplant."

"Perhaps, if I travel abroad? Perhaps, get a second opinion?" I had interjected.

"Travel, go around the world, but you will come face to face with the same eventuality. It will sit there waiting for you, like some grinning toad, when you come back."

I digested his words.

"Go the way everyone has to go," the voice inside me said to me, even though I could see nothing but a deep, all-encompassing darkness. "Go forward, and somewhere, somehow there will be a light, an exit, an end to all this complexity. Some day, everything will become quiet and simple again."

And now, I faced my wife. I took her hopes and crushed them with my words. I told her that soon, very soon perhaps, the path would narrow into dialysis. For this she must be prepared, because everything pointed that way. Eventually there would come a *yeshuah*, a salvation — but only along this path.

I was twenty-three years old, by the way, when these conversations transpired, when I sat in our peaceful kitchen, speaking quietly for fear of waking the children already asleep in their bedrooms off the hallway in our apartment.

**Ruchi:**

I AM BACK IN THE HOSPITAL AGAIN. I AM LYING ON MY BACK. BUT still, oh, how can I describe it — the reality hasn't hit me yet. In my mind it was only another stage connected with pregnancy and childbirth: an extension of the painful things one has to go through to have children. I admit the word biopsy, with its connotations, had shaken me a little but not too deeply. The conviction still remained embedded deep within my psyche that, "This will pass. Of course it is unpleasant, something to be got through, but no doubt it will pass, blow away into the more substantial air of my real life, which I must, by the way, be getting on with." This here — see this grayish hospital wall, that is all I saw as I lay face downwards — hard, cold, blankness; a maze of doctors and nurses carrying on conversations over my downturned head. Quick, the pillow — bury your head in its welcoming whiteness. Buried feelings wash over me like waves: Don't move, dangerous, cold, gray steel, anaesthetized, punctured, clenching fingers so tightly the blood stops flowing — hands turn white. Over soon — back to the apartment, back to the children and the daily routine and all its multi-layered exigencies. Better that than this. All over now, lying against a rolled pillow as the minutes tick by. Oh, the endless waiting, the pain, the waiting to be given permission to do something as inherently simple as getting off the bed, putting on my coat and shoes, and going back into the street of trams and shoppers and solidly real life.

❧

As we waited for the results of the biopsy, our lives continued as normally as possible. This had to be. Why should the bloom of our children's lives be tarnished by the long shadow which now touched ours? We knew we were waiting for a moment of truth of sorts, but for the time being, this thought had to be pushed far into the back of our minds, like Pesach dishes into their concealing closets. When the results finally came, we were half expecting them.

During this waiting time, too, we undertook a journey to America. We thought that in another country, another doctor would wave a magic wand and take back all the cruel things that had been uttered. We actually visited a prominent professor in Manhattan and were given the same opinion.

As we said goodbye to my mother and my Aunt Bracha, at the airport, ready to leave America, I ran back to my mother, threw myself on her shoulder and sobbed and sobbed. My mother was overwhelmed. She hugged me and started crying with me.

Upon looking at this scene my aunt cried out, "What is it, Malka? Why is she so hysterical?"

But it was as if I already felt that something horrendous was looming over us. It was as if we felt we were living in a black cloud. We would run as far as possible from the doctor's words, to the end of the earth perhaps, and we would find a way out, an escape route. We were like those famous tunnelers from German prison camps, whose task extended over many months, and who worked against all odds. In their story the supports of the tunnels fell in, or if they succeeded in leaving the parameters of the camp, they were shot by guards stationed in the watchtowers. In the same way, in reality, we were in the hands of the Master Planner, and all our efforts to evade what was clearly mapped out for us in the years ahead were like the squirming of a trapped insect.

Winter, 5748
1987/88

THAT PERIOD DRAWING INTO WINTER, WAS ONE OF WAITING, waiting for one door to open and another to close. What can I tell you about how we lived through those weeks, as the days began to shorten and snow fell through the crisp air? These were weeks in which we adjusted ourselves to our new future. We understand suffering to be a tool which puts everything in the right proportions at a stroke, and more adequately than any philosophical notions or rationales in the world. It is as swift and non-sparing as the operation of a child's magnetic drawing board. The child draws a picture with a special pen, painstakingly filling in the strokes, and eventually he achieves a total effect. Then, he pulls down the shutter and all his work disappears in one fell swoop. The picture is changed irrevocably. This is suffering. We busy ourselves with our little schemes, our day-to-day small-minded preoccupations. Suddenly a new situation arises, which quite simply shrinks everything into the right proportions. So that what is important, what unimportant, significant or trivial, all becomes clear as daylight and at a stroke. Suffering is truly not marginal to life, not a tacked-on addendum, a hasty afterthought; it is a gift from Hashem. It allows us to see the truth. It enables us to achieve purpose. But first one must learn to read the language. This is what we were trying to achieve in those weeks leading up to dialysis. We understood, "G-d is talking to us, He has given our life a totally new and inconceivable direction. What does He want from us?" (Our Rabbis refer to Tishah b'Av, the day of utter and historic destruction as *mo'ed* — a meeting, because paradoxically, it is within the extremes of destruction and tragedy that Hashem's Hand in history can most clearly be seen. So, too, within the lives of individuals. Tragedy is *mo'ed* — a righting of priorities, a meeting place within one's own "little" fate, with Hashem.)

**Yanky:**

YES, THIS IS PERHAPS SOMETHING OF WHAT WE FELT DEEP DOWN. BUT despite all this, don't think that this was an easy or simple time. There were so many pressures. I prepared our respective families for the almost inevitable likelihood that my wife would soon have to go on dialysis. But they refused to accept this lying down.

"Why think of the worst? Perhaps it will never happen!"

"One never knows, there are new medical developments taking place every day."

"Nothing is ever sure. Why be a pessimist?"

"Why make her depressed? This is not what you as her husband should be doing. You should be raising her spirits."

As a result of these pressures, I reflected long and often over whether I was actually taking the right line. Were they right? Was I being a cruel prophet of doom? Was all this talk of the inevitability of dialysis unnecessarily pessimistic? I was driven at this time, torn by doubts. Sometimes at night, I would awaken suddenly, shaken by strange dreams. Then the heated voices and counterarguments of the day would return to haunt me. Right or wrong? This way or that? The long road or the short?

There is a famous parable about a traveler who comes to a crossroads. There are two options open to him: Either a short path, which is strewn with thorns, wild animals, highwaymen, all conceivable dangers of the roads, or a longer path, which is nevertheless straight and open.

This is something of how I viewed our predicament at this point. The way forward was surely the long path of dialysis, which would ultimately happen, if not tomorrow, then the next week or month. I resolved not to listen to any more arguments to the contrary. Despite the family's cheerful prognostications for the future, I prepared my wife for the worst.

Purim | As it happened, the change in situation occurred quite suddenly. A week before Purim, the creatinine[5] level in her blood began to rise quite sharply. At this point, Ruchi really felt quite ill. Her skin was yellow. She felt persistently nauseated. By the time Purim had passed, she was feeling little short of awful. Now she was admitted to the hospital to be trained for hemodialysis. However, in order for hemodialysis to take place, a fistula or shunt had to be made. This means a connection between an artery and a

---

5. *Creatinine is a normal waste material produced in the body and removed by the kidneys. A quick and fairly accurate guide to the filtration efficiency of the kidneys is obtained by measuring the amount of creatinine in the blood.*

vein to allow access to the bloodstream. This is usually made in the arm, but must be carried out under general anaesthetic.[6] Meanwhile, things were rapidly deteriorating with regard to my wife's condition. Her creatinine level indicated that she had now reached the stage where dialysis was urgently necessary for her. In other words, she was in advanced renal failure.

❦

## Nurse:

EIGHT BEDS IN A LARGE, SQUARE ROOM, FOUR ON EITHER SIDE, TOO close to one another. All beds are occupied.

Two or three are fairly new patients of several months' standing, the others are pretty much veterans. For them, dialysis holds

---

6. *Vascular access: Before hemodialysis can be performed, a way must be made to connect the dialysis machine to the patient's bloodstream, so that blood can flow to the machine and back to the patient. This is called "vascular access." Vascular is an adjective meaning "of or having vessels." There are two main forms of vascular access:*

*1. Fistula*

*A fistula is a direct connection under the skin between an artery and a vein. Some of the blood that previously flowed to the hand then passes directly into the vein. Over the next month the vein grows larger, due to the increased quantity of blood passing through it. When the vein has enlarged, it is then possible to pass special needles into the fistula, to carry blood to and from the dialyzer each time dialysis is needed. In a right-handed person the fistula is made in the left forearm, and vice-versa. This allows the patient to use his better hand to insert needles for himself. Fistulae are used all over the world for vascular access for dialysis.*

*2. Shunt*

*For the person who requires urgent dialysis, there is no time to develop a fistula. Instead, rapid vascular access can be made by placing a shunt in the leg on the inner side of the ankle. A shunt is an artificial connection between an artery and vein. A shunt can be used for dialysis within minutes of its being made. It continues to be used for some time, while a fistula is created for longer term use.*

*Rapid short term access to the circulation can also be obtained by inserting a special catheter into a large vein which passes behind the collar bone.*

almost no terrors. They know every knob, every pipe, every hitch possible in the routine. In the corner old Thomas is at his machine, book in hand. He acknowledges me as I enter the room, by lowering his book ever so slightly, and winking with his left eye. He looks so solid, weather-beaten and healthy, his checked shirt open at the neck, that I have to remind myself each time I see him that he is in fact, a very sick man. In the other corner sits Fraulein__, retired schoolteacher. She is reading. She is unmarried. She comes and leaves alone, although on rare occasions, a middle-aged niece accompanies her and sits nervously through the first half-hour. After this she makes some excuse and leaves.

Every few months, there is a change as some patients leave and others arrive. Perhaps one is liberated from dialysis — whisked away to be "transplanted." Very occasionally there is a death. For a while after this, the atmosphere in the square room becomes more subdued. The desultory chatter that normally hangs in the air seems to peter into nothingness and an awful silence descends on the ward. The others look soulfully out through the windows, like survivors of a great catastrophe. Everyone is alone with his thoughts. But by the next day, the atmosphere has begun to lighten. Patients on dialysis seem to be hung in a strange balance. They are ill, but the machine keeps them alive. For the hours they are on dialysis, they are in communion with the machine which is, strictly speaking, an artificial extension of their own bodies. Sticking needles into yourself and watching your blood flow out through rubber tubes goes against all basic human instincts, as does sitting in a chair for hours on end, in one position. Also, many patients nurse a secret fear that the needles will fall out. But the human spirit is remarkably adaptable. Most patients, given time, learn to adapt to these new exigencies. Then dialysis becomes, if not exactly normal, a way of life.

I qualified as a nurse over twenty-two years ago. After a few years in general nursing, I decided to specialize as a dialysis nurse.

People often ask me why — why this particular area of nursing? I suppose part of the answer is the intensity. In other wards, short-term relationships develop between staff and patients. There is a constant ebb and flow of humanity. Patients enter the hospital, they remain there for weeks, sometimes months, but eventually, the treatment they are having comes to an end, the scars of the operation heal. They leave the hospital environs, arms full of flowers, full of fond goodbyes and promises to keep in touch. These have mostly flown from their heads by the time they have reached the bottom of the brownstone steps and entered the waiting taxi. They have been reabsorbed into the world outside the glass doors, where cars come and go, where there is ordinariness and health. But the dialysis unit is something of a different category. Patients attending a dialysis unit are not ill, in the extreme sense of the word, but then neither are they well. They are hung in a precarious balance between health and sickness, life and death. The thing that swings the balance is the machine and the skill in using it. Over the months and years, a strange sort of three-way relationship develops between the patient, the nurse and the machine. The machine is always at the center, all-knowing, all-seeing. One flick of the switch, one misplaced needle, and all is lost. This is the underlying drama enacted almost daily in the oh so calm square room of the eight beds. This current trickles beneath the bright, brittle chatter, and intermittent laughter. And then you get to know these patients, more than intimately, almost inside out, while they're chained to their machines. You begin to recognize all their quirks, fears, small acts of courage. You know just how each of them would react if the needle refuses to penetrate, or the machine begins to bleep. You have seen Mrs. Guttfreund slumped forward on her chair, in a faint, countless times. As you bend over her you know at which exact moment , her eyes will flutter open and she will murmur: "Ah, nurse... so sorry, so very sorry...."

It is in my square office too, leading on to Professor Bindzwanger's room, that I have seen enacted so many human dramas, when patients have come face to face with the inevitable, the blank, staring, dumb-as-stone fact that they will be unable to live through another week, another month without the machine. These are patients who have just been told that they have reached end-stage renal failure, or put another way, the end of the difficult tormenting road that they have traveled to this point. In this small space, crammed between cubicle and wash-basin and my desk, partitioned off with graying net curtain, I have risen and caught countless patients in my arms. Have you ever seen an adult cry and cry — until like a child, there is no more fight; they have cried themselves into silence and a sort of wearied resignation?

Every night, when I return to my quiet apartment, shaded by quiet trees, I cannot quite divest myself of the images of that partic-ular day. They are with me still, like a shadow that stalks your every movement, as I enter my small kitchen and begin to prepare supper for myself.

Rather a strange occurrence today. As I sat in my square office, attending to my paperwork, I could hear the sound of voices ris-ing and falling in Professor Bindzwanger's office. It sounded like a couple, youngish — for the man's voice was quite firm and vig-orous. The woman's voice rose and fell melodiously. Then a sud-den silence, and a sound of heartfelt sobbing. I have seen such sit-uations too often, I reflected, as I looked out onto the square of green beyond my window. The new shoots were beginning to push their way through winter-hardened soil, in preparation for spring. Outside, new beginnings — a new cycle of rebirth was enacting itself; inside that office, I reflected, a young couple's hopes perhaps were being obliterated into nothingness, like waves dashed against a cliff wall. I heard the creak of chairs against the polished floors. The interview was at an end. I sat on the edge of my chair, rigidly waiting. They might need a shoulder to cry on so I positioned myself, ready to provide just that. The door opens. A man steps out. He is young, fairly tall, red-bearded and bespectacled. His clothing looks as though he has stepped out of the nineteenth century — a walking anachronism, dark, immaculate frock coat, dark hat. Now, I notice he wears sidelocks. In my mind's eye, something clicks. Those countless newsreels I have watched, alone in my darkened apartment, footage from concentration camps and prewar Poland. Germans — scissors in hand, brutally hacking off a beard or sidelocks. Those children with shaven heads, covered with oversize skullcaps, large, mournful, half-starved eyes hanging in pale faces. This man is a Jew, and a Hassidic Jew, if I am correct, a member of an ultra-Orthodox sect. Simultaneously, the word associations form almost unwanted in my mind — Hassidic Jew — other-worldly, ethereal. All this flashed through my mind so quickly that I hardly noticed the tall, well groomed young woman a step or two behind him. Her appearance, in contrast to that of her husband's, presented nothing out of the ordinary. A young woman, such as one might see any day, in a smart department store or strolling, pushing a baby carriage in the center of town. But I saw her eyes were red-rimmed with unshed tears. She had obviously been crying, quite copiously and had somehow, at the expense of great effort managed to stop. That is, the tears were not flowing at the moment, but she looked as if the slightest word or touch would unleash them all again.

"Good afternoon Mr. and Mrs. Guttfreund," I said in my best professional voice. "What seems to be the problem?"

The man began to speak in a soft, rhythmic voice.

"This is my wife, Rachel. As you can see," he paused, "she is a young woman. It has just been confirmed again by Professor Bindzwanger that there is no hope. She will soon have to begin dialysis. Obviously we are both very upset. We have three small children at home..." he spread his hands in a gesture of utter helplessness. At his mention of the children, the wife began to visibly tremble. She was about to burst into tears again. I stepped forward — I remember noticing the faded gray patch of floor just where she stood — and caught her tallish, slight figure in my arms.

She cried and cried — tears from true gut — not just falling from the eyes, but deep tears, from within her splintered heart. "Sha, sha," I cooed, as if to quiet a child whose toy is broken or who has grazed his knee, as if my comforting could put it all to rights. Meanwhile, the husband had stepped to the window and was looking silently out. At length, her body seemed to still itself; she was all spent, like a broken spring. At length she disengaged herself from my shoulder, and with a deep sigh, straightened her skirt, her blouse.

"So sorry," she muttered, almost ashamed. To have cried in front of a stranger, her eyes said, a temporary aberration — it won't happen again.

"Wait, sit a moment," I said, motioning her husband to a chair. "And there is no need to apologize. This is my job. I am here to give comfort. You are not the first and, unfortunately, I don't suppose you will be the last to cry in my arms."

She nodded wordlessly, her dark blue eyes translucent with her recent crying.

"You know something," I began, seeking for the right words (for in each case, the "right words" are different), "dialysis is not the end of the world."

At this, the young husband turned to his wife, as if with an imperceptible nod.

"We have patients who have lived this way for years, yes, many young people too. It takes some getting used to, some emotional and physical adjustment and of course, there are always teething problems, but ultimately, with a bit of willpower, we get on top of it. And you'll find this a very friendly unit, our patients feel almost like" and I searched for the word "a family."

"But to live, to be dependent on a machine," she shook her head "it seems so — so...." her voice trailed off.

"Let us be practical," her husband spoke to her in a low voice. "We know, we know how hard this is for you, for all of us, but believe me, there is no other way. If this is what the Almighty wants from you, now, at this moment in our lives, we must learn to cope with it, as well as we possibly can. For all our sakes," he added on a lower note.

She nodded wordlessly and I nodded, reinforcing his words.

"I personally am willing to give you any support you need — day or night. We have an excellent team here, who in time will explain every detail of the dialysis process to you. As you get to know the procedure, it will all become less strange, I promise you."

At this, they rose and I rose too. I stretched out my hand to the husband, in the usual gesture. To my surprise, his arm did not leave the side of his frockcoat.

"I am sorry, Nurse, but Jewish Law forbids any physical contact between men and women, even the slightest touch. However, please do not consider this as any impoliteness or slight on your person. I am more than grateful to you for your kindness to us today. It means so much to us to know that there are people who understand, sympathize and will be there to guide us when the time comes."

I was forcibly struck by the richness of his expression and also by the unusual sensitivity of emotion that it displayed.

"We will meet again," I reiterated. "Until then, take care."

At this I sprinted down the corridor, towards the patiently waiting ward.

## Yanky:

AS WE TURN TO GO, RUCHI MOTIONS THAT SHE WISHES TO SPEAK. "I feel that there are good people here, this is a good hospital, and with Hashem's help, all will be well."

With that one remark, I enter her inner world. For know that I am essentially an onlooker, however intimately connected to the events transpiring. She is the suffering, feeling party, the one who must face it all alone ultimately, despite the care and lovingkindness lavished on her by those who surround her. I see her suddenly as a lone, shrinking figure. I remember all those nights that I have heard her pacing the hallway of our apartment talking to herself, exhorting herself to be strong: "Hang on, this will soon pass." I see her literally clinging to the *mezuzah* of our bedroom. What prayers pass her lips, I wonder. That is why, when she says: "This is a good hospital," I do not challenge her statement. I just smile a little.

I know that in the darkness of this ever-thickening *nisayon*, she clings to every ray of hope, every tiny splinter of good feeling. To put yourself into her situation or that of any suffering individual, picture yourself in a very dark cave with a group of people. Everyone is silent, totally helpless in the all-enveloping blackness. Suddenly, someone reaches into his pocket and removes a small candle. He fumbles around for a match, lights it and then lights the candle. Despite its size, the tiny candle lights up the entire cave for everyone. Nothing is more appreciated than that little candle. But when the group finally finds its way out of the cave, blinking in the sunshine, the light from the candle, which but moments before was so appreciated, has paled into total insignificance. In much the same way, one is intensely aware of the Divine Presence, the *Shechinah*, while one is in the throes of some *nisayon* or terrible era of suffering. Then everything has greater intensity. Each word of compassion or kindness, however random each particle of hopeful feeling, assumes both new proportions and significances. However, it is a mistake to think that when the suffering passes, with it passes the extra intensity of the *Shechinah*. It is there, radiant, all-enveloping like the daylight. The fact is simply that we are no longer aware of It. It largely goes unrecognized.

**Ruchi:**

TODAY, IT IS TIME TO VISIT THE LAST HOSPITAL IN THE LINK — THE low two-storied hospital on the other side of the city. If we go by public transport, it may take us just under an hour, changing trams and finally waiting for a small private bus in a suburb high above in the city. As the bus chugs up to the top of the hill, and the driver calls out the name of the hospital, we catch our first glimpse of the hospital complex. This, in a way, is the place most saturated with memories for me. This waiting area, for example, is a corner in a busy corridor, with some green chairs laid out in a square. Here I paced after the operation was over, in a mood of deep uncertainty bordering on despair. I remember too, the good feeling I had had when I first entered this hospital, that nothing untoward would happen to me here. Perhaps it was something to do with the absence of the typical smell which characterized the other hospitals for me. Well, at any rate, this good feeling I spoke of proved to be utterly false. For my time in this "low-walled" hospital was checkered with confusion, despondency and a feeling of hitting rock bottom. After the episode of the fistula operation, it was also the place where the very first dialysis was carried out. You see those lawns, beyond the patio door? Round and round these grounds I would walk, as if to escape from the inevitability of going on the machine. Of course, ultimately there was no escape possible. But that's another story, belonging to a later epoch. The operation itself was carried out under local anaesthetic. I was also given a tranquilizer, but since I already did not feel too well, was nauseous and weak, also dreadfully apprehensive, it was all a nightmarish haze. I remember the ever-returning pain and also the sense of immobility, with my arm wrapped like a hot loaf of garlic bread. I prayed over and over again for an end to all this, when all the while I knew deep down that this was but the beginning of a long and arduous road.

# Yanky:

BY THE TIME RUCHI WAS OFFICIALLY ADMITTED TO THE HOSPITAL, her physical condition was rapidly deteriorating. Her creatinine level was now such that she should have undergone dialysis there and then, but she was not ready. Her lungs were full of water. She was vomiting and felt continually nauseated. Her color was yellow and her skin was what I can only describe as transluscent. After the operation, which was carried out one spring day under local anaesthetic, she was confused and disorientated. She had no feeling in her arms. She could not keep food down. The arm could not be used for dialysis for two weeks, for the wound was too fresh and needed to be allowed to heal. Her condition continued to give grave concern to the doctors. When the cretanine level rose to one thousand, they were thoroughly alarmed. Let me explain at once that a creatinine of one thousand is not just a number. What it means literally is that the blood is full of poisons. The kidney is now simply unable to clear the urine. Drugs were prescribed to lower the level, but these proved ineffective. At this point, Uncle Chayim offered us a Kabalustic cure consisting of some pounded flax. She drank this mixture and, miraculously, the level dropped from over eleven hundred to eight hundred. The doctors were astonished. Inevitably it then began to creep back up again, but nonetheless, in this way we had gained a few days. As it began to rise steadily again, a gray-haired doctor approached me one morning as I entered the hospital corridors.

He began abruptly, not beating about the bush.

"Look here, I'm afraid we really cannot delay any longer. If your wife's creatinine gets any higher, we simply cannot afford to wait until her arm heals; we must pass a catheter into the large vein in her neck, and carry out dialysis that way. I am afraid this might prove uncomfortable and even painful, but nevertheless, you must prepare your wife for the possibility."

A cloud of blackness passed before my eyes. It was as if a great sob broke on some inward shore of hurt and I cried out within me: "*Ribbono shel Olam*, what do you want from your children? We have accepted the fact that my wife will not get better, that she will have to sit at the dialysis machine, despite her comparative youth. But now this — a dialysis which will shatter any peace of mind she might be able to muster? How do I tell a young, once untroubled wife such news?" How I walked down the corridor and found myself at her bedside, I shall never know. But there I was, sitting in her small hospital room, which should have held two beds but held only one. She must have been drowsing. She looked up and said immediately, with some terrible insight: "What is it? Please, tell me at once!"

"Ruchi," I began. "You know your blood is now full of poisons. That is why you feel so desperately sick and unwell. The doctors say they cannot afford to wait, for your arm to heal."

"They must start dialysis," she resigned.

"Yes, but since your arm is not ready...." my voice trailed off.

"Then how?"

"In the neck..."

She began to sob — noiselessly, but the sobs shook her whole being.

"It's so difficult..." she sobbed at last.

"You will be given the strength...." I articulated weakly, scarcely knowing what I was saying. To this there was no audible reply.

When Ruchi and I talk about this period of our lives, we discuss one point. What was the worst moment in the entire saga? I always state that those few days, when we feared that the worst would take place, in the form of dialysis in the neck, when every day brought a worsening of her condition, physical and mental, when I drove back and forth through the city traffic to this hospital, not knowing how we would get through the next day, the next hour, when the prospect of Pesach loomed through all the confusion and uncertainty, this was the very lowest point for me. I felt an awful looming sense of darkness, as if my whole universe were about to cave in and crumble to nothingness. If your house is burning down, you say to yourself, maybe at least one room will be spared. Then as the flames continue unabated in intensity, you realize, "No, all is lost." All at once you feel stripped, denuded of all those symbols and supports with which you have so carefully forearmed yourself. No, in this moment, you are conscious of the true all-destroying force of the fire — and also of your utter helplessness in the face of it. Your only consolation is prayer.

*"The second level of trust in G-d is distinguished by the addition of one's hopes and expectations of an internal seeking of G-d with one's heart and an external one in the form of prayer." The difference between hoping with one's heart and seeking with one's heart is that he who uses the former only waits for G-d's salvation or help, but does not turn his heart to Him pleadingly or imploringly. The latter however, exhibits a greater level of trust, because his prayer fortifies his trust in G-d; his outward expression strengthens his inwardness. In addition, since man shows his submission to G-d through prayer, by recognizing that only He can help and save, it automatically strengthens his trust, expectations and hope in G-d's salvation — for the more man depreciates his own ego, the more he appreciates his reliance on G-d.*

Unbeknown, our prayers must have pierced the Heavenly Veil, for somehow my wife managed to get through ten whole days. At this point, her arm was examined carefully and pronounced fit for dialysis to be carried out. The very next morning, she was to be dialyzed. This would be *erev Pesach*, and the situation would now necessitate another Pesach to be spent in hospital. This took place not a moment too soon, for by now she was in a dangerously weakened state. Her life itself was threatened by further delay.

I remember well a conversation I had with my mother-in-law the night before this dialysis took place. This transpired around our kitchen table, which had been freshly scrubbed in preparation for Pesach. In the kitchen everything gleamed as the last rays of the sun filtered through the long rectangular windows and slanted off faucets, work surfaces, tabletop. It was a scene of domestic orderliness, but within our hearts, all was blackness and confusion.

"Perhaps," she began, "she will recover now. Yes, there will be a miracle, and why not, we believe in miracles. Her condition may yet be reversed and she will emerge as she was."

I looked at her across the table. I saw that she was not speaking out of any sense of the reality of the situation but that she had erected some kind of fantasy in which she floated, cushioned from the truth of what was transpiring. At this point, I came to the realization that the parents of a child who is diagnosed with a disease, build a protective wall that does not allow the truth to penetrate, as it is too painful to face the facts. Other relatives can generally face reality much quicker, since they are a bit removed.

"Listen," I said, "we can only get through this thing if we face facts. Your daughter is in advanced renal failure. Nothing, and I repeat nothing, other than an open miracle, can reverse this reality or make it go away. Believe me, we have pursued every option, every alleyway, every obscure line of hope. There is no hope along this path. Do not think this is not painful for me, just because I speak in this bold way. It is worse than pain. It is a drowning out of my whole world. But deep within my bones — I feel — I trust that just because we have reached a point of ultimate blackness, when we no longer know which way to turn, the light of salvation is close at hand. Imagine a dark tunnel. As one enters and travels further, the light from the tunnel entrance grows dimmer. Then, one reaches a point of total blackness and disorientation. But here is another light — a light from the exit. This can only be reached by the one who is moving, when one arrives at the very darkest point in the tunnel. At this very instant, one is closest to beginning to see the infiltration of the exit light."

But my mother-in-law began to cry — even as she nodded in assent to my words. For, I had forced her to let go of the light of hope for a return to normal life, and reach towards another unknown light, which would only become apparent as we progressed through this *nisayon*. And this was an agonizing wrench. In truth, she had had to let go of the entire past.

**Ruchi:**

NOW, WE ARRIVE AT A NEW ERA IN OUR PROLONGED JOURNEY, A NEW milestone, a new stopping place. Dialysis is not just a medical procedure. It is a way of life. Anybody who has been on dialysis for even the shortest spell of time will attest to the overwhelming truth of this statement. This is the way the medical textbooks describe it:

Dialysis

> Some people have a few months or years of warning that their kidneys are failing. Thus they will have some time to get used to the prospect of dialysis and gain some idea of the restriction that it will place on their life. However, advanced chronic renal failure may creep on unknown, so that dialysis may be necessary shortly after the diagnosis is made. For people in this group, the sudden change in the way of life may be a major shock. Over a period of a few weeks a person has to change from independent life to one of frequent visits to a hospital and treatment by a dialysis machine. Even for patients who have had warning, this period may prove to be a worrying and stressful time.

But first let me explain what dialysis is. It is not a cure for kidney failure. It is a procedure that replaces some of the kidney's normal functions and is performed when a person's own kidneys can no longer function adequately to maintain life.[7] Treatment with dialysis is necessary when a person experiences kidney failure ,when both kidneys are working below five percent of normal. Dialysis, like healthy kidneys, keeps the body in balance by performing the following functions: removing waste products, including salt and excess fluids that build up in the body; maintaining a safe level of blood chemicals in the body, such as potassium, sodium and chloride, and controlling blood pressure. There are two basic kinds of dialysis, hemodialysis and peritoneal dialysis. The type of dialysis that we chose, for several

---

7. *In the United States today, more than ninety thousand individuals undergo dialysis treatment to stay alive.*

well-considered reasons, was hemodialysis. With this procedure, an artificial kidney (hamodialyzer) is used to remove waste products from the blood and restore the body's chemical balance. In order to get the patient's blood to the artificial kidney, it is necessary to create access to the patient's blood vessels. This requires surgery on an arm or a leg. Once healing occurs, two needles are placed, one in the artery and one in the vein side of the fistula. In this way the patient is attached to the dialysis machine. The artificial kidney has two compartments, one for the patient's blood and one for the cleaning solution called dialyzate (filter). A thin porous membrane separates these compartments. Blood cells, protein and other important substances in the blood remain in their compartment because they are too large to pass through the holes of the membrane. Smaller waste products in the blood, such as urea, and creatinine and excess water, pass through the membrane and are washed away. Needed substances such as calcium or dextrose (sugar) can be added to the dialyzate, and can move from the dialyzate through the membrane into the patient's blood. The time required for each hemodialysis treatment is determined by the patient's remaining kidney function, fluid weight gain between treatments and the build-up of harmful chemicals between treatments. On the average, each hemodialysis treatment lasts approximately three to four hours and is usually necessary three times a week. These are the bald medical descriptions of dialysis. And in truth, by the time we reached this point in our long *nisayon*, we were quite familiar with the technical terms. We thouroughly understood the meaning of kidney failure, dialysis, and even transplantation. What one can never visualize is the true bone-deep knowing that comes only from undergoing this thing, step by halting step, knowledge on your own person, in your bones. This runs like an undercurrent beneath the medical descriptions, so that later you turn the terminologies over in your mind and say: "Yes, but it's not really like that — it's different, in so many subtle ways."

My husband was not present at the first dialysis. He was too exhausted, washed up on a shore of deep physical and mental weariness. So that in the hospital of the long hallways, in the square sunny room, I was dialyzed for the very first time.

# Nurse:

DO YOU REMEMBER THE YOUNG JEWISH COUPLE, OF WHOM I SPOKE? Today, the wife was dialyzed for the first time. She was weak with the typical yellow translucent glow to her skin. Ten days ago she was operated on, and a fistula made. At first, when I arrived at the ward to take her to the dialysis room, she seemed resigned about the prospect, nonchalant almost. I was surprised. Normally, patients express quite a high level of apprehension and anxiety. From what I remembered of her in my interview room, she was obviously deeply emotional. This calmness seemed unreal. This time she had come without her husband. I took her arm. She was much taller than me, and normally imposing, I imagined. Now she looked like some shrunken wax, doll. We approached the room together; the patient being wheeled there with her mother and father-in-law at her side.

She was so weak, so skinny and at the same time bloated from the excessive water which was retaining in her system, that my heart went out to her. She had an almost otherworldly look at times due to the translucence and pallor of her countenance, and at other times, she looked more like a frightened bird. During the first dialysis, she clung to her mother's hand as she flittered between consciousness and darkness, like a drowning man to a raft. She was muttering, odd phrases too, in a low, scarcely audible tone.

Leave me alone were three words, I managed to decipher. Then her voice would trail and she would be in a dead faint or vomiting violently. I do hope, for her sake that things will improve.

Of course, I often feel a sense of emotional involvement with my patients, but this case seemed to me particularly poignant. She seemed so young and at once vulnerable, but also with her life outspread before her — a husband, three young children. It seemed to me immensely sad that her life was being curtailed in this way. And then, this was a couple that seemed somehow a little 'out of step with the world. Perhaps it is the strangeness of their garb and customs that suggested this to me, but at any rate, Jews and Judaism have long held a peculiar fascination for me.

The secret of Jewish survival in history against all the odds seems to me to be a remarkable example of overwhelming faith, loyalty to an ideal, self-discipline and sheer pluckiness. They have survived, as has been said, 'with their hands tied behind their backs', showing no weakening nor infirmity on their parts."

This interest has stimulated me to read books by both Jewish authors and those dealing with aspects of Jewish culture. Now, strangely enough in this cosmopolitan city, with only a small Jewish population, these two people have been washed up on the shore of my daily working experience. It was strange, or yet another example of the mysterious workings of Providence.

### Yanky:

THIS WAS THE SECOND YEAR THAT I FACED THE PESACH PREPARATIONS alone. I was beginning to dread this particular Yom Tov, which I had always loved and looked forward to. However, by some miraculous turn of events which proved to us — if proof we still needed that our Father in Heaven was watching over us in our ordeal — my wife was dismissed from the hospital in time to join us at home for seder night. At a seder table laden with silver and crystal, light from the chandeliers catching the light from below and playing with it delicately, the entire family gathered: parents, children, grandchildren. It looked like a conventionally joyous family gathering. That is, until one glanced at the sofa, where a pallid, yellowish, gaunt young woman, a veritable bag of skin and bone, lay prostrate on the comfortable couch. She had been fixed up like a doll to make her appearance more acceptable, more palatable. But she slept virtually from the opening words of *Kadesh* to *Leshana habo'oh biYerushalayim*. All the timeless questions, discussions, songs, symbols — all passed over her consciousness lightly, stealing over her like a thief at night, grazing her but not really touching her.

"Where is she?! Where is she?!" I asked. What troubled dreams are passing behind her eyelids? She spoke not one word during the entire seder. And when I asked the question: "The bitter herbs that

*Pesach*

we eat, what is the reason?" my tears began to flow and would not stop. In truth, I made little effort to control or wipe them away.

I remember silently asking the question:

"Master of the universe, here is a young woman who can enjoy nothing — not even the laughter of her own young children! Is this how You want us to give *shevach* (praise) to You? Is this really a progression from slavery to freedom?" The more these questions chased their way in my head, like clouds darkening for a storm, the more I had the feeling of being somehow left behind, of being incapable of continuing to the end. I felt almost helplessly that there is always a zone of silence, a zone of darkness, which, we can never pierce. Also, that we were unbearably close to this place of no questions.

Seemingly miraculously, by the next evening, my wife's condition had improved slightly. She managed somehow to sit with us briefly. A happier mood descended on those around the table. She is here among us once more. She speaks. She even smiles a little. It was like a crushingly heavy stone positioned over one's heart was being rolled away a little.

Meanwhile, dialysis still had to proceed at regular intervals. The next morning therefore, I did not return to the synagogue (shul), as did the others. No, I set out on an hour's long walk to the other side of the city. Here I would meet my wife — who had been driven there by a non-Jew, for the purpose of being dialized. Every second day dialysis would have to be carried out. You will not be surprised to hear that Pesach passed, therefore, in a spirit of intense pain and bitterness.

After Yom Tov, dialysis began to assume a certain air of routine. It was carried out three times a week. Ruchi was assigned a personal nurse, whose task was to teach her the main aspects of dialysis. It was necessary for her to understand the procedure thoroughly, for safety reasons.

In fact, she was encouraged to feel that **she** was in charge of her own treatment. She had to insert the needles and take an active part in dialysis throughout. She would then later be able to teach me and I would assume the role of her helper. However, should I have to leave the room for a few months, she was more then well aware of how to handle the machine.

However, the first few weeks were exceedingly difficult. She was prone to anxieties and vomiting. The idea of being attached to a machine was still proving extremely difficult for her to accustom herself to. Just imagine you are told to sit on a certain chair for three or four hours without getting up. You would find this challenging. The urge for freedom of movement is strong and after a certain amount of time, it would reassert itself. You would have to be free of this chair. You would have to break the shackles of what would seem to you a dreadful imprisonment. But should you **choose** to sit on the self-same chair for the same amount of time, well, that is a different matter. Sometimes, when I thought that she was well settled on the machine, I would manage to slip away to my business. More than once I received a phone call from the hospital.

Before I left I would have to calm her down. To her pleas, to let her be free of the chair, I would have to add my own:

"You know how important you are to us all. And this machine is keeping you alive. Please, complete this treatment for all our sakes...."

❧

My original intention to carry out home dialysis had not abated. It still lingered in my mind, like the scent of rain on a humid day. However, at the moment that I made that instinctive decision, I knew less than nothing of what this entailed. But my resolve strengthened as dialysis proceeded, and my wife's state of mind did not improve. She continued to become tense, merely on entering the hospital's swing doors, and being assailed by the now familiar sickly-sweet smell. The entire impersonal atmosphere of the hospital, from its neon lights to the flurry of white-coated figures, seemed to make her feel: "You fit in with us. You, the patient are no longer a feeling, thinking independent entity. You are merely a cog in a vast functioning machine." I became increasingly convinced that it was these feelings which exacerbated her physical symptoms. Every day, I pressed the nurses and doctors on this point. "When will I be able to begin training to carry out home-dialysis?" But first she would have to be thoroughly trained, for should something untoward happen to her helper, she would have to know how to disengage herself from the machine. The teaching-time required would be about three or four months. Whilst this teaching would take place, it was decided that I was not allowed to be present. My wife was assigned a special nurse who would train her.

THE FIRST FEW DIALYSES HAVE BEEN CARRIED OUT - WHAT I REMEMBER is the sense of deepening nightmare! I lay on a bed in what I can only describe as a semi conscious state. I was wheeled to the dialysis bed, as I was too weak to sit on a chair, my father-in-law paced back and forth. The procedure began and the little I do remember was of intermittently fainting and vomiting violently. I was floating somewhere in a comatose state, but I remember trying to begin sentences and never managing to finish them — such was the weakness of my physical state. Alongside with this, was a point of mental and psychological despair and what I tried to tell those clustered around my bed, including my mother, whose hand I gripped so tightly that it must have turned black and blue, was: Go away all of you. Leave me alone — don't expend so much effort on me. For if this is what I must endure, it is beyond my capability to endure it, and so just leave me alone — and whatever the *Ribbon shel Olam* wishes in His infinite wisdom will come to pass....."

This was the gist of what I attempted to say over and over again, but always the darkness of fainting enveloped me and I would find myself back at the beginning of the same sentence.

"I don't care any more what they do to me, as I feel as though I'm only half alive. Anything must be better than this semi-alive state." This is what I remember of the feelings with which I approached dialysis.

⟡

# Nurse:

THE TRAINING HAS BEGUN. TODAY, THE YOUNG JEWISH HUSBAND brought his wife to the door of the dialysis room. Her brown eyes pleaded with him: "Stay. Stay here — I need you." I watched the dumb show in a seemingly disinterested way. He hesitated. She was willing him to enter the room and remain at her side. But he had had strict instructions from Dr. Zaruba. The previous day he had ushered him into his office.

"Mr. Guttfreund," he had begun. "We have decided, since we intend to begin training your wife in the techniques of dialysis, that you can no longer remain with her during this time. You may bring her and you may pick her up — but you must leave her there alone."

The young man seemed to examine Dr. Zaruba's features for a long moment. I thought he would acquiesce immediately. But no, he evidently thought it was worth a try.

"Please, Dr. Zaruba," he said. "I will not disturb you. I will be as quiet as a mouse. But I must sit by her side. She must know that I am in the room. Otherwise I know she will never undergo dialysis."

"It is out of the question."

"But I know my wife," he repeated with quiet desperation. "I know her secret fears. I am the only one who can reassure her enough to help her through. And I will be in no one's way, just a silent shadow at her side."

"I am sorry," Dr. Zaruba persisted. "It is totally inadmissible. We have our rules here and, like everyone else, you must abide by them. I must warn you quite seriously that if you attempt to stay on I will personally escort you off the premises."

So here was the young man, still hesitating, although he knew quite clearly what must be done.

Now he summoned all his courage and also all his power to be cruel — and like a parent leaving his child on the first day of school, he turned his back on her smartly and walked off. Only I saw the tears spilling down his cheeks as he moved quickly down the green floored hallway.

"Now, now," I said to my patient, "he is gone and we are going to be brave and begin to get to grips with this thing."

As he disappeared out of the swing doors, a single tear rolled down her cheeks.

All the time I was offering the usual words of encouragement. She seemed not to be listening to me at all. Her mind was focused indifferently. "Now let's just get you comfortable and I'll explain everything," I murmured in a low voice. Suddenly she just bolted — flew off like a startled bird. She was walking, running almost, with a strength of which I would not have considered her capable. She was through the glass doors, out into the garden beyond. She seemed to be walking with a certain intensity and ferocity, as if she could somehow outwalk the immobility into which she was being cornered. All the time she was talking to herself, in a dull undertone, words of exhortation or reproof. Towards what was she driving herself, I wondered, and also simultaneously being driven? I kept pace with her at first, like a shadow at her elbow. Then I just stood in the center of her path, and watched her turn in ever-decreasing circles. She would walk herself out, I thought, and turn wearily with resignation back to the chair and the machine.

Now I turned to address her. "You mustn't run away, dear. We can beat this thing together. You know you must learn so that you can help yourself and later go home with the machine. That is what we all want now, isn't it?" I said, as if talking to a child.

She returned to the chair as if unaware of where she was.

"But I feel so nauseous, so sick. How can I be bothered with all these names and technical terms? All I want is to be left alone."

"Now, now — don't carry on so," I said, putting an arm around her shoulder. "I have seen hundreds of patients and just like you: At first they say they can't be bothered and they'll never learn. But learn they do. And do you know something? They're usually the ones that learn the quickest. Now, let's begin..."

Why did this particular case touch me so? I've asked myself this question, time and time again. And in the light of what later transpired, I must find an adequate answer to this question. I live alone, have never married. There were one or two opportunities in the dim reaches of the past, but I suppose you might fairly say, I've always been too "married" to my work. In the wards, donning my starched white uniform, I felt a deep and genuine sense of identity. It was here that I came alive, as it were, became Nurse Julia, a person of a certain importance and not a little influence. And maybe this was enough for me. Do I regret the missing dimension in my life? I suppose I do — sometimes in the dark recesses of the night or on a bus crowded with giggling schoolchildren. And perhaps that is part of the reason why this particular self-contained family nucleus, struggling against the encroaching odds to maintain itself as a cohesive unit, gnawed at my sense of identity. As I have said, I am alone in the world, except for a host of growing nieces and nephews. Should I contract a serious illness, I might be missed professionally and socially, but no one's life would be seriously disturbed, no one's equanimity would be threatened. But this young woman, married and far from the country of her birth, was needed by her family, her obviously devoted husband and three young children, and needed desperately. She was the keystone of the archway which, if removed, would cause the whole edifice to crumble. Her illness was not a tragedy for herself alone, it was a tragedy for them all. And so her plight must have touched in me, I suppose, something deeply buried under the autumn leaves of many years' regrets and unfulfilled hopes.

At any rate, I cannot pinpoint the exact moment that my sense of compassion crystallized into something quite other — a desire to help her and her family, with all the resources at my disposal.

**Ruchi:**

So here we are back in this room again, but now quite alone. Yanky has gone. Nurse Julia sat me down on the dialysis chair, that much I remember. This room was occupied, I suppose, by other patients, perhaps five or six. The machine was waiting. But suddenly I knew I had to get away, delay the moment. I walked or rather ran out into the gardens beyond. There is someone at my arm as I walk, in ever-decreasing circles.

"Just give me a moment or two. In a moment I will be ready. But not yet. I want to remain free."

Birds circle the wide arc of the sky, in an exact transformation. They know where they are flying to — and I? I have lost my way somewhere in all this.

The voice is urging me. "Return — go back. Sit in the chair, be attached to the machine. It is the next step in the *nisayon*! At this moment, you may not understand why — but somehow this is the way forward now."

Then the other voice. "Wait. Give me time. I am so young. I have hardly lived. All those bright hopes of the seventeen-year-old-bride; so young, so innocent, so unaware. Where are they now? Everything has become so unbelievably complex and intricate. Please, Hashem, make it simple and clear again."

"In the nurse's firm touch there was an air of quiet authority, and something else too — genuine human compassion. Her square homely face, kindly brown eyes, capable hands — all seemed to suggest the words: "Don't worry — I am here. While I am here I will see that nothing unpleasant happens to you!"

"But I feel so tired, so drained, and now they want me to concentrate on this seemingly chaotic mumble-jumble of tubes, knobs, needles and the function of each tiny part in the intricate maze. What do they want from me? Is it not enough that I have to sit for hours in this room, attached to this machine, marooned on this island, away from those I hold most dear in the world? Now they are asking me to assimilate this information, too, to absorb it with my intellect. *Ribbono shel Olam*," I pleaded "give me strength for this also!" Now I would have to summon the physical and mental strength to begin to learn to read those foreign signposts, but as a child does, from a position of total lack of knowledge — and in a spirit of utter humility.

❦

## Yanky:

WHEN I TURNED TO LEAVE RUCHI ALONE IN THE DIALYSIS UNIT ON THAT spring day, I experienced a feeling of total desolation. The doctor's words and my proud retort still echoed in my mind.

"Sir, I will never leave my wife alone."

On and on they echoed in my head as I moved swiftly down the hallways. "Rules and regulations, disturbance..." I felt sullied, like a criminal when he is stripped of all his possessions and photographed from every angle for police records. When Nurse Julia finally motioned me to go my feet turned in the direction of the exit, but my heart would not let me.

"You will manage it...." I shouted noiselessly back over my shoulder. "Be strong, we must endure this also...."

Would it be too dramatic to say that I saw in the image of her blue, softly pleading eyes an image which haunts me always – retrieved from my parents' generation — of a group of Jewish women transported by Nazis on a lumbering army truck. From behind the wires, everything in their eyes and hands is pleading as they are wrenched, torn away in an instant from all that they hold dear: husbands, fathers, little ones.

"Stay, turn back, don't leave her," the voices pummeled me like a frail boat on a stormy sea. But in my heart of hearts, I knew that this too was for the best. She must now be left alone, to piece together the fragments of her life, to gather her own courage in her hands, to muster her own resources of heart and intellect. This she could only accomplish alone, if I let go of her hand, metaphorically speaking, and let her find her own depths. Up to this moment, in our shared *nisayon*, she had leaned on me, she had allowed me to think, to negotiate, to plan for her. Now it was time for her to find her own, if deeply changed, sense of self.

Nurse Julia began to teach her on that day. The main purpose of the instruction was for Ruchi to be able to disengage herself from the machine should anything happen to me, once home dialysis began. There was a psychological aspect to this also, which was to have her get a grip on herself and come to terms with her disease, to enable her to be involved with the healing process. This made things easier for herself, as she herself was physically involved in the technical details. The learning process proceeded agonizingly slowly. April turned into May, then it was June, and suddenly summer arrived. Now the trees were swollen with blossoms, as I made my way to the hospital daily, either to bring my wife or to pick her up.

Each time I asked her, "Are you ready yet? Have you completed your training?"

"In a little while; Nurse Julia says I need a few more weeks. Just give me a little more time..."

She knew why I was urging her, for I could hardly contain my desire to begin learning dialysis myself. The sooner I could begin, the quicker would arrive that day when I could bring the 'machine' home and resume some semblance of normal family life. Meanwhile, these weeks crawled on, in a tortoise-like fashion. No two days were exactly alike or predictable. Some days, she would return home and go straight to sleep for hours. On other days, she would return home and surprise us all with her energy. At these times, she would be fired with an unnaturally active spirit. She would want to go with her children to the lake or to the park or to go shopping and meet with her friends, anything but to remain at home, or in bed.

One late June day, I was finally summoned by Nurse Julia to the dialysis station.

Folding her strong arms, she said cheerfully, "Well, your wife Rachel now knows everything there is to know about dialysis. So I think it is time for us to begin..." These words, so long, more than eagerly awaited echoed on and on soundlessly in my head, before I could assimilate their meaning. "Your wife and myself, we will be your instructors" and at this she smiled a little.

"How long might it take me to learn?"

"Well, in my estimation sir, about three months...."

So I began. I attended the dialysis unit daily and learned the technicalities of dialysis in intricate detail. I also had to be made aware of what might go wrong and what to do in those eventualities. There is a Rabbinic saying: "There is nothing which can stand in the way of one's will." And this is the only possible way to describe what now occurred, for undoubtedly, it was something beyond the norms of human ability or understanding. I can attribute it only to Hashem's help, and not one iota to my own skills. For in two weeks, I had mastered dialysis utterly. One day, Nurse Julia watched me complete the entire process, then in a state of some agitation called the doctor. Again, I was put through the whole procedure, and neither nurse nor doctor, experts of many years' standing, could fault me, in any one detail. I can only say that once again, through the intensity and purity of my desire, I had been granted no less than Heavenly Assistance!

The Maharal, in connection with a Gemara which states that when one visits a sick person, one must sit lower than the sick person because the *Shechinah* is over his head, makes the following explanation. A healthy person is (or at any rate feels himself to be) independent. He walks about unaided, he conducts his day-to-day affairs alone. However, a person who is ill requires outside help. Thus, he is very much aware that his existence is dependent on the One Above. The sick person has therefore progressed from an awareness of Hashem as *Kail Shakai* (Hashem Who lets nature run its seemingly independent course) to an awareness of Hashem *Havayah* the G-d Who constantly interacts with creation.

By the time this momentous pronouncement had been made by doctors and nurses alike — that I was capable of operating the machine — like a thief stealing up unawares, suddenly it was summer. I felt that it would be beneficial for all the family to have a change of scenery. But the ever-looming problem of dialysis remained. We became once more painfully aware of how dialysis now permeated every facet of our daily lives. No longer were we free to choose a holiday location on the basis of its mere prettiness. No — we were now governed by one all-pervading imperative, and one only, the need to be near a dialysis station! Once due inquiries had been made, our arrangements were then made around this information. The weeks passed and merged into one another — in a flurry of walks, outings, and of course, the inevitable journeys to and from the dialysis station. A change of dialysis station always carries with it a certain degree of risk, and a feeling of uncertainty crept over us like a chill wind.

At this time too, a strange interlude occurred in the long history of our *nisayon*. A young couple who had a very sick child contacted us. They had to spend all their time in the hospital with the child, and were very weary and dejected in spirit. We extended what little hospitality we could to them. They ate their meals with us and joined us on our outings. Looking back at this episode, I am lost in amazement. How, I wonder, could we have shown such strength at a time which was so shaded with darkness for us? How resilient is the human spirit — that very spirit that can whisper to you: "Their problems are yet greater than ours. Are we not, on the ultimate scale of things, relatively fortunate? In their case, it is a child who is sick, a child who cannot rationalize and accept his *nisayon*. In ours, it is a mature adult." And, of course, this helped us too, to see our troubles as if from without, with a new level of detachment and therefore acceptance.

## Ruchi:

WE RETURNED HOME FROM OUR VACATION TODAY. I FEEL SOMETHING akin to relief — to be back to our familiar surroundings, and the now familiar dialysis room in the hospital. Nurse Julia was delighted to see me. She pinched my cheek and cried, "Ah, that good mountain air! My dear, we will soon have you built up!" All the others in the square room greeted me in their various ways. One raised a hand in greeting, another simply nodded. Mrs. Keller, motioned me a little nearer when I stopped by her chair, saying, "Well, and what's this I hear? That you will soon be leaving us poor creatures — and taking your machine home."

I nodded in assent, thinking, "News travels fast."

"Well, yes," I answered. "We are hoping to take the machine home. But I'm sure I'll be looking in here often enough." I felt like someone about to abandon ship.

Mrs. Keller took my hand. "Well, dear, I wish you well. Be brave. You are young and things have a habit of turning out well — you'll see..."

Tears welled in my eyes as I withdrew my hand and turned to leave.

The dialysis room possessed an air of something akin to a family spirit, for when one sits for hours on end with fellow humans equally renstricted, one develops a sort of instinctive and profoundly felt bond. Outside, in the wide world of free entities, one is something of an anomaly, a peculiarity: "Look, there is so and so; she lives on a machine..." But here, in this room, all those barriers melt away — young or old, Jew or gentile, we are all bound by the same contingencies — the chair, the needle, the pipe. (It was nowhere near the family spirit I felt when I visited the dialysis units in Israel and America. In Israel, we shared a common bond of being Jewish, and the warmth and friendliness that the Israelis and Americans portrayed was a stark contrast to where we lived, where people were cold, distant and intimidated by our Jewishness.) Now I was about to leave the cocoon, and although I felt anticipation, there was undeniably a deep groundswell of terror. Did we realize what we were undertaking? Would my husband cope with the responsibility? And what of our young children? Would the sight of the machine frighten them? Was it even right to subject them to such knowledge, when up to now, all they knew in their childish ways was my absences?

## Nurse:

WELL, MY YOUNG COUPLE RETURNED FROM THE COUNTRY TODAY, AND things are moving quickly. All the formalities will have to be gone through, the customary checking of the apartment and facilities for suitability, and then, quite soon, they should get their machine. The husband can hardly contain his eagerness — and I think this is due both to a desire to get his wife back home, and also to a deeply felt need to become an active participant and not just a bystander. If I had ever married, and had known the closeness of that bond, I suppose I would recognize what I am witnessing here is a natural consequence of that closeness in its most extreme expression. "Your pain is my pain, when you suffer, I suffer by definition" — it is all quite awe-inspiring in its way. I hope for their sake it all works out, and looking further into the future, that they can soon be placed on that never-ending list for transplant. I see this as their only long-term hope for a return to normality, for them and their young family. But, oh that list, it reminds me of something I once read. It is said that on the Jewish New Year two books lie open before the Almighty, the book of life and the book of death, and one's misdeeds or meritorious actions decide in which book one is to be inscribed. The transplant list seems to me to possess something of that weightiness, the book of life or the book of death. For all too often we forget that the prospect of a transplant really holds out to a dialysis patient nothing less than a new lease of life...

**R**uchi:

TODAY, WE HAD SOME VISITORS: A GROUP OF DOCTORS DROPPED BY THE apartment. Their assignment was to ascertain our facilities and see if our apartment measures up to the rigid guidelines laid down for hygiene. They inspected every nook and cranny of our home, firing questions at us in rapid succession.

"Where do you intend to place the machine?"

"Where will the nearest sink be, in relation to the machine?"

There were other questions too, which I prefer now to forget for they were of a more personal, probing nature. I remember the feeling of indignity, as though the cloak of privacy surrounding our lives was being mercilessly torn asunder.

To our responses, they just nodded in a noncommittal sort of way, so that we had no idea if what we had answered was acceptable or not. When they finally concluded their investigations and were ready to leave, there was still no clear indication of what conclusions they had reached. We looked at each other in bewilderment. Were we acceptable or not?

A day or two later, Dr. Zaruba summoned my husband to his office.

"We find no reason," he began, "to withhold permission for you to carry out hemodialysis at home. That is, provided you are prepared to carry out the necessary adaptations."

My husband nodded rapidly. "Dr. Zaruba, we are prepared to do anything, anything at all to get my wife home."

He did not react to this statement, however, but instead began listing the necessary adaptations to be enforced.

"Yes, yes," Yanky said impatiently. "Consider them all done. I will begin making the necessary arrangements immediately."

We left his office with a new lightness of heart — something we had not felt for many months. Perhaps, perhaps after all, we would come through our *nisayon*, if not unchanged, yet somehow spiritually whole. Perhaps now, for the first time in months, the tide was turning — it was no longer running against us.

Much thought now had to be given as to where to position the machine. Undeniably, it was a big machine (as large as a refrigerator in fact) and the thought farthest from our minds was to turn our home into a kind of hospital. This would run counter to our entire aim in bringing the machine home. The main living areas were therefore automatically excluded. But the machine would have to be positioned near to a sink, as only soft water[8] could be used for dialysis. This necessity then excluded the guest bedroom and second bedroom and left our bedroom, which was in fact a very large room as the only other option. Once we had decided on this — everything else seemed to fall into place, as if orchestrated by an Unseen Hand. For we immediately realized that our bedroom would in fact provide the ideal location, as there was a small shower-room containing a sink adjoining to it. Also, this was positioned at just the perfect distance from where the machine would stand, neither too near, nor too far. The reclining armchair too, was ideal for dialysis purposes, as it could be tilted to a lying position should I feel unwell or faint. In this way as we proceeded through each item, each contingency, we realized with a kind of exultant joy that it was as if this very room had been designated for nothing other than this very purpose, from the beginning!

Every month a truck arrived at our home to deliver the necessary items, about ten to fifteen cartons of dialyzer fluid. The truck was marked with the name of the drug company but was otherwise quite inconspicuous. I had a gentile neighbor to whom I hardly spoke apart from saying, "Hello, how are you today?" One day, she stopped me on the stairs and said, "I don't mean to be nosey but it seems that someone in this building is unwell. A drug company truck stops here every month.

"It is me," I said on impulse. "I am on 'dialysis'.

"Oh my dear, why did you not say?" she asked me. "My mother is on dialysis."

---

8. *Soft water, i.e. water that has been treated to reduce the calcium content. This is needed to rinse through the machine before dialysis can begin.*

How well I remember the day the machine arrived at our apartment. Though in truth one can hardly call these acts of remembering, inasmuch as you cannot say a concentration camp victim remembers the number indelibly tattooed on his arm. No, these inky blue dots which once formed his identity mark now never leave his consciousness, neither by day nor night. So, too, all my memories of this time, the tears of grief or frustration, the shared laughter, the little triumphs, every nuance and innuendo, all these are etched into my every waking moment. I will never again be totally free of them, nor they of me. So, I see it all again in my mind's eye, as in reality I see it all again at every moment, the transport truck arriving in the street below, the struggle to negotiate the machine around corners and up the stairs, and finally the machine crossing our threshold. This is the climax of so many weeks of preparation and thought, every contingency has been thoroughly thought through and planned. Nothing has been left unprepared, no stone unturned.

I will sit on that comfortable chair over there. We have cleared a space in our large bedroom here, by moving out a two-seater settee into the living room. The machine will stand just so, in the light, and there the room opens into the balcony to give me some air if I require it. A sink in our private bathroom has been adapted to provide the specially filtered water necessary for dialysis. A protective polystyrene sheet has been carefully laid over that section of carpet on which the machine will stand. These and so many other details have been planned and replanned, until we are certain that everything is in place. But as the machine is finally positioned precisely onto the specified spot in our bedroom, why does my heart seem to break into two?

For was this moment not designated to be a joyous one, signalling a freedom of sorts? If this is so, why then does the machine suddenly look so big out of its normal hospital environment and placed in the confining space of our bedroom? Why does it look once again so unfamiliar and daunting? Why does my heart seem to break in utter desolation? And once again, like waves breaking on the same shore, why are the old doubts of my worst nightmares here again, resurrected in all their full and pompous gravity?

Doubt is endemic to the human condition. We can never be sure of anything, for what seemed to be so wise and discerning in the dead of the night might not bear close examination in the harsh, unrelenting light of day. And what if we were wrong, what if...?

## Yanky:

NOW ALL MY FAMILY'S SMOLDERING OBJECTIONS, OVER THE PAST FEW months, return with an almost malicious vengeance: "Think of the responsibility... You are not a doctor... Why turn your home into a hospital?... Why frighten the wits out of your young children?... Why tread a new path and take on what others in your situation have never attempted?... Foolhardy, daredevil, presumptuous.... And finally, I recall the prefatory remarks of the doctor who instructed me in dialysis: "Young man," he said a little jauntily, "let me tell you straight away, there are at least fifty different ways to kill a person on this machine...."

"*Ribbono shel Olam* — if you have helped me reach this moment, surely, surely this is part of your all-encompassing plan for Your children? Surely, if the machine is here now, it is only because it is and was meant to be here all along, and because this will ultimately turn out for the best? But if I ever needed strength, a superhuman strength almost, of will, heart and mind, I need it now, as I prepare to take my wife's fate literally into my hands...."

## Ruchi:

THE DAY THE MACHINE ARRIVED IN OUR APARTMENT, MY AUNT BRACHA and her husband were staying with us. At the sight of the cumbersome machine coming to rest in our bedroom, they both paled visibly.

"Oh my dears," they cried, "such a thing, such a thing..." they muttered, and then, "Oh so young, so very young..."

Then they involuntarily clapped their hands over their mouths, as if to still the restless thoughts that came spilling out almost unbidden...

As if on some unknown cue, we both turned to reassure and comfort them! Amazing — here we were, embarking on new and uncharted territory in our long and arduous *nisayon*, bolstering up the courage of our more senior relatives.

"Aunty, uncle," we cried, as if with one voice. "This is not a sad day for us. No, no, quite on the contrary, don't you see? Now, we will be able to have the benefits of treatment without going to the hospital and the unpleasantness that it implies! You must see it as we do... no, don't cry, don't cry — see, we are not crying, we are happy! This machine is not our enemy."

As these last words were uttered, the thought sprang into my head, "No, this machine is not my enemy. No, not at all. This machine is my **friend**." This machine is my best friend, for through its agency G-d has literally kept me alive and will continue to do so."

I remember a new and vast determination sweeping through me, and in a sense it was a kind of watershed.

If I had been weak and frightened in the past, I was determined from now on with the Almighty's help to be stronger and stronger each day. Did I ever ask that most universal of questions — that one that may spring immediately to one's mind and lips: "Why me?" — the answer is a clear and unequivocal: "Never!" Never, in the darkest moments of pain and bewilderment did I pose this question, and if I now felt fear, fear of the unknown, even then the fear was not punctuated with this haunting question, for I was raised with the knowledge that everything that Hashem does is for the best. We have to accept all the trials and tribulations that come our way, and there is no room for questions. This upbringing helped me overcome the natural urge to ask this question when trials arose, for it is only human to ask it. Dialysis — I was determined, now with a new and fierce determination, turning a corner into this new era — was something to be mastered. But that this was a necessary component of the All-knowing master plan for me at this juncture of my life, that I should have to undergo these very *yisurim* and this very *nisayon* — that this was the type of pain I had been chosen to know and know again — this I never once doubted. I am reminded of a parable I once heard. A young child walks hand in hand with his grandfather, along one of those endless tree-lined boulevards which you find in many European cities. To the child it seems that at some distant point, the trees actually meet. He is afraid. He cries out: "Grandfather, let us not continue walking along this road, for can you not see in the distance, the trees come together and we shall doubtless be trapped?"

The grandfather reassures the frightened child.

"My child, do not fear, but let us continue walking on this path, a little way..."

Presently, it seems to the boy that the trees are opening up, and they are in fact able to advance further. The grandfather turns to the child. "My child, so it is on life's path and you would do well to remember my words. Sometimes it would seem as though we can no longer continue on our appointed path. The way is blocked, insurmountable difficulties rise up one after another. But if you remain strong and you continue walking, what happens? That which was seemingly insurmountable will dissolve, like so many specters in the night, and slowly, slowly at each stage, the path opens up before you..."

This simple tale, encapsulated all my most deeply felt emotions at that moment. Looking back, I could see that at every stage, even the blackest of the blackest holes of despair, what had happened? I may have thought, no, this is the worst, I will never scale that wall. "But have you tried," my inner voice would interject. "It might not be so bad after all." What happened? I took a few, at first faltering steps, and then with Hashem's help, the path opened up a little, and those seemingly massively looming obstacles of a moment ago had disappeared and faded into insubstantiality one by one.

**Yanky:**

THE DAY THE MACHINE ARRIVED — BY CHANCE ONE, WOULD SAY colloquially, but what we really imply by this is the mysterious working of *Hashgacha pratis* — a small package arrived in the mail. It was a small book of stickers which I received from time to time for business purposes. Leafing idly through it, in a quiet moment, I came across the following drawing. A caricature creature was depicted, wearing a hat, and next to the head a red arrow, pointed upwards. Above, a short caption read: "Hold your head up high." A sudden flash of inspiration ran through me, like a molten arrow. I hurried to the machine and placed this sticker right in the center of all the pompous knobs and dials. I turned to my wife and said:

"This will be our motto, for however long the machine remains in this house. Heads held high, and with heads held high, we will carry out dialysis for as long as necessary. We must view this machine, not with bitterness, but with joy and gratitude, for through the medium of this machine and its sophisticated technology, the Almighty is granting you the gift of life. Although you have been stricken with a serious illness, *bechasdei Hashem*, in G-d's infinite goodness, you have been granted a way to live, which was not available in previous years. And now, as a further *chesed*, you will be able to remain in your own surroundings of cozy and comforting domesticity. My dear, this machine was created for you, only for you... and as such we welcome it in our midst, as a dear and cherished friend..."

In retrospect, we had brought the machine home not a moment too early. For over the last few weeks, I had noticed a marked deterioration in my wife's state. Something inside her was not tranquil, not at peace; a restless spirit was tossing and tearing her apart from within. Her feelings of claustrophobia and being trapped on the machine increased in intensity until they reached fever pitch. (Here, I must explain that these feelings are very commonplace. They were intensified in this case by the overwhelming sensation of being dislocated from her natural place at home with her young children.) This all came to a head one day, when an aunt who had been visiting us left for the airport. After taking leave of her, my wife grew more agitated than I had ever seen her. The drug the hospital had administered to calm her a little seemed instead to increase her excitability: She had experienced an adverse reaction, actually having been erroneously administered the drug twice by a young nurse. At that moment she seemed utterly lost, hardly in control of herself or her emotions. Watching her that day, I vowed to do everything in my power to bring her home as soon as it was safe to do so. (Shortly after this, I was given permission to begin training for dialysis.)

On the first day the machine was connected, my wife took her place in her comfortable sitting-chair and I carried out my first home-dialysis with Nurse Julia in attendance as an extra precaution.

**Ruchi:**

FIRST HOME DIALYSIS CARRIED OUT... IT IS LIKE A WHOLE NEW WORLD opening up for me. No feelings of nausea — no familiar stomach wrenching at the sickly hospital smell, no feelings of claustrophobia on the machine — no, all that is vanished, like so many bad dreams that dissolve at the first touch of daylight. My husband seems so confident, so sure. He connects and disconnects pipes, turns knobs, carries out the whole procedure in a calm and assured way. From a cart, he picks and discards pieces of equipment with great confidence. I was so afraid that he might waver, and had he wavered even for one instant I would have been lost. I look up and say to him, "Do you remember when you couldn't stand the sight of blood? When even having a simple blood test would make you pale and shaky?"

At this, we both laughed. It seems so long ago, a whole world ago, and on looking back, what strikes me now is how much we have both grown in such a short time. We have grown and matured beyond all recognition. I marvel at the intricacy of Hashem's ways — "My ways are not your ways..." — and their hiddenness. Who would have imagined that we could reach a stage where we could really say: "This experience has changed us unalterably," and even, "I wouldn't want to go back to where we were before..." And we have grown so much closer, my husband and I. Should one surmise, according to all mortal logic, that such an experience — coming as it did so early in our married life — would tear us apart, would overwhelm us one would be wrong. No, we have developed I think, a special sort of closeness which would not have been possible had things remained "normal." Not only have we formed a deep sort of interdependence one on another, for we are thrown together emotionally — like two climbers yoked together on a sheer cliff face: "If you lose your foothold I am lost. If I make a misjudgement you are lost," — we are inexorably bound together for better or worse and we know it, in a way which some couples never in a whole lifetime of living together gain a true awareness of. My children run in and out of the room as this first dialysis takes place. They come up close to the machine, but what I feared most, that the sight of their mother attached to a machine would frighten them out of their wits, does not appear to take place. Children are so much more resilient than we give them credit for, and they can accept difficult realities in a more genuinely truthful way. Once again, I thank the Master of the Universe, who in His infinite kindness has allowed me to be reunited, after so many trials and tribulations, with my husband and children.

**Yanky:**

As the days passed and things began to fall into an identifiable pattern, we derived our own ways of achieving the maximum possible benefit of having the machine at home. Gradually, we worked out that the best time to carry out dialysis would be early evening, shortly upon my return from work. The preparations preceding dialysis and clearing away and disconnecting the machine afterwards could take as long as an hour each (and I had been taught that the longer the dialysis, the more effective); to begin later than eight o'clock in the evening would risk the treatment stretching on until the early hours of the next morning. So I would return home about seven o'clock at night. I would say "hello" to my children and kiss them, but there was simply no time now to play or chat with them. Nor was there time to put my feet up and relax for half an hour, as I might have felt inclined to do. No, I would make my way directly to the bedroom, where I would immediately begin preparations for dialysis. These preparations were exceedingly time consuming. It was extremely necessary to be punctual in starting these preparations, for should I begin late, dialysis, which lasted for approximately four hours, would be delayed. At these times I felt the full gravity of the burden I had undertaken, for it all depended on me — and me alone! From the bedroom doorway, I would almost bolt straight to the machine. I would begin by adjusting certain buttons. The next step was to clip the artificial kidney (dialysis) to a stand, and to connect the lines carrying dialyzate to and from the machine to the filter. Dialyzate was then allowed to flow through the dialyzer. Next, the blood lines needed to be unwrapped from their packets (a fresh sterile set is used at each dialysis) and connected to the entrances of the filter. Using clips which were rather like plastic scissors. Further procedures included attaching a one liter plastic bag of saline solution to the arterial line and switching the blood pump on. When the bag was almost empty, the blood pump was switched off and the lines clamped. They were now ready for use.

While I was carrying out these preliminary procedures, my wife was weighing herself and making a note of her weight. She would then measure and record her blood pressure, both in the lying down and standing up positions. Next, I had to check that all the "needling" items were in place on a specially prepared sterile tray. These included: gauze swabs; a few small dishes in which are placed a skin antiseptic solution; and a dilute solution of heparin. Heparin, a liquid drug, is introduced in order to thin the blood and stop it from clotting. Blood outside the body will clot. Clotted blood will not flow and cannot be returned to the patient. Since Heparin's effect wears off fairly quickly it has to be used continuously during hemodialysis. The exact amount of heparin needed during one dialysis varies from patient to patient, for should the blood be thinned too much, this would also prove extremely dangerous. (In order to determine how much heparin was needed, a small cut was made in Ruchi's arm and a test was performed to see the amount of time it took for her blood to clot and how much Heparin was needed. She still has the scar from this test on her arm.) Accordingly, I prepared a large syringe of heparin, and during hemodialysis an intravenous line slowly delivers the heparin into the line. The actual process of dialysis has been compared, in laymen's terminology, to that which takes place when dirty laundry is placed in a washing machine. This is the way in which several doctors at varying times have tried to explain this seemingly complicated process to me. The patient's blood, filled with creatinine and other poisonous materials, is analogous to the laundry to be cleansed. The blood is cleansed by passing it through a semipermeable membrane which filters out waste products and poisons, and it is then returned to the body. Dialyzate is the mixture of water and salts which is used for the dialysis process. This water has to be heated by the machine to the same temperature as blood, so that the necessary exchange can be made.

The next stage which was carried out was possibly the most traumatic both for my wife and myself. It is called "sticking" and means that two needles, the arterial and the venous needles, would have to be inserted into the fistula. These two needles are extremely thick and long with an oval opening. First, the arm is cleansed with antiseptic. The needle is then pushed through into the vein. The line from the needle is then clamped and the needle and line secured to the skin with a little sticky tape. The whole process is then repeated for the second needle. This is the stage which my wife possibly found the most difficult, both physically and emotionally. If one ponders a little, one soon realizes that it goes against all basic human instincts to take a needle and insert it into your own skin. Yet, without her accomplishing this, the whole process could not begin. It also had to be carried out with great speed as the needles would produce a large opening and blood might begin to spurt forth. Not infrequently my spotless white shirt ended up spattered with Ruchi's blood. Her skin actually became quite tough and in doing it herself it was somehow less painful — for she was fully focused on her task, as if playing "nurse" to herself. At such times, a little flushed from my exertions to get the machine ready and all necessary preparations made, I would exhort her:

"Please, please, Ruchi, just stick the needle! It will hurt for a moment or two, and I know it is difficult for you, but then it is over and the dialysis can continue."

My urgings and her pleadings for time would extend over many minutes. Sometimes she would stick the needle, but apparently miss the exact spot, and no blood would flow. Then I would take a non-toxic pen and mark the spot for her on her skin. Encouraged by this, she would then try again, until eventually, like someone drilling for oil, she would strike the right spot. This is a bald description of what transpired at these times, but obviously, in human terms, these few minutes cost us both dearly in heart-wrenching pain, and are some of the moments we would both most dearly like to forget.

With the needles in place, the clamps are removed and the blood pump switched on at low speed. Several more technical points ensue, but eventually, if all is well, the heparin pump is switched on, dialysis is considered begun and a note of the time made. Blood pressure is measured and recorded at the beginning and at the end of dialysis, and at every hour during dialysis. Before and after it is measured both sitting down and standing up, but during dialysis, obviously only sitting. There now follows a period in which although the patient is relatively restricted, he or she can carry out some normal activities, such as reading, listening to the radio, sleeping or eating. In order to conclude dialysis, the approximate reverse processes of those carried out at the beginning are enacted. Ruchi would remove both needles from their places with me standing with some gauze dressing. She would have to press fairly firmly over the puncture sites, but not too firmly so as to create too much pressure. Her blood might flow quite drastically as she was taking heparin to thin the blood! After a rest of some minutes, my final procedures would be to remove the filter from its stand, wash and sterilize it, throw way the lines, wash down the machine and set it to self-sterilize. Meanwhile, my wife would again measure her lying and standing blood pressure and weigh herself. This weight would represent the post-dialysis, or dry weight and would tell us how successful that particular dialysis had been in terms of removing fluid.[9]

*Ruchi:*

THE FIRST FEW DIALYSES HAVE BEEN CARRIED OUT AT HOME. ONCE everything is in place, I can sit in a fairly relaxed way and read or have the children wander in or out. As each dialysis lasts approximately four hours, it is fairly late when I can finally be unhooked from the machine and go to bed. For my husband, it is even later as he has to finish cleaning the machine, and make sure that everything is back in its place. "Needling' is always a painful process for me. I cannot explain why, for I should have become inured to this most necessary part of the procedure by now, but for me, the sight of the thick-ended needle that I must thrust through my fistula and into the artery below, is hard, oh, so hard to accept. Yet, I fight constantly to

---

9. *Patients on dialysis usually produce one or two cups of urine at the beginning. At a later stage, urine is no longer produced. Water is removed during dialysis by ultrafiltration (the method by which fluid is removed from the blood during hemodialysis), but in between dialyses only one or two cups of urine are produced daily. This means that the patient is not allowed to drink more than about one pint of fluid daily. Drinking more than this will not have the effect of "forcing" the kidneys to get rid of the excess. The extra fluid remains in the body and the pre-dialysis weight will be too high. If a patient has been foolish and drunk more fluid than is safe, the extra fluid may accumulate in the lungs. This may not only cause increased shortness of breath before dialysis, but could, in extreme cases, be very unpleasant or even fatal. Restriction of fluid is perhaps the worst feature of the whole way of life.*

remind myself how **fortunate** I am to be home, in my own pretty bedroom and surely here, in these surroundings, even this most soul-wracking of moments must lose some of its awesomeness. *Ribbono shel Olam,* always at this moment, I would ask You for more strength, more strength than I would be able to muster of my own free will, for since You have given me this test then most certainly it is also Your will that I pass the test with flying colors, so to speak. Help me now, help me, now — I would cry out — let the moment be quick, let it pass, let the needle reach its target below my flesh and skin. But frequently, I was literally drenched in sweat after this needling process had been accomplished. It is at these moments too, that I see my husband is closest to losing his customary, almost miraculous equanimity. He is so flustered from rushing in from work, no time to rest or put his feet up, hurrying to the machine to start preparations. Sometimes I feel heartily sorry for him, sorry to the very core of my being. He is, after all, such a young man and now he has to carry this massive, all-consuming burden alone. He has to, literally, take my life carefully, ever so carefully, in his hands, like holding a quantity of water in one's upturned palms and making sure that even one drop does not spill. So, every minute to him is precious and he is, understandably, a little tense.

"We must start precisely on time," Yanky always tells me; otherwise, he is afraid, dialysis will stretch on to the early hours of the morning. For by early morning he must be up again, hurry to *Shacharis* (morning prayers) and his place of work and then begin the entire, endless cycle again with just a day to rest and gather his thoughts in between so, when I hesitate, needle in hand, he cries out, "Please, please I beg you, just 'stick' and be done with it." I do not blame him, he does not say this out of anger but out of *ahavah*, the intensity of his anxiety and concern for me. But something in me always shrinks back, pleading for time. Then he takes a pen from his pocket and marks the exact spot for me, with a black dot. Psychologically speaking, had he plunged the needle into the artery for me, it would have hurt me far more than doing so myself. This is why we decided early on that I would needle myself. Sometimes though, the needling would not proceed quickly enough and I would watch with absolute horror as spots of blood quickly spread in all directions on his white shirt. I felt each spot like a blot on my very soul, for was it not enough, I reasoned, that he had to take this enormous burden on himself — must I also sully his outward appearance? How or from which untapped source I did eventually find the necessary inner strength to stick myself, not once, but probably several thousand times during my years on dialysis, proved to be the *Yad Hashem*. But I did accomplish it, and in so doing, I proved to myself that even this most feared of moments could be faced, if not with equanimity, then at least with a fierce determination not to be beaten.

※

## Nurse:

I HAVE JUST COME FROM THE GUTTFREUND HOME... I DON'T SUPPOSE they would have mentioned my presence at the first few home dialyses. For I was present, but taking no active role — I was, in truth, more insubstantial than a shadow. Sometimes the husband would turn to me, a half-smile playing on his lips — sometimes, the wife. But I am amazed at how well they are coping with all the intricate procedures involved. The husband seems to know the machine intimately and to display an extraordinary degree of confidence in handling it. It is at these times, when he has got dialysis well under way — his wife is settled comfortably in her chair, the children run in, their hair washed and neatly brushed to kiss their mother "goodnight" — that he permits himself the half-smile of which I spoke before. "See, Nurse Julia," he seems to be saying, "I can handle this. I told you I could. No other family members are involved, no nursing staff — just me. I am doing this for my wife, and I am doing it alone." And the wife? The wife smiles a smile that seems to come at unexpected moments, lighting up her young features, a smile that says: "I'm not beaten yet. I am going to master this inexplicable thing that has happened to me." And this smile seems to occur so much more frequently here than it did in the hospital, when she sometimes had the look of a frightened, cornered animal. Now, I feel like an outsider looking in — like someone caught outside on a stormy wind-lashed night, pressing her nose up against a windowpane and watching the fire burning merrily in the hearth, at the cozy, domestic scene within. And is there, I ask myself sometimes, the tiniest, ever-so tiniest feeling of autumn-tinged regret, when I reach this stage in a patient's supervision and care, of becoming more or less superfluous? I don't think so. I sometimes see myself in the part of a director, whose greatest joy is to watch the performance from the wings at opening night. As the play has advanced, he has slowly been sidled further and further off stage — but by the same coin he has achieved his self-avowed purpose — the consummate and seemingly independent performance of the actors under his supervision. But I have the deep-seated intuition too, that in this case, I will still somehow remain connected and entangled in some very profound way, with the fate of those two young people....

**Ruchi:**

SO DIALYSIS BEGUN AT HOME CONTINUED IN ITS SET PATTERN. BUT LET me explain to the reader in a little more detail what life on dialysis involves. It has been said that dialysis is not merely a treatment, but nothing short of a way of life. This is no exaggeration. The phrase "way of life" perhaps comes closer than any other description to indicating something of the all-encompassing nature of dialysis. In truth, there is no facet of one's life that it does not seek out and touch or distort in some way. One "lives," it is true, but a life governed and shaped by the machine and its exigencies. Let me explain what I mean with a practical example. Diet on dialysis is restricted in several aspects. The major aspect is the strict limitations placed on fluid intake.[10] But what did this mean to me on a daily basis? Fluid does not only mean what we think of as actual fluids but also foods pos-

---

10. *This is at the beginning. As dialysis proceeds — than the machine actually takes over the function of the kidney completely and the kidney shrinks and dies out.*

sessing a high water content such as soup, yogurt and fruits such as apples or watermelons. This restriction was difficult at all times, admittedly, but imagine a long Shabbos afternoon in the summer. The warm hours stretch ahead languorously and there you are with your yearning. Thirst creeps up on you, and suddenly you realize it has become all pervading, a sine qua non shutting out thoughts or images of all else. You balance your glass of water or lemonade carefully on the table in front of you. Then begins the all too familiar circular inner dialogue. "Shall I drink all of it now, and quench my thirst in one fell swoop? But wait. What will happen later? In an hour or so I will be thirsty again. No, don't be rash. Control yourself. Drink half now and a half in two hours time. Or better still, divide it into quarters."

"Drink now — can't you see your tongue and the roof of your mouth are dry."

"Delay, drink — drink, delay!"

In this way, a simple glass of water becomes transformed into a veritable battleground of desire and will.

Imagine having to attend a *simchah,* and one's mind refuses to focus on anything other than the brightly colored bottles of soda on the table. You know its not proper to stare, but you just cannot help it.

Sometimes, when the thirst was not too overpowering, I sucked a candy or a slice of lemon. But these were temporary measures, for, sure enough, my thirst returned.

Connected to the issue of fluid intake was the restriction on salt intake, as salt retains water. I therefore had to learn to use other spices rather than salt in cooking. The only time the restriction on salt was lifted was during dialysis itself, during the first two hours when the washing of the blood actually took place. During this time, and especially during the first hour, I could eat olives, pizzas, pickles, tomatoes and pretzels. I wanted to have finished eating by the time my visitors would normally arrive.

Foods high in potassium are also restricted. Potassium is quickly removed by the filter, but after dialysis the quantity in the body slowly increases. If the blood concentration of potassium rises too high, this can prove extremely dangerous. Potassium is to be found in a variety of foods, ranging from bananas and apricots to chips, baked or roast potatoes, beans, chocolate and cola. All these restric-

tions had to be incorporated into my dialysis lifestyle, but obviously this required a mixture of both iron will power and a deep sense
of acceptance of one's situation. (And this acquired sense of self-con-
trol spilled over to other areas of my life at a later date.)

**Yanky:**

A PATIENT ON DIALYSIS MUST SEVERELY LIMIT HIS OR HER FLUID INTAKE.
An indication of how much fluid needs to be removed on dialysis is
obtained by recording a pre-dialysis weight. If the machine starts to
pull too much water out of the body, this will result in fainting or possibly even coma. With this bold statement of fact, you must, dear reader, understand another facet of the enormity of the task we faced each
day as we undertook dialysis. For dialysis is a treatment which requires
not only exact technical skill, but an astute level of observation of the
patient. At moments such as these, the machine mastered, apparently
functioning as it ought, patient seemingly alert and well, in the back of
a mind numbed with an ever-recurring profound sense of fatigue —
business, wife, machine, children all over squeezed into their allotted
spaces, in a waking day always too short — I may have been forgiven
for lapsing into a sort of semi-comatose state of stuporous self-satis-
faction. But, wait — in the darkening lamp-lit room, I notice my wife
has suddenly become very still, her eyes half shut. Is she sleeping or has
she fainted? I rush to the side of the chair: "I don't feel good, I don't
feel good," she murmurs. This is the critical hour — when the machine
can pull too much water from the body. I open a clip, allowing salt
water to circulate straight into the blood stream. (Salty foods would
take too long to achieve the desired effect.) Each time this happens, I
am astounded at how quickly she is restored to full consciousness, as
if the fainting of a moment ago had been nothing but a well-rehearsed
mime by a child seeking to frighten his parent. Dear Ruchi, forgive me;
I do not doubt for one moment your integrity, but the speed, the
alacrity of the change, would throw me off balance every time it
occurred. And at these moments, too, I understood in a sort of instinc-

tive fashion what an awesome "super" machine our bodies, fashioned by our Creator, really are. One slightest ingredient off balance and we lose ourselves and all our vigorous perception of the world — in an instant! In these seconds, too, as I rushed to her side, I felt the seemingly vast control I now exercised over my wife. "*Ribbono shel Olam*," I am sure I prayed in those seconds, "direct my hands, let me unclip just the right amount of what is necessary to restore her consciousness. Guide my hands in this, for I know that each time there is no surety, no automatic guarantee of success — only Your all-pervading Will."

The only time my wife could eat certain foods freely and drink without fear of restriction was on dialysis. So this too became part of my onerous task, though lovingly undertaken — to prepare interesting foods for her to tempt her appetite. How well I remember one evening preparing a salad of asparagus and tomatoes, and suddenly at a whim, arranging it all into the face of a clown. "Let this make her smile a little," I thought as I completed the picture, and the clown smiled back a shallow, grotesquely happy smile from the plate. Tears suddenly blurred my vision, for that is how it was in those days. At moments when you least expected, sadness, grief even, there it would steal up and touch your shoulder lightly, as if to say:

"You think you're so clever, you think you've got this situation all tied up. You even allow yourself a smile, a little happiness. Well, you're a fool. Look into you heart — isn't it broken....?"

"No, No, I would shout, "I refuse your sadness.... I **can** be happy, in spite of all this, happy and poised and well balanced..."

And did she smile at this simple instinctive gesture I made on that day, and others? Yes, I remember her smile on that occasion lighting up her dark features, making her look for a fleeting second deceptively like that carefree young girl I had married, not so many springtimes ago...

TODAY THE ALARM ON THE MACHINE WENT OFF. IN THE PAST WHEN THIS has occurred, my husband has hurried in from the front room where he has been learning, not unduly alarmed, but eager to locate the problem. Mostly the problems have proved easy to solve, and with a few deft pushes of such and such button or adjustment of pipes, order has been restored. The machine has returned to its normal functioning, my husband to his learning partner patiently waiting in the front room, I to my book. But this time I watched him pushing all the customary buttons, making the usual maneuvers. By now, the machine had ceased functioning. Silence reigned in our bedroom — only the ticking of the clock on the wall can be heard and now the ever present throb of traffic from the main road beyond. Next, he dials one of a number of the telephone numbers he has written down in preparation for just such a situation. The technician at the other end transmits his information yawningly, for it is just half an hour away from midnight.

"Try adjusting such and such needle," he apparently tells Yanky, for this is what he begins to do. These measures have always been successful in the past — but now, they do not appear to help. The problem must be deeper, somewhere in the heartland of that tangled maze of pipes and buttons which we call "our machine." He returns to the phone. He now calls an emergency number.

"It must be something technical. Open the machine," he is instructed.

"Open it?" he repeats open-mouthed, as if the machine is sacrosanct and such an action would amount to violating holy ground.

"Yes, open it."

He locates a box of tools, picks out a particular size of screwdriver and unscrews the machine. The machine gapes open — a tangled mass of wires and joints. He returns to the phone for directions once or twice more. Within ten minutes the machine has been mended and is apparently functioning normally. But somehow our perception of the machine as something of an entity beyond reproach or repair has been irrevocably broached.

# Tuesday Club:

DIALYSIS WAS NOT ALL THE DESPAIR WHICH WE HAVE HITHER TO PAINTED. Every Tuesday, for example, a set of friends would gather to sit with me. These occasions soon became quite an occasion of merriment.

The following is a description of the "Tuesday Club," as it soon became known by one of its participants:

"Hello, Shira, it's Tuesday night again. Pick you up at eight for this week's Tuesday club? Be seeing you!"

For the uninitiated, the Tuesday club is an informal get together, which was unique in many many different ways. Firstly, the venue itself was remarkable. There we sat, my friends and I, facing Ruchi, on her dialysis machine hooked up to various tubes, a miracle within a miracle.

The intriguing thing about walking into Ruchi's was the atmosphere. We were not overwhelmed by a feeling that we were entering a sickroom, but rather sensed immediately that Ruchi was delighted to see us, that she was genuinely interested in us and that this interest overrode all those tubes and needles. And the conversation? One hundred percent lashon hara-free! I can hear some cynics, "How boring! What on earth did they ever find to talk about?" Truthfully, we were never at a loss for the next topic to discuss. Energetically, we tackled everything. World events were covered with gusto. Subjects close to our hearts were also hotly debated. Should our children be required to wear school uniform? Should *kiruv rechokim* take precedence over family life? With participants from America, S. America, Britain, Israel — and of course Europe — these issues were considered from every angle. The debates were sometimes fast and furious and, more often than not, side-splitting. How many times did the blood-pressure indicator rise as Ruchi giggled uncontrollably, or became excited or indignant. When one of us made a purchase, the dress was brought to Ruchi and laid out for her opinion and expertise. Ruchi concocted monograms and suggested color schemes. No, we were never at a loss for words!

Perhaps the *Piece de Resistance* of the Tuesday Clubs was the show. It was decided that the ladies of our town should put on a performance, with the proceeds being donated to the local *cheder*. Accordingly, a script was written; costumes, props and scenery were designed and created; and choirs and dances were prepared. Friendships were forged, new talents were discovered (sometimes to the great surprise of the talented ones themselves) and a new *achdus* and sense of purpose permeated the activities of these ladies. At the heart of it all was Ruchi תחי׳ and the Tuesday Club. There, ideas were born, plans were laid and problems were ironed out. And Ruchi תחי׳ was always there with fresh ideas, with know-how and with the conviction that the show was going to be a success. And with the help of the *Ribbono shel Olam*, it was!

We always left Ruchi feeling so much richer than when we came. Being a member of the Tuesday Club, with Ruchi as its chairman, gave us another dimension in life. We saw greatness in the face of adversity and it never failed to move and inspire us. When the news finally came, after many years, that the kidney transplant had taken place, and with it the realization that the Tuesday Club was disbanded, we knew that we had been privileged to accompany Ruchi תחי׳ along certain stretches of her path to recovery *b"h* and we rejoiced that the Tuesday Club was no more.

⊱✦⊰

## Nurse:

APPARENTLY, THEY ARE DOING WELL, MY JEWISH COUPLE. MANY MONTHS, almost a year now into dialysis. They tell me they will soon attempt a journey — perhaps to the Holy Land. I visualize it as a sort of pilgrimage to their holy sites, a spiritual recharging of batteries. I feel they are mentally ready now for such a journey, for as the months have progressed on dialysis, so has their confidence. There have been few problems, either technical or otherwise. In fact, the wife has fainted remarkably few times and seems in increasingly better health, both physically and mentally. Her husband tells me he likes to prolong the dialysis as long as he is able to, for he has been told that the longer the dialysis, the more effective it will prove to be. He has proved remarkably assiduous, too, on gathering information about dialysis and kidney disease, and seems intent on exploring all possibilities available. I look in on them from time to time. This is how it usually occurs: Sometimes, after my long hours at the hospital are finished, I find myself possessed of a sudden urge to visit these young friends. Then, almost without knowing how or why, I find myself on the other side of the city, at the outskirts of what passes here for the Jewish quarter (an area not intensely inhabited by Jews, but where one is likely to see the rare traditionally garbed old man using his cane, or a young boy, earlocks flying pass, on his bicycle), and inexplicably at the door of their second floor apartment. The door flings open, the children rush to greet me.

"How goes it?" I ask each member of the household in turn. Have patience, my young friends, I murmur to myself as I enter the bedroom door and see the young woman's face light up in greeting. This will not last forever. Keep your spirits up and we will surely find a way out. Sooner, much sooner than you dare hope...

TODAY, I CONSULTED WITH NURSE JULIA ON THE ADVISABILITY OF undertaking a journey to Eretz Yisrael. I think, in some profound way, we are more than ready for this step, and perhaps we would be afforded the opportunity of pouring our hearts out at the holy sites and graves. Since this *nisayon* began, we have had little time to catch our breath spiritually as it were, to truly appraise our situation. We have been fully occupied simply coping with the endless daily demands of my wife's condition. She feels ready, too, a little nervous perhaps, a little apprehensive at leaving her own machine for something unknown, but if she wants to expand her horizon a little, she must learn to face change. (There is a psychological danger that she will become in some subtle way dependent on her machine and the familiarity of her own surroundings. Difficult as it may seem, she must take those first tentative steps back into the world at large.)

Ruchi:

Upon arriving in the Holy Land we immediately made our way to Tel Aviv, where we attended a modern dialysis unit. It was so strange, for dialysis has come to be associated in my psyche with my home country and gentile faces, some stern and unwelcoming, others friendly. But never among Jews. Every unit necessarily assumes something of the nature of a family — for it is usually attended by the same patients two or three times a week. This was a large airy room, and sunlight slanted in from the tall windows and cream-colored blinds — not the pale insubstantial sunlight of my home country — but strong Israeli sunshine. In the light gray chairs sat six or seven Israelis, ranging in age from a youngish-looking fellow in his twenties, apparently a taxi driver — a thick gold chain dangled from his neck — to a matriarch of about sixty. There seemed to be some sort of discussion raging, but when I entered the room there was an immediate and palpable silence. I knew they were assessing everything about me carefully, including my appearance as an Orthodox woman. They continued to eye me a little warily and from a distance, as if stalking someone who might turn out to be an enemy. The tall nurse with whom we had conversed previously entered the room breezily.

"Everyone, please show respect to this young couple from Europe. This young man here has been carrying out home dialysis for his wife for nearly a whole year...."

One could almost hear the sharp intake of breath at this announcement. All at once, the swirl of voices broke out again, but this time directed towards us, and in friendly tones.

# Yanky:

IT SEEMS LIKE PART OF A DREAMLIKE SEQUENCE THAT WE ARE HERE IN THE Holy Land, together as a family. Psychologically, my wife has succeeded in breaking a seemingly insurmountable barrier. She has left behind the womb-like familiarity of her own four walls and her own machine. I believe that she must learn, however painfully, to sever this cast-iron link at regular intervals. She must resume living in the wide open spaces of the world and not in some sort of quasi-imprisonment, which holds her fixed immobile to one spot as effectively as iron railings or the prison guard tapping on the windowless cell. I say this perhaps a little glibly, because possibly not even I can imagine how many self exhortations, fortifications of will, restless nights pacing up and down our carpeted corridors, this costs her. But somehow she is here, at my side. We have attended several dialysis sessions in Tel Aviv. She says herself that she feels she has broken an impenetrable barrier. How we travelled the length and breadth of the country in between dialyses, I cannot explain. It is one of those facets belonging to those years which supersedes rational explanation. But I remember wanting beyond anything to prove to ourselves and others that we could live a normal life, we could travel without restriction, other than the need to attend dialysis. I remember Massada in the shimmering heat — stone-hewn steps, the bone aching climb upwards and suddenly the summit. The palpable aura of human suffering and self-sacrifice in that place threatened to overwhelm our equanimity. In any case, I think that during the entire visit we were always close to tears. I had rarely felt so exposed, so raw, as if all the long-held emotions were barely held in leash below the surface. In our home country, it seemed throughout our ordeal, emotions or tears were to be suppressed, not at any rate anything to wallow in. But here, on the contrary, they seemed to be part of the rich texture of life itself — laughter, tears, pain and human loss, that one felt less ashamed to be what one really was — a feeling, vulnerable bundle of humanity.

Yes, of course, we prayed at the *Kosel*, we added our requests to the mountains of pleas pressed into the crevice-ridden wall. Yet strangely enough, although I had imagined this moment so many times during my years on dialysis and how I had prayed: "Would I could just stand before the *Kosel's* ancient stones — oh, how my tears would flow" — alas, as I stood faced with its reality, it was as if I had become as frozen as a rock. I simply could not find one word of entreaty or prayer to the Almighty and this inarticulateness was in itself an agony. So after a few moments I simply said, almost out aloud, "*You, Ribbono Shel Olam,* You know my innermost feelings and thoughts these last hours. Now take them and form them into the proper words." When we finally withdrew from this holy place I was therefore uplifted, yet disappointed too. We travelled north on bumpy, noisy buses, and prayed at gravestones there. On one occasion my three children joined hands and prayed out loud:

"Please Hashem, make our mommy *gezunt* (well) again...."

Spiritually and emotionally spent, we returned home, hoping that somehow our prayers had changed us in some profound way and perhaps, found their mark.

This was the beginning of a series of journeys, not lightly undertaken, but purposefully, carefully, intricately. Plans would begin weeks or months before the proposed journey, for I would have to ascertain the best facilities available for dialysis in our intended location. On arrival, our first port of call would be not the local sights but a clinic, hospital or dialysis unit. It was a strange, backhanded way of familiarizing ourselves with the capitals of the world. Each dialysis unit, we soon realized, had its own quite unique flavor, and hand in hand with that its advantages and disadvantages.

Our journeys broke the monotony in what had now become an established routine of dialysis and its intermittent interval of fairly normal life. In addition, I acquainted myself with dialysis units throughout the world. Each bore the unique character of its inhabitants. In Eretz Yisrael, our Tel-Aviv unit was noisy, quarrelsome, had something of the irreverent nature of a group of ill-assorted relatives, who both envelop you in their warmth and irritate you with their impertinent probing questions or remarks. Harley Street in London clinic was sedate — its members cooly polite, welcoming you with a steely nod, rarely affronting you with their curiosity. Even my husband's outlandish appearance did not occasion more than a barely perceptible raising of the eyebrows. Here, the prime feature was restraint. My parents accompanied me on some occasions as they were in England for my brother's *sheva berachos*. It was tormenting for them having to endure the joy of marrying off their son and the agony of attending their sick daughter simultaneously.

Next stage was the planning of a journey to New York to attend a family *simchah*. I spent three weeks in New York and attended the Staten Island clinic. The unit I attended in New York was positively garish by comparison. Nurses wandered in and out, addressed us by our first names. Patients were rarely quiet for long, there was a constant hum of chatter or activity. In the far corner of the room sat a young black man, oblivious to the world, swaying to some pulsating rhythm perpetrated by the headphones which sat squarely on his curly head. Usually, the change in machine did not seem to cause me any ill effects once the initial emotional adjustment of a change of scenery had been made. Looking back from my new vantage point, these journeys were desperately important, serving as commas, in what would otherwise have proved years of unbearably monotonous waiting...

## Yanky:

THROUGHOUT THE PROLONGED PERIOD WHICH MY WIFE SPENT ON dialysis we were privileged to witness many instances of obvious Heavenly Assistance — *siyata diShmaya*. Looking back, these happenings seem nothing short of miraculous, for had happening A and B not fallen into place in just such a way, the ultimate outcome, we now realize with the spurious wisdom of hindsight, may not have been achieved.

One such example which springs almost instantly to mind is that of our usage of the newly developed drug, eprex. The most obvious function of the kidney is to produce urine. However, the kidneys have some other essential functions. They are involved in regulating blood pressure. They also affect the amount of calcium in the bone. Finally, they influence the production of red blood cells in the bonemarrow. Thus, when the kidneys cease to function, the hemoglobin level automatically begins to drop. In the past, therefore, kidney patients have had no choice but to undergo frequent blood transfusions. These transfusions created new and very serious problems, as they increased the risk of contracting viruses such as hepatitis or HIV. An additional problem was the creation of new antibodies in the blood. These would considerably lessen the chances of a successful transplant being carried out, as the more antibodies found in the blood, the greater the chance that they would attack and ultimately destroy the new organ. This was the dilemma in which kidney patients routinely found themselves. However, shortly after my wife began dialysis, a new drug was developed. This was hailed as one of the major medical breakthroughs of the last hundred years. The wonder drug, named eprex (or Erythropoietin), which would radically alter the prospects of thousands of patients on dialysis, would imitate the function of the kidneys in giving the command to produce red blood cells, thereby more or less eliminating the need for blood transfusion. For us this was to prove a *nes galui* — an open miracle, because had my wife been forced to go to the hospital for blood transfusions, not only would she have been prone to the physical problems mentioned before, but I am convinced that many of the emotional problems she had experienced in the hospital would have returned to haunt her, so that much of the benefit of home dialysis in respect to peace of mind and spirit would have been lost. This medication was initially very expensive. It was provided as a capsule which I put into the line, and a set dosage would be administered during dialysis, thereby eliminating the need for Rachel to stick herself again. Thankfully, with the aid of this wonder drug, her hemoglobin had begun to rise and rise. Some months after we had begun administering this drug during dialysis, we journeyed to New York, attending our chosen dialysis station. As dialysis neared its end, I approached a nurse and told her that at this point I would have to administer a certain drug to my wife, as I was accustomed to do at home. (This drug was newly developed in our home country and was not yet available in America). Uncertain, she beckoned a passing doctor.

There was no blood bank here which would alleviate our concerns over the source of the blood. This created a problem.

"Doctor, this man wishes to make a formal request to administer a drug to his wife."

He eyed me, in a long hard look.

"What's the drug called?" he asked somewhat off-handedly.

I gave him the full title. We watched his eyes bulge with wonder over the fact that we already had this new drug.

"Sir, I have to tell you that this drug has not yet been approved by our FDA (Food and Drug Administration of America), and as such I cannot allow its use in this unit."

"Well, what should I do?" I asked in a tone bordering on despair.

"Your wife will need a blood transfusion.[11] Let me see, she can call in the day after tomorrow for that..."

"I cannot agree to this," I countered. "She has never needed a blood transfusion and I will simply not allow it... Just give me a needle and I will administer the drug myself. I assure you I am quite used to doing this."

"I am afraid I simply cannot allow the administration of a non-approved drug in this unit."

With that he turned on his heel, leaving me staring at the receding whiteness of his back.

Two days later we returned to the same unit for dialysis. I still had not decided what course of action to take, and the nagging worry was

---

11. *Blood transfusions can only be given in a hospital because they can have strong reactions — including fever and some problems. Sometimes it can be even be fatal if not tested beforehand with some of the patients own blood. This mixing of her blood and the transfusion blood could only be done in a laboratory.*

smoldering within me like an autumn fire. I had secretly determined to avoid this particular doctor; however, as soon as we entered the unit, I saw him approaching out of the corner of my eye. There was little hope of turning away for he seemed to be moving directly towards me.

Such was one instance in a long series of stupefying "coincidences." For what we had now trained ourselves to do was to play a kind of "glad game," convincing ourselves to find the good in every situation. Had my wife, for example, become ill before the advent of this wonder drug she may ultimately have had more difficulties in receiving a transplant because of the build up of antibodies caused by the blood transfusions. In illness as much as in health one requires a certain degree of *mazal*. The "good" that Hashem wishes for us can be traced like fingerpatterns on a rainy day, even within the bad, but one must achieve the right frame of mind to seek that good... and this made life easier to bear.".

"Good morning, Mr. Guttfreund," he proclaimed heartily, all the sullenness of the previous day seemingly vanished. Before I had time to answer, he continued:

"I have a very interesting piece of news to offer you."

I coughed, not knowing what to expect.

"The drug eprex, which you mentioned to me the day before yesterday — well, it seems it has just been approved by the FDA as recently as a day ago. I can now allow you to use it here without any qualms... In fact, would you please leave some with me here as we are unable to obtain it on the market."

Another instance of astonishing intervention by the Master Planner came a little later. This is included in the section of our story which I mentally labeled "the list." Let me explain. Throughout the whole period that my wife remained on dialysis, the idea of an ultimate escape from the constant need for this treatment burned on in my mind and heart. It was there, during every waking hour and minute, and probably inhabited our dreams, too. It simply never left us — this one overwhelming thought — how to get on "the list" and then ultimately "the transplant." If I say it was a thought or an idea, it is because I have no better words in my vocabulary with which to describe it, but in truth these words do little to summon up the all-pervading nature of the idea. Perhaps, obsession would be a better word or obsessive thought, because it was quite a rational idea (as opposed to what we normally think of as obsessions), perhaps fixation, perhaps all-consuming goal. It matters little what we call it, but while occupied with pipes and needles and pre- and post-dialysis weights, the thought would frequently come over me unbeckoned, "One day we will be free of all this, one day, soon, whatever it takes..." And if, sometimes, in an unguarded moment, looking down into my wife's dark eyes, the habitual cheerful smile frozen on my lips, I would fancy I saw there just the self-same question: "How much longer?" or "When will it come...?!" But we rarely shared these thoughts with one another, for it took all of our poise and courage just to maintain our equanimity, to cope with that one moment and then the next. We were like tightrope walkers, deeply aware of the safe grassy haven just a few feet away, but needing all of our concentration for just the next step and then the next....

That's how it was for us in those days, and that is how we lived with a supreme effort of will.... One escaping sigh, one tear rolling down one's cheek, and all might well be lost. Tears, certainly for my wife, were a luxury she allowed herself only in the shower, with the water already flowing or for me at a rain-lashed window in the early hours of the morning. I could see that she did not want me to see her crying, as this would "rock the boat" of normality which we tried so hard to maintain. True, she was not always in the best of spirits, yet she rarely allowed me to see her in tears.

Our all-consuming thought was how to get ourselves onto the transplant list and with as much alacrity as possible.... Once on the list the waiting-time was still seemingly endless, the odds were still frighteningly small, but at least one lived with an ever so tiny sliver of hope, for one was after all on the list... This is what the list represented to us, so that quite possibly we would have given all that we possessed, all our cherished little treasures, just for the privilege of inclusion on the list. But it would seem this was not at all such a simple matter. The list was housed at the university hospital. When a patient has decided to have a transplant, his name, details of his blood group, tissue type and other information are registered. When a suitable kidney donor dies, the tissue type and blood group are transmitted to the transplant unit. Then an elaborate system of crossmatching is put into play, the details being fed into a control computer. The computer then produces a number of names of people who would be ideal matches for this particular kidney. The choice has then to be whittled down to one ideal recipient. In fact, each hospital has its own system of choosing this one recipient. In some parts of the world, one patient is called from a waiting room holding ten people whose names have been drawn from the computer. Thus it happens that out of ten waiting individuals, nine are sent home. This system has its obvious drawbacks — the call out to the hospital, the raised hopes, the ultimate disappointment — all conspire to produce an aura of deep depression in the dialysis patient. In our home country, however, the system enacted was that only one person was called. The fateful choice really and truly rested in the hands of the head of the department. We must keep in mind that they are only messengers of Hashem; their powers are all G-d-given. He would decide after a period of the most careful analysis — based on a number of consideration such as age, family conditions, how long one has been waiting — who should have the kidney. But all this presupposes that one is already on the list. However, we had not even reached that most tenuous of footholds...

## Ruchi:

NOW THAT DIALYSIS IS WELL-ESTABLISHED, ALTHOUGH I TRY NOT TO divulge these thoughts too often to Yanky, the thought of a transplant seems to consume the substance of my thoughts more and more thoroughly. I do not want to impart the strength of my feelings about this to him, for he has already taken on so much in bringing the machine home, that I feel to add to his anxieties would constitute a sort of betrayal. But, in truth, it is a dream of freedom which has seeped into all the nooks and crannies of my consciousness. I dream of a time when dialysis and its myriad needs and preparations will not steal up to thirty hours of our time each week. I dream of a time, and this can only be truly understood by someone who has been on dialysis, when I can eat and drink what I like, and be healthy and strong; I dream of a time when I am not attached to a machine, and when I can function as a healthy individual for the sake of my husband and children. Simple enough dreams, you might well whisper to yourselves, but to me they existed only on the other side of what appeared in my nightmares as a gray impenetrable wall. How could I scale it? The wall appeared forbiddingly high and featureless, entirely without footholds. I was a tiny shivering figure at the bottom, I could not even work out a way to begin my ascent for it seemed to defy human logic. Sometimes, too, I would visualize a list of names in my dreams — the list itself was nondescript enough, a gray sheet of paper, typewritten names, neatly spaced out in alphabetical order. I would begin to scan the page; when I reached the letter with which my surname begins, I would look and look again. It was not there. The list continues to other successive and meaningless names. "There must be some mistake, there is a mistake," I cry out like a child, "I have been left out, passed over..." Then, I would awake to the bald realization that not only had my name not been summoned — it was not even included on the imagined list....

❧

Yanky: ANOTHER PESACH PASSED, THEN THE MONTH OF APRIL WAS GONE, then May. Outside our apartment the trees were bursting into bloom, business at the flower shop at the corner had begun to be brisk again, as the owner set out the earliest summer plants, their rich trailing hues spilling over onto the city pavement.... I notice all these things but not with a lightness of heart, rather with a melancholy dragging down my spirits, for there had been no reply to my request, now some months old, to place my wife on the list. This worry nagged at my equanimity. I did not know whom to consult about how to proceed from here, for perhaps, I thought, forcing the issue would somehow imperil her chances. I felt almost paralyzed with fear. Wait a while, a voice told me, no, you must ask, wait, have patience... I was thrown from one opinion to the other helplessly. Finally with the end of May in sight, I gathered my courage and approached a doctor at the university hospital — the doctor who had promised to mark her name down all those months ago.

"Did he remember me?" I asked somewhat naively. "It's for my wife that I ask." I spelled out the name twice, as he noted it down. "Would you happen to know," I asked with a desperate casualness, "would her name happen to be on the list yet?"

He scanned the names on computer.

"No, her name did not appear to be there... But isn't it a little premature, Mr. Guttfreund? Let me see, I would say that in about a year or so, you can expect her name to appear on the list. After all there is a long waiting list and these things just take time."

I struggled to retain my composure, while inside everything was raging. A year, a year without hope? No, it is impossible to live like that. The thought of days spent in endless preparations for dialysis stretched on interminably, week after week, month after month without respite. No, I simply could not wait it out. Once she was on the list I was quite prepared to fully exercise my *bitachon* and leave things in the Almighty's hands, but there must be a way to get her on the list initially. I worried and fretted around the problem, my mind returning to it constantly like a mother fussing over a sick child. I listened to advice. Some said I should not risk contacting the professor in charge. Others said: "Phoning would be useless. Write. What could you lose? It must be through the medium of a lawyer. He will formulate your request in official terms. If you write it yourself in layman's terms, you have little chance of success."

I considered the matter. I prayed for guidance. Somehow I believed that in every dark corner Hashem would show me the right way to proceed, as He had in the past. Now, this instinct told me: "Seek out no expensive lawyer. Take a pen and write a letter yourself in the language of your own heart. Perhaps your words will find their true mark...."

So one evening I closed the door of my study, took out a blank piece of paper and began. If I tell you that I did not write the letter myself, but **it** wrote itself, it would be no less than the truth, for the facts speak well enough for themselves. My hand flew back and forth, back and forth as though an unseen hand was guiding it, and in little more than twenty minutes the letter was composed. This is the substance of the letter which I wrote in my wife's name:

"Dear Professor Lagfeld,

"Let me address a few chosen words to you. I, Mrs. Rachel Guttfreund, have been married for four and a half years to a European young man. Our marriage has brought three healthy children to the world; one is three and a half, one is two and a half, and the baby, a girl, is one and a half years old. Fate decreed that despite my youth — I am but twenty-one and a half years old — I should have to sit at the dialysis machine. I was pregnant with my third child when it was discovered that I had the symptoms of nephrotic syndrome. Eventually, this developed into glomerulonephritis, and it soon became apparent that there was no help for it — I would have to go on dialysis. After some time, we were able to carry out home dialysis, and now this has been established three or four times a week.

"Initially, when I heard that I would have to go on dialysis, you can imagine perhaps a little of how I felt. My whole world seemed to break into little pieces over my head. You see, professor, I was always such an active young woman, and also I desired with all my heart to give the proper attention to my little ones. They are, thank G-d, normal healthy children and as such are noisy, playful, tiring, messy — all the things that very young children are, but most of all, I think, they need and are entitled to a fit mother. When I had to spend weeks at a time in the hospital, you can well imagine the chaos which reigned in my home. I had to ask other people to look after them, and they became confused and more than a little resentful. My husband runs a full-time business. Now, in the evenings he has to help cook meals, give attention to the children and carry out dialysis for me, which takes endless hours of his time and energy. The only way, in my humble opinion, for us to extract ourselves from this mess and return to some measure of normalcy, is transplantation. I know that nobody can tell me how long I would have to wait for a transplant, but it would be far easier for me to accept this mentally, knowing that my name is already on the computer list.

I have heard, dear professor, so much good said about you. It is well known that you are a person with a truly kind heart. It was this thought that prompted me to take the extraordinary step of contacting you since you are "the person in charge," who ultimately makes the decisions. I hope I have shown no impertinence or effrontery in so doing, but I simply beg you to assist me in eventually returning to being the healthy young woman that I once was, and more importantly, a healthy mother for my heartbroken children. I pray every day that G-d send me a kidney speedily and may the Almighty send you also many healthy happy years.

"Sincerely, Rachel Guttfreund"

I read this letter through once or twice, made some minor changes, then copied it straight off, in my own handwriting. When I was satisfied that I could not improve on it, I folded and sealed it, affixed a stamp — then walked the block and a half to the nearest mail box. I imagined it fluttering inside the mailbox to join the pile of letters. I imagined it falling like a delicate autumn leaf onto the professor's porch floor. More than this I dared not imagine. But as I walked home, the steady roar of traffic ringing in my ears, I felt that at last an iron band had been lifted from around my heart...

❧

## Ruchi:

YANKY SEEMS DIFFERENT IN SOME SUBTLE WAY, PERHAPS A LITTLE lighter in spirit than he has been lately. Not that he is depressed and melancholy normally, no, on the contrary, he is always extremely cheerful and optimistic. And he finds so many little ways of raising my spirits — but only I know how much real weariness of heart this brittle cheerfulness costs. We are like participants in some extraordinary dumb show, each one trying at all costs to conceal his true feelings from the other. But this is a necessary component of the way we live our lives at this time, for neither of us can afford the strength of our true feelings to upset our hard earned balance.

If this was one of the positive aspects of the whole episode of my illness, then the enrichment of spirit this afforded me was, dare I say it, worthwhile? Sometimes I reread some words I jotted down on a piece of paper detailing my feelings. These words were written one year after Yom Kippur had passed:

"These are just some thoughts, some very private thoughts of my own, and not *divrei Torah* or *mussar*. But they are not just theoretical words, but words drawn directly from the rich taproot of living.

"I have been sick for some time now, so you can understand that I constantly grope for ways to keep both my spirits up and my *bitachon* unwavering. This entails finding things for which to be truly thankful. This Yom Kippur I felt I had reached new heights in achieving a new understanding in the meaning of the words in *Shema Koleinu*: '*Avinu Malkeinu shelach refuah sheleimah l'cholei amecha*.' This year I found that on uttering these words, quite contrary to what one would expect, I could not bring myself to cry for myself, as I felt so young and self-conscious among all the older people praying around me. My tears or any other sign of undue agitation might also attract their curiosity and pinpoint me as the target of many curious eyes. Also, it somehow felt wrong to ask for a *refuah sheleimah* for myself, although this is not necessarily what one ought to feel. Today I know that one is supposed to pray for himself just as well. The *Avinu Malkeinu* having been said, it bothered me that I had not been able to express myself about that which I wanted above all else: a *refuah sheleimah*. Continuing the verses I arrived at the words *Al tashelicheni milfanecha v'ruach kodshecha al tikach mimeni*. As I repeated these words, a middle-aged woman two rows ahead of me burst into hysterical sobbing. I could see her shoulders bobbing up and down, her chin trembling as she finally subsided, completely burying her head deep into her *machzor*. The sight of her distress moved me beyond words, and made me think: 'Why am I standing here apparently unmoved? Something is passing me by, here; I am missing something.' So I read the words again, but this time slowly and deliberately weighing each word. *Al tashelicheni milfanecha v'ruach kodshecha al tikach mimeni....* — 'Do not cast me away from you, and do not remove your holy spirit from me.' Suddenly, it was as if a new, hitherto unseen world opened up before me. Each of us encounters some or other *nisayon* in life. Some of us are allowed to see it clearly, some of us less clearly. However, my *nisayon* was unequivocal and bore no possibility of error in detection. After all, my kidneys had stopped functioning, I was on dialysis and was now desperately in need of a *refuah*. Then and there, I 'struck a bargain' with the Almighty. I said: '*Ribbono shel Olam — yode ha kol*, You know the heart of every human being. You know what it is that I pray for most dearly, and that is quite simply, to become healthy again. But at this point, I dare to ask you for something quite new. I entreat you, *Al tashelicheni milfanecha*, grant me Your special *Ruach* of holiness, always to enable me to undergo and surmount the obstacles placed in my path — in my case, my kidney disease...'

From that moment onwards, I would repeat this verse as often as I could, whether holding a *siddur* in my hand or just in my head. To the extent that I was sincere in asking for this "holiness of spirit." I feel that I was granted just this. For strength was granted to me not just to get by from one dialysis to another, nor for the time, please G-d, when my name enters the list, nor for the time the call for the transplant comes, but here and now, feeling with all my heart, when I look at the faces of my three innocent children, when I consider that I am still alive to watch their upturned features quicken to my smile — that my salvation is in the present, has already touched me on the shoulder. And also in the achingly hard trying to really live my life and not live my life in the waiting, I must say that all this trying was not just "I tried," but the receiving of a special "gift" of the Almighty's love, as if I were already floating, somewhere warm and cushioned from the reality of the pain surrounding me...

**Yanky:**

SOMETHING UNBELIEVABLE HAS HAPPENED — AS I WRITE THESE WORDS, I am still stunned by the alacrity with which events seem to have moved. Ruchi has received a call from the hospital and she has been asked to bring along some blood samples, for tissue typing. We both know what this means — that she is about to be placed on that almost mythical list. Is it possible that my simply written letter could have touched a chord within Professor Lagfeld's heart and that he then acted spontaneously to place her on the list? Of course, that is what I hoped for in writing to him, but I made my request as a child does — a little fancifully — little expecting it to be fulfilled. I would like to know how this actually transpired — to see the gray wheels turning behind the facade. The only person I can think of who might be able to shed some light on all this is Nurse Julia...

**Nurse:**

MY JEWISH FRIEND PHONED. HE IS IN A STATE OF SHOCK — PLEASANT shock as it were. It seems his wife is about to be placed on the list and he cannot fathom how this objective was achieved so quickly. As it happened, I knew the inside story. Professor Lagfeld had in fact not been in the hospital for two months. Rumors abounded in the hospital as to the reasons for his absence. Some suggested a leave of absence, others that he had travelled abroad. However, I was perhaps one of the few people who knew the true story. He had suffered a mild stroke — a fact which he and his family had taken pains not to publicize. On the first day that Professor Lagfeld returned to the hospital, recovered but not yet fit to operate, the letter written by my friend was lying upturned on a large pile of unopened correspondence on his desk. So that when he reached out and picked it up in his right hand, which still betrayed signs of a slight tremor, when he opened it and read the handwritten letter inside, this was the first impression of his hospital responsibilities to imprint itself on his mind. The letter itself was simple and undeniably moving — but it was when he came to the final words: "May the Almighty send you also many healthy happy years..." that a strange feeling took hold of him, shaking him to the core. He had taken such care to ensure that very few people know of his illness, that it did not become public knowledge, that these words seemed now to take on an almost prophetic nature. It was as if some invisible power in the world was communicating itself to him and that he, insignificant though he felt the fate of one individual to be, was nevertheless part of a larger plan. He swivelled his chair to look out on the familiar lawns and trees beyond his office and felt quite uncharacteristic tears streaming down his round face. He picked up a pen and painstakingly copied the name on the bottom of the letter.

IN FACT THIS CONSTITUTED AN AMAZING EXAMPLE OF *SIYATA DISHMAYA*, that my letter should have come to Professor Lagfeld's attention so soon after his illness. This made him more sympathetic to the sufferings of others, especially a young woman, for he had in actual fact had a 'close call' with death. This is how Ruchi came to placed on the list so speedily.

THE DRAMATIC WAY IN WHICH MY NAME WAS ADDED TO THE LIST SOON dulled into grayness in our minds, as one by one the weeks and then the months rolled by without any apparent change in our situation. Dialysis continued, the day-to-day fabric and constituents of our daily life now proceeded much as before the incidence of the seeming hiatus, so that now the list began to assume an almost mythical nature in my imagination. If it was true that my name had been inserted in what was to my mind a long "graying sheet of papers," it seemed to me as outrageous a chance as winning a prize in the National Lottery that my name should now actually be summoned forth from all the others. In my dreams, I visualized this as some sort of strange award ceremony. "Mrs. Guttfreund," I imagined the master of ceremonies calling out, "your name has been drawn out of the hat — you are the lucky recipient of such and such prize..." I would step forward a little shakily towards the outstretched arm... Then I would awake, but the overwhelming feeling of somehow waiting to be summoned lingered on...

TIME IS PASSING SO ACHINGLY SLOWLY AND STILL NO WORD... I AM beginning to despair. Getting on the list is not the salvation I had hoped it would be. I have heard so many stories of people waiting years for a kidney. There is just no way to predict the waiting period, but I feel instinctively that neither of us could endure much longer in this state, patiently weightless. "There must be a way, there must be another way out of this" — this was the refrain which throbbed and pulsed ceaselessly through my temples. One quiet, nondescript evening — the children long asleep, the apartment still — the doorbell rings. My wife and I look at each other questioningly across the kitchen table. We are not expecting anyone and it is too late anyway for uninvited visitors. I go to open the door. There, framed in the doorway is Nurse Julia. She looks a little uneasy, a little unlike her usual, solidly good humored self.

"Come, come in," I welcome her. "We haven't seen you for some time, Julia. How are you?" She enters. "Sit, please." I say, drawing out a chair.

"No, no, I am in something of a hurry — I was just working late and happened to be driving this way, so..." Again the slight edginess in her voice, as if she is concealing something.

"Well, we always appreciate seeing you, even for a few moments..."

"Well, no," she continued, as if she had not heard my last remark. "That is not quite true, I did not just happen to be passing this way at all. I came here quite expressly. There is something I must show you both." And now, she produced from her briefcase a few sheets of official looking papers.

"Do you know what these are? Well, these are photocopies of your wife's medical history. She will need them if you are to succeed."

"But, Julia," I interpolated, scanning the photocopies briefly, "I don't understand — why should we need these? My wife is already on the list. These would only be necessary should we decide..." my voice trailed off.

"Listen to me, my dear, dear friends" she continued in a low and urgent voice. "I must tell you both something. You well know that your wife's name was entered on the list about a year ago. I must tell you that in my experience and judgement you are in for a long wait..."

At this, I heard my wife let out a tiny, hardly audible gasp. I did not turn round.

"Is it hopeless then?" I repeated, like a child learning a new word, "Hopeless?"

"No, not hopeless, but I believe it could well take years for her to receive a kidney here, and meanwhile your wife remains on dialysis with all the difficulties that that situation brings. But all is not lost. I will tell you what to do — but first you must swear to me never to divulge what I have advised you to do. My whole career would be in danger, I am sure of it, especially if it became known that I have secretly photocopied this information for you." She tapped the photocopies lying on the kitchen table.

"We promise, we promise," we both rejoined, almost at once.

"Your wife is an American citizen. You know very well that in this country, we have the regulation that your name cannot be included on two or more lists at the same time. Strictly speaking, should you decide to enter a list in another country, you ought to withdraw your name over here... However, I personally think this to be another of those petty-minded regulations with which our system is riddled. You want to put yourself in the best possible situation for your wife to get a kidney. Well, what I would say to you is — get your wife's name on a list in the USA, as well as retaining it on this list here, for I honestly see this as your best chance — and that is why you will need your medical history... But again, I must seek your confirmation on this point — not a word of this breathed to anyone, as I could be in serious trouble for this breach of regulations. However, I trust you both implicitly. Now I really must be going," she added almost lightly. In a flash, a flurry of her dark winter wrap, her scarf, her briefcase — she was gone, and we were both left sitting, holding our breath as it were, afraid to utter a word or comment on what had just transpired.

## Ruchi:

A REMARKABLE EVENT HAS TRANSPIRED, ONE WHICH WHEN WE ARE OLD and gray, please G-d, I am certain we will look back on as one of these seminal, earth-shaking moments which changed our lives at a stroke. Nurse Julia arrived late on our doorstep. She has advised us (and not just advised us but taken practical steps to help us to this end, even to the extent of endangering her own position) to register as soon as possible on a list in America. "It is simply not enough," she stated most forcibly, her hand striking the table, "to rely on your name being on the list in this country." We were both shaken to the very core, trembling as we struggled to come to terms with this event that seemed to us, as soon as the door has shut quietly behind her, more like an apparition than an actual day-to-day happening.

"What does it mean?" we turn to each other, both with the same question dying on our lips. Surely the same wonderment which we saw in one another's eyes meant roughly this:

"We can read the signs. It is one of those moments which has punctuated these dark times, and which we grope towards and then take our direction from." And then we both mouthed silently: "We must do as she says." For it has come again, this category of *Na'aseh Venishmah* — the heart leading the mind, the not unthinking but deeper than thought intuitive knowledge that this, and only this is the way forward without anything remotely approaching understanding of what the following of that way entails. My husband now spoke out loud, for the first time voicing merely the practical outcome of all this silent rumination. "You know that this means we must go... and as soon as possible... Are you ready for this?"

I nodded.

"Well," I mouthed soundlessly, "this is the sign." Let me explain exactly what I meant by that... In the past eighteen months, we had felt ourselves to be utterly confused and disoriented, perhaps more than at any other time. Why? you might ask. Dialysis was progressing almost routinely, and I was now on the list. But that was just the trouble. Punctuated throughout the all-enveloping darkness of this *nisayon*, we had often been privileged to feel the comforting proximity of the Master of the universe to us. This sense of inspiration would guide us when all seemed confusion and despair, speaking to us in a "small still voice," directing us as to which path of all those opening up before us to take. But in all these months, when things appeared to be stagnating, with no discernible movement in any direction, there was no sudden flash of inspiration, no lightning-like intuition. Nothing — no sign how to proceed. Silence, blackness, supreme aloneness. How often during those months and months of gray ordinariness, of simply living the *nisayon,* did I pray, "*Aibishter*, I am lost. Send us a *siman* (sign) how to proceed."

In this context, let me relate the following parable. There once was a man who was stricken by constant troubles and illness. Such was his despair that at moments when he felt most alone and forsaken, he would lift his eyes to the One Above and cry out, in all sincerity: "*Keili, lamah azavtani* — My G-d, why have you abandoned me?" One night, he had a rather strange dream. He dreamed that he was walking on a seemingly endless path. When he looked back, he saw two sets of footprints, but when the path narrowed, he observed only one set. As he reflected a little on this phenomenon, he realized that this path was actually symbolic of his own life. Starting at his birth, he had passed the milestones of childhood, youth, middle age, finally reaching old age. But throughout his journey, Hashem had accompanied him and lit up the way. However, now he realized that the good times were represented by those places in which the path was wide, and the difficult times by those where it narrowed. Now, it seemed to him that Hashem had been beside him in the good times, but that in his difficulties he had been compelled to walk alone. At this realization, he cried out in bitterness: "Oh, Hashem, why did you abandon me? Why did you leave me on my own, at my most difficult moments? Surely those were the very times in which I most needed your support?!" Suddenly he heard a gentle voice saying: "My beloved son, you err. It seemed to you that when the path narrowed, you walked alone, but in truth, quite the opposite is true. At those times of hardship, there was no need for a broadening of the path accommodating you and I alongside each other, for at those times **I carried you**. What you must realize therefore, is that when you feel most forsaken, I am in reality closer to you than at any other time!"

Thus ended the dream and the man woke up. But he felt a changed person. He had learnt to rely on faith to help him shoulder his troubles, and would from that time onwards repeat in all sincerity: "Even when I walk in the valley of the shadow of death, I fear no evil for You are with me."

This is something of how I felt at those times when I found it difficult to see clearly that the Almighty was indeed "carrying me."

※

**Yanky:** NOW THIS HONEST, PLAIN SPEAKING, NO-NONSENSE NURSE HAD ARRIVED on our doorstep, unbidden, and confessed to having done the unthinkable, placed her career in jeopardy, to give us some heartfelt advice. Why, why should she do this? Logically, rationally, it made no sense. This highly qualified, long trusted nurse, had literally put her future into our hands. There was nothing but our loyalty to her and conversely her supreme trust in us, standing between her and the collapse of all that she held most dear in life, that which constituted almost entirely her identity. For with the starched uniform, the badges of office, stripped away, what little, I wondered, would be left of Julia? No, there was no other possible explanation, a phenomenon so astonishing that it cannot simply be explained away, but that this was the long prayed for sign. We must follow her instructions, and with as much alacrity as possible.

So here we are — in America. But now again the clarity which we felt so potently on the night of Julia's visit seems to have dissipated. Things have become confused and bewildering again. There are so many options theoretically open to us that we ask ourselves, "Which is the right path?" We traveled from place to place like nomads, our stopping places being hospitals and clinics. We spend endless bone-wearying hours carrying out routine tests, filling out forms, answering questions — the same ones over and over again. Sometimes, there were harder tests which leave my wife physically and emotionally drained. And the ceaseless probing, the questioning, doubting looks:

"Mr. Guttfreund, if we enter your wife's name on this list, how long will it take you to get here should a kidney become available?"

I felt a sort of distrust, as if what they were really saying was:

"Now, what on earth do you think should induce us to put your wife's name on this list — when there are plenty of people living in the vicinity, or at least in this country, who could be here within hours of our summons?"

However, we registered our names in several places. In one far-flung location, I felt a deep sense of unease. There was a Jewish community of sorts here, but a very small one. Should I have to spend perhaps half a year here, what would happen to the children's Jewish education? Again my heart told me: "Don't stop here. This is not the culmination of your search. Take the straight road…" Yet it seemed that in the major metropolis all avenues were closed to us. The days ticked by, relentlessly — our stay would soon be over….

## Ruchi:

WE ARE BACK ONCE MORE IN AN ERA OF TESTS, OF WAITING, PROBING, answering questions. I feel as though I have been thrust unceremoniously back into a terrible gray time when everything was undetermined. Alone in a cold, impersonal hospital room somewhere in America, I experience again some of the feelings I underwent when that very first biopsy was carried out. I had to lie perfectly flat, while machines and cameras whirred above me. It seemed that my body was once more no longer my own, but something I had to make as prone and unfeeling as possible. For it would better tolerate the intrusion if my mind was not truly there, if my mind was floating somewhere away from all this, thinking of good moments, playing with my children all dappled in sunlight, their quick, happy features turned towards me. For how else could I have borne this steel coldness near to my heart? Yanky was waiting alone in the corridor and I knew he was pacing up and down, unable to sit still for long. We both felt a lack of clarity here. "Is this the direction from which the *yeshuah* will come?" No, since coming to this country there has as yet been no moment of certainty.

"Wait," my husband's eyes seemed to be telling me.

"I can't hold on..."

"Wait a little longer. Have trust. It will come..."

During this time, we travelled to both Cleveland and Boston. We were also put in touch with a woman named Rina who had undergone her third kidney transplant. "Coincidentally" she had to travel to Cleveland for a checkup and she offered to accompany us.[12] The hospital was a huge complex and I felt as though I was walking streets and streets of hospital corridors. The actual tests I had to endure were not only hard but in a sense humiliating, since I began to feel that my body no longer belonged to me. I then underwent a series of tests and scans, in which a large machine is brought down right over one's face. At this point, my nerves would always begin to play tricks on me, and I would become extremely claustrophobic. As I awaited the final test, I turned to Rina and said, "Well, what does

---

12. *She gave us great encouragement and we remain close friends to this day.*

this one involve?" Not wishing to add to my pain, she just said: "Ruchi, trust me, it's not too bad." When I entered the room, I was strapped to a machine and my whole body rotated. I was literally hanging upside-down. The young doctor who was carrying out the test seemed to be completely nonchalant about it. Now somehow, in my deep fear, my humor came in to play. So I screamed out to him:

"Hey, put me down right now! Where do you think I am, Coney Island or something?"

He paused — recognizing the level of profound fear within me as I pleaded more quietly: "Look, I just cannot take this — it's just too hard."

Now acquiring human characteristics, he said: "Well, would you like to take a rest now? But then we'll have to go back to the beginning."

This more compassionate human interchange gave me courage. So I said, "No," quite firmly, "Please continue."

When the test was concluded, I was so exhausted that I simply **fell** into my friend's waiting arms, crying out: "Why didn't you tell me?"

"Ruchi, believe me, it would only have made it harder for you! *Baruch Hashem* you endured this test too."

She left us to take her plane back to New York that night, but we remained in Cleveland so that I could have a partial dialysis. By the time I arrived back to my parents' house in Boro Park I was literally in an animal-like state. I crawled up the stairs on all fours. My mother and a cousin who had watched me enter the house were both aghast. Later, as I lay on my mother's lap, the long-suppressed tears finally flowed.

THE DAY BEFORE WE ARE DUE TO LEAVE, WE SIT IN MY IN-LAWS' HOUSE. Time is ticking down — we all know that, though we try as best we can to conceal it from one another. Although my wife's name has been noted down in several places, nevertheless we both feel with a bone-deep knowledge that we are about to return home empty-handed. It is at this point that a friend[13] presses a small piece of paper containng a phone number into my hand. I am not surprised, for this has been the pattern of the last few weeks here. We are like private detectives following obscure leads. Leads that were literally thrown into our hands. Leads which we followed, and actually saw pieces of Divine Providence falling in together.

"What's this?"

"This is the phone number of a young woman. She lives nearby. A friend of a friend. She had a transplant a few years ago. In fact, since the transplant she has had a child — her only child. Call her up. Perhaps she has some advice to offer you from her own experience."

My wife and I look at each other doubtfully. We shrug our shoulders as if to say: "We have nothing to lose — but then again, there's probably nothing in it. We know of and have explored most of the likely avenues...."

I take the piece of paper and retreat to the next room, where it is quiet. I dial the number.

"Hello, is that Ethel H.?"[14]

"Speaking," the voice sounded calm and self-assured.

"This is Yanky Guttfreund — you don't know me. A friend passed your phone number on to us. To be brief, my wife is on dialysis. We are here on a short visit from Europe. We have already tried several hospitals and clinics as we are seeking to enter her name on a list over here. Can you give us any advice?"

A slight pause, a cough.

"I will give you just one name. Butt. B-U-T-T" she spells out, as if to a child.

"Dr. Butt?" I query. "Is that all?"

"Yes, that's it. He is the man who performed my transplant. He is nothing short of a genius in this area!"

---

13. *The friend was Chani B., a good friend of my mother's, who had been to interview Rina F. about her ordeal.*
14. *Ethel H. oleha hashalom was a wonderful human being. She was also a kidney transplant recipient. Later when Rina F. married off her son, Ethel, Rina and I danced in a circle at the wedding. We were "kidney-sisters" so to speak. Sadly, Ethel is no longer with us.*

"Well, what do I do? How do I get to him?"

"Quite simple," the voice answered. "Call him up. I have his phone number right here. Give him a call. May your wife be well."

I struggled frantically for a pen, smoothed out the small scrap of paper with her number and, underneath it, inscribed this new number.

"I must warn you," the voice continued. "You must be prepared to be persistent. As you can well imagine, he is an extremely busy man. Do not allow yourself to be put off and eventually you will reach him. When you do, I feel confident he is the man who will be able to help you. I wish you *hatzlachah*. May your wife be well and may you enjoy many healthy years together."

This is the first time that we heard the name Khalid Butt and it was like a pebble thrown into a fathomless, dark pond, the ripples of which spread outwards in ever increasing circles. And there I felt it again, at that moment — Divine Providence, the sense of destiny, returning in spectacular fashion like a pillar of fire at nightfall. For why else would my heart be beating so loudly, as if it were about to jump out of my dark frock coat. I looked out of the narrow window onto the street outside. A solitary tree stirred in the wind as the light began to thicken into a gathering translucence. On the sidewalk, men returning from work or study with purposeful steps — the women and the children long inside their houses, ears straining for the eagerly awaited purposeful footstep on the stairs, along hallways. I paused for a long moment, and I realized my hand was shaking, still holding the receiver. I was deeply afraid. Afraid that perhaps this would transpire to be nothing other than another false start. Afraid of a rebuff for daring to approach Dr. Butt without the benefit of any formal introductions. And yet, and yet, I knew that this was something I had to attempt, if only to discount it as a real possibility.

I dialed the number. A voice answered. It was a man's voice, I remember thinking, with not a little sense of surprise, but unusually sonorous, unusually mellifluous.

"Yes?"

"I would like, if possible, to speak to Dr. Butt."

"Speaking."

The shock I felt at that moment was indescribable. It was like being admitted to the king's throne roomwithout any proper preliminaries or preparation. I felt my tongue dry up and cleave to the roof of my mouth.

Again, the voice said:

"Speaking," but with an ever so slight edge of impatience to it.

I gathered my wits and plunged straight into the story. I told it clearly and honestly, without attempting to hide or gloss over anything. When I had finished speaking, he said:

"At this moment, Mr. Guttfreund, I am at my office in Brooklyn Downstate Hospital. How long would it take you to get over here?"

In a single breath, I let out:

"Roughly twenty minutes?" and then as if I had not really understood: "You mean you would see us now?" incredulously.

"Well, Mr. Guttfreund, there's an old saying: 'There's no time like the present.'"

I literally flew into the next room blurting out to my wife:

"Quick, we're going. Now, get your coat."

Poor thing, she stared at me incomprehensibly.

"Someone, anyone, call a car service."

The car service screeched up to the door. I managed to maneuver myself and my wife into it and make the necessary explanations to her, all within minutes of saying to Dr. Butt, "Roughly twenty minutes." The neighborhood began to change as we sped along. As we left the Jewish district we entered almost abruptly a dilapidated, run-down area. Lining the sidewalk were multi-storied brown brick houses, fire escapes creeping down their sides like spider's webs, some with their windows boarded, some windowless, exposed to the elements like eyeless sockets. Everywhere along the pavements and clustered more heavily around the houses or tenements was scattered garbage. It lay there boldly, almost as if it had a right to be there, as if it was making some kind of statement. Half-opened bags, stray cats licking at the contents, decaying, discarded mattresses, broken and gutted radios, dismembered bicycles. The road was an obstacle course of pot holes and ruts over which the car lurched uncertainly. A light drizzle had begun to fall. The primordial chaos of the scene matched the disarray of our feelings as the taxi raced along, radio blaring. Presently, we drew up at an unlikely looking building. The district we now found ourselves in was dilapidated, if a little more orderly than its neighboring one. Groups of out-of-work youths were gathered, heads down on corners, looking over a single newspaper or talking in animated fashion. One or two jogged in rhythm to an oversized radio. Again, we looked up at the building where we had stopped.

"This is impossible." I said to the taxi-driver. "I think we must be at the wrong address."

"You want ..." and he rattled off the address I had jotted down on my piece of paper.

"Yes."

"Well, this here is it. Now it is up to you as to whether you get out here or not, but I ain't personally going no further." And at this he folded his arms, as if prepared for a long wait.

So we alighted, still dubious, still uncertain. In Europe, we were used to hospitals being located in suburban districts. We entered and, finding someone who looked like a lone member of staff, were told to take the elevator to the sixth floor where Dr. Butt's office was situated.

Ruchi:

THE PAST HALF HOUR HAS JUST VEERED INTO A SORT OF SPEEDED UP version of a silent movie. One moment we were sitting with our relatives and conversing congenially — the next, my husband darted from the room where he had been telephoning, begged me to put on my coat and gloves and follow him into the street.

"But why, why?" I kept asking him.

"Later," he said, "later," motioning with his hand.

"But where are we going?"

The car service drew up — we got inside.

"Listen," he began by way of explanation. "The lady I called, she gave me a number — a Dr. Butt. He performed her transplant."

"Yes," I said doubtfully.

"Apparently, he is **the** top man in this field. I spoke to him..."

"Wait a minute. You spoke to him? So quickly?"

"I called the number, and he himself happened to answer the phone. He asked me how long it would take us to reach his office."

The entire sequence of events sounded extremely dubious to me, from the idea of a highly placed specialist answering the phone himself, to his asking to see us immediately in his office. We were accustomed to the concept that the more prestigious the specialist, the more inaccessible he would prove to be. These gnawing doubts were matched by the unlikeliness of the location we now found ourselves. I could see my husband was also having his doubts. It would seem that this fellow was some sort of joke, not the individual, who would lead us to the culmination of our long search.

WE RODE THE ELEVATOR TO THE SIXTH FLOOR OF WHAT LOOKED LIKE a partially disused clinic. We saw and spoke to no one. We knocked on an innocuous looking door upon which hung an unimpressive cardboard sign: Professor Khalid Butt.

"Yes." Again the voice I had heard on the phone.

We entered. There, surrounded by boxes and piles of papers, sat Dr. Butt himself. An imposing man, when he rose to greet us, I could see he was of commanding height and build.

He extended a hand and then motioned us to sit.

"I must apologize" he began, "for the state of the office. You see I am in transit, just now. We are all moving upstate to Westchester, hopefully within the week. Half of the stuff has gone ahead, including most of the staff and my personal secretary. So I'm reduced to answering the phone myself." At this, he let out a hearty laugh.

At that moment, I understood it all — my picking up the phone just at that moment, my reaching Dr. Butt himself immediately, without any recourse to defensive secretaries. It was like some unseen hand was rolling out a red carpet for us to tread on — only for us!

"Let us just recap again, Mr. Guttfreund" he continued.

So I repeated the entire story from beginning to end.

"Well, I personally have no problem with that," he said — and this reply was so unbelievable, that it held a totally unfamiliar ring in our ears — after the distrust we had encountered in all other quarters which we had visited.

"You say that you can be here within twenty-four hours?"

"Yes," and I went through our proposed travel arrangements. "I have mentioned all possible routes; if necessary we would even travel by Concorde."

"Well, that sounds just fine," he said again, obviously impressed.

"Now, would you just pop downstairs and take a couple of blood tests. Nothing elaborate. Oh, and one more thing. Would you be so good as to leave me a copy of your papers?"

So it transpired in this strange fashion that within fifteen minutes of arriving at his doorstep, we found ourselves once more, downstairs, in the unprepossessing lobby — our business, so it would seem, concluded.

❧

Upon leaving Dr. Butt's clinic, which was in the final stages of abandon, we found ourselves in the lobby looking for the laboratory in which to take the necessary blood tests. We entered a room and saw two or three people lolling about. They were all of young age and were talking and laughing animatedly. The principal actor had his feet on the table.

"Hello," we said, feeling we were witnessing some kind of comical Shakespearean interlude.

"Yeah."

"Dr. Butt sent us down to take some blood tests. My name is going on the transplant list shortly."

"Yeah, we can take blood. Just how much do you wanna give us, lady?"

The blood tests taken, the principal actor began again.

"You wanna see a kidney? Well, we don't have a kidney right now, but you can see a pancreas." And with a flourish he opened the refrigerator door and produced a glass jar with a pancreas floating in it. We were in shock. For all the time we had been discussing transplants, we had never actually visualized the organ itself as a reality. Then reality really hits you.

My husband and I looked across the middle of the room at each other, hovering uncertainly between laughter and tears.

"You cannot take seriously what just took place up there?" I began, when we were safely on the drizzling gray sidewalk.

My husband made no sign of assent or dissent.

I did not articulate it, but in the words, "What just took place in there," I mentally included Dr. Butt, whose afterimage palpated softly around us like a mysterious residue. Surely, surely all my rational faculties told me he had just played out for reasons best known to himself, an elaborate charade. This and this alone could be the only possible explanation of what had just occurred.

WE RETURNED HOME AND A GREAT SENSE OF UNEASE AND UNCERTAINTY seemed to have returned with us, hovering over us like a cloud-like thing, difficult to explain. What transpired in America seems to us now like so many fevered imaginings of an overstretched brain, which bears little relationship to the reality of our day-to-day lives. Dialysis resumed, but now it became a wearying, routine procedure, as our minds were focused differently. At each dialysis there were the words which lay between us: "Maybe this is the last time. Perhaps this is the last time I watch you insert the needle just so or adjust these knobs and pipes. Perhaps tonight, or on just such a quiet unprepossessing night like this night, the call will come..."

So let me tell you a little what it is like living your life in the waiting: This waiting was like nothing else that I can describe. It is not like waiting for something fairly trivial or subsidiary to your needs, so that you wait but meanwhile your life is taken up with a myriad of other demands and exigencies, and when the waited for event transpires, it even catches you off your guard a little. No, that is not the way of it with this waiting. Here you wait but your whole being is totally and utterly subsumed with the waiting. You wait — but with every fiber of your being exposed, with every nerve stretched taut. As you wait from morning till nightfall — everything is utterly sucked in to this act of waiting. What we were waiting for essentially was the phone to ring and a receptionist to drawl in a nonchalant way: "Mr .... This is ..... clinic calling. We have to inform you that we have a kidney for your wife. How soon can you be here?" Yet although we knew that this was probably the way the waiting would be resolved, our nerves were stretched to such a finely tuned point that anything unexpected, a ring on the door late at night, an unidentified car drawing up outside our apartment, made us literally jump out of our skins. In this fashion the days drew into weeks, as summer gave way to autumn.

⁂

WHEN WE LEFT AMERICA AND RETURNED HOME — WE KNEW SOMETHING had been accomplished, but it was hard to determine what. It could have just as easily turned out that no significant advance had been made and we had returned home empty-handed. It was simply impossible to say. But our lives had to resume their normal pre-journey state. The phone became a center of intense speculation for me. If it rang, I did not now rush to pick up, thinking lightheartedly, "Oh, it will be so and so from down the block, phoning about something to do with the children or just for a chat." No, now every time the phone rang it could well have been the phone call that would change our lives, or it could have been at the other end of the scale — nothing, nothing at all of importance. I reached a stage where I could not face answering it at all — why risk the disappointment, the inevitable raising of hopes and the subsequent dashing of them? Better, I argued, to remain in ignorance. But then another voice intervened, the voice of reason: "If you don't take the risk, you will never find out what happened" — the end of the story as it were. So, inevitably, I lifted the receiver with a heavy heart. When the phone — as it did occasionally — rang on Shabbos, we became literally torn, ridden with doubts. Although, halachically speaking, should this be the kidney we were allowed to answer it, what would happen should it be merely a wrong number? The inner turmoil that this caused was indescribable.

Medical textbooks describe our condition at this time in the following terminology:

> "All things come to those who wait," they say. But there is waiting and then... there is waiting. Waiting for a kidney to become available can be stress-provoking. Fear of the unknown is very normal... On the other hand, many resources are available to help you cope with your stress, and to channel your energies correctly at this time....
>
> "... the period of waiting for a matching kidney to become available may be months or years, during which the patient is maintained on dialysis. Throughout this time the patient must remain readily available to be contacted by telephone at home or at work, day or night. He should know how to get to the hospital at any hour..."

# Yanky:

I HAD A GUT FEELING, RIGHTLY OR WRONGLY, THAT IT WOULD BE beneficial to keep in touch with the various clinics where Ruchi's name had been noted down in America. These included Westchester, Boston and Cleveland. Every month, therefore when I was required to send blood samples to these medical centers, I would take my opportunity and pick up the phone:

"Hi! This is Yanky Guttfruend here. "I sent you such and such blood samples today. What's new?"

And then a week later:

"Have you received the blood sample I sent out on such and such date? Were they in the proper condition?"

I cannot explain why, because nobody told me to do this, but again it was one of those instinctive feelings which arose within me of its own accord.

I felt that since thousands of miles separated us from these hospitals and clinics, had I not maintained some cursory form of contact, it might well have been a case of "Out of sight, out of mind." And I was firmly determined not to let this happen, not to let any avenues which we had so fought to be opened to us, now close their doors in our faces. Now, the days and weeks flew by, in this cold interim, no-man's land of time. The leaves began to yellow, the days to shorten, ready for the decline into winter. We felt this speedy passage of time even more keenly, more bitterly than others, my wife and I, for it marked the anniversary of my wife's third year on dialysis. We both felt at a particularly low ebb, drained by the emotional turmoil of the past weeks and the seemingly interminable waiting.... Still we tried to encourage one another: "Things will look up," we would say. But we said these optimistic things merely allowing them to trip off our tongues — but in furtive fashion, never allowing our eyes to meet, neither wishing to see the desolation which so obviously lay there. During this time too, I undertook to have all our *mezuzot* checked. This took a period of some weeks beginning in Ellul. The last *mezuzah* was changed on *Chol HaMoed Sukkos*, with the suggested addition of a *mezuzah* on the basement door. This accomplished, we felt in some inexplicable way that all human efforts had now been expended — now we were simply biding our time waiting for events to turn a Divinely orchestrated corner....

As a postscript to this era, I must add, that on that Yom Kippur, my two sons, who were then very young children aged about five and four respectively, accompanied me to the *Kol Nidrei* service for the first time. On the way home, I began to speak frankly and openly to them and also as though I was speaking to much older children:

"My dearest *kinderlach*, I want to tell you something. It may be important now, it may only be important in a year or two. Nevertheless, I will tell it to you now, for then you will have the necessary understanding to deal properly with the things of which I speak, whenever that time comes. You know that tonight is Yom Kippur, and I want to tell you that should the telephone ring in the middle of the night, I am allowed to be *mechalel* (desecrate) this holiest of days and answer it. You know why? Because it will probably be a phone call from America saying that they have found a kidney for your mother. Should it be the kidney, then you will both go with your sister to stay at your grandparents, and we will travel to America for your mother to receive the kidney. I want you to be brave and good children for your grandparents, and those that look after you, and in this way you will help us to get through all this. Sometimes you might be a little homesick, but try to remember always the reason why we had to go away suddenly, perhaps in the middle of the night. And above all, remember that it will not be long before we become a proper family again — with a healthy mother to look after all of you."

**Ruchi:**

THE CHILDREN HAVE BEEN VERY QUIET FOR THE LAST DAY OR TWO. I think their father has spoken to them about what may happen when the call finally comes. They have been sticking very close to me, looking up at me with eyes that say: "Is it true that one morning we might get up and you will be gone? So now you are all the more precious to us."

Still, in a way I pity their precociousness, their too deep knowledge, because they have had to learn so many harsh realities barely out of infanthood. This too, this illness has done to us, stripped them of their right to a healthy mother. How I long for the day, for all their sakes, for all our sakes, when this situation will revert back to some semblance of normality, when we can both be simply parents, no longer self-absorbed in our own struggles, when the need for them to step delicately about me becomes superfluous. I want nothing more than for us all to become part of the real rough-and-tumble of daily life.

❧

**Yanky:**

YOM TOV WAS OVER, OUR RELATIVES HAD RETURNED TO AMERICA AND WE began to feel the inevitable sense of anti-climax as the winter sets in. In our situation it was important not to allow ourselves to become depressed. So we tried oh-so-hard for childrens' sakes to make Shabbosim happy occasions, as we were more afraid of facing Shabbos than any day, having more time to think. And thinking at this point was perilous. It was *Rosh Chodesh Cheshvan,* October 20th, a Friday night, so we forced ourselves to enjoy a relaxed meal — we sang *zemiros* — in an unusually happy fashion with the children. We went to bed early as was our custom on those already lengthening Friday nights. Almost immediately I fell into a deep, quiet sleep. I was dreaming — and it seemed to me, as had happened frequently in the past few months — that the phone was ringing. Then I would awake and slowly the almost palpable silence would fill my mind, drop by drop. This time, I awoke, and I judged by the darkness of the room that it was about 4 a.m.. Then I glanced towards the phone. It was still ringing. By now, my heart was beating, almost in time to the phone's still persistent tones. Ruchi stirred. She turned on her side — then sat bolt upright.

"The phone," she said. She picked up the phone — after what I could see was an immense struggle — to do so on Shabbos. "I can't hear anything," she said. "It's a poor connection." She put down the phone. Then it rang again — the tones persisting once, twice, three times. By now, I was sure, by the persistence of the caller that this was not a wrong number. Also, this ringing on *Shabbos kodesh* could portend only one thing — the kidney.

I ran for the phone — not wishing to burden my wife with the trauma of picking up the phone again. My hand was trembling.

"Yes..." I said breathlessly, a little abruptly.

"Good morning," a cheerful voice sounded at the other end. Is this Mr. Guttfreund?"

"Speaking." I said, trying to sound calm and nonchalant.

"This is the Westchester Medical Center, Nancy speaking. We have some good news for you. We have a kidney for your wife. What is your wife's general condition?"

"She is fine," I blurted out. "She was last dialyzed Thursday night."

"Any colds or other infections?"

"No, absolutely nothing."

"Which is the quickest time you could be with us?"

"We'll leave within the hour," I said. "Give us till tomorrow morning."

I had memorized the quickest routes to New York. I had called the airports to confirm the information and it then dawned on me that Concorde would be our best possible option. If we left the house at 6:30 to go to Paris we would arrive at 9 a.m. (European time). We could then take the Concorde and expect to arrive in New York at 9 a.m. (American time). Thus, we could then be in Westchester by 10:30 a.m. their time.

"That's fine. See you over here then and good luck."

I remember thinking — hold on, hold on, we're coming...

I felt like saying: "Dry up the oceans, fold away all the highways and intersections, they are not needed here." I felt like saying: "Let me take a giant leap out of our bedroom, directly into a small hospital room in upstate New York, where I see Dr. Butt's face relax into a familiar jovial smile, as he stretches out his hand to greet us..."

But Ruchi was at my shoulder.

"Nu, Yanky," she urged in an alert voice. "What is it? What is it?" and then in a whisper, "Is it the kidney?"

I nodded and as I turned to face her I felt a wave of nausea hit me, knocking me sideways, like an unexpected stampede. Never have I experienced such a sick-to-the-very core feeling as in those few chilling moments. But my wife was calling to me, her face slowly coalescing into a pallid whole.

"What do we do? What do we ever do?" she cried in utter panic. And then, she began to tremble:

"I don't want the kidney," she almost gasped out the words in a terrible wave of fear of the unknown. "Leave me alone, I'm fine as I am. What do you all want from me?"

I looked her squarely in her eyes, for there was no time now for feelings, even though the pent-up emotions of the years now developed into a tremendous tidal wave.

"Listen, Ruchi" I said, in a voice trembling with the effort to be realistic, "Just listen to me. If you don't want this kidney — fine, just say so. I'll go right ahead, I'll call New York. I'll say: 'I'm terribly sorry, but my wife has changed her mind.' And do you know what will happen?"

I watched her eyes — two dark, terror-stricken pools enlarging.

"They'll say: 'Is that so? Well, thank you very much for informing us. That's no problem. We have a second choice for it.' And then you'll go right to the bottom of the list and will begin the waiting all over again. Who knows — another year or two or three? Is that what you want? Because, if it is, that is what I'll have to do."

"No, no," she cried out, like a frightened child. "Don't do it. Wait, wait. Give me time...." for she was afraid. Afraid of the change in her situation, afraid of the unknown, for she had now spent three years on dialysis.

Again, the plea for time, time in which to come to terms with the tossing tumultuousness of her feelings, just as she had pleaded for time in those difficult early days of dialysis. I had rarely ever felt more real pity for her, as she was then so afraid, so vulnerable, so alone — part of her wanting this with all her heart, yet another part not wanting it, not daring to step towards it.

"Ok, ok," I said slowly. "Take your time..." although I knew that if there was one commodity we were short of just now — it was time. I waited a minute, maybe two.

"Well, what have you decided? Do you want me to ring Westchester and refuse the kidney or do you want me to book our places on the airplane?"

"Yes, book the places...." She cried tears streaming down her face.

I lifted the phone. I booked two places on a flight to Paris, and then two places on the Concorde from Paris to New York. I had pre-notified the airline company of our plans, so that everything now slid quickly and quietly into place. Meanwhile, the noise of the phone calls in the quiet night had woken the children.

They stood at the door to our bedroom, one clutching a little blanket, one a precious stuffed doll. The oldest said in a knowing way:

"Tatty, *emess*, it is the kidney? The kidney has come?"

Again, I nodded wordlessly on the edge of tears.

"Go back to bed, my darling little ones, and I will call your Bubby and Zaidy right away."

**Ruchi:**

THERE WAS NO WARNING OF WHAT WAS TO COME — NOTHING UNUSUAL in the events of the day or the evening. But I suppose that is how these things usually transpire — stealing up on one unaware, like a thief in the night. The first intimation of any change in our situation was the sound of the phone in what seemed like a dream. Then I lifted the phone and it went dead. When it rang again, I realized that Yanky was now speaking on the phone. The moment I saw him, standing, receiver in hand on *Shabbos kodesh,* a dim shape in the darkened room, I knew that these very seconds signaled a new beginning, the start of a new era. How did I know this? Oh, but I knew this with a sudden stark sureness and clarity, after all the false starts of the last few months. But, then came the fear, drip by drip, — it permeated my brain, my heart, my core, my essence. This fear was soul-deep and chillingly relentless — like gray, cold rain on a dark November day. I pulled the covers around me.

"I can't go, I can't go," the fear screamed within me. It was then that I asked my husband, "What is it? Is it the kidney?" and just minutes later cried out: "Leave me alone...I'll stay as I am.... I'm afraid, so of the unknown..."

I wanted — but what? Oh, I wanted to go to sleep — and sleep undisturbed for a thousand years. I wanted to awake from the anaes- thetic — Dr. Butt's face floating gently above my own, saying kindly: "Its all over now. You're going to be fine...." I wanted to go back to the way I was before all of this muddle — carefree, healthy, no treacherous terrain to traverse. I wanted never to hear the word kid- ney or dialysis again. I wanted to wake up at last from the inter- minable nightmare of the past few years. I wanted not to be asked to endure or undergo anything difficult ever again. I remember holding my head in my hands and weeping, weeping for everything — for my spent dreams, for my young husband's intolerable burdens, for my children's disturbed childhood, for my youth, my inexperience...

I wept and wept until there were simply no more tears — and then as my husband waited, turning to me with a simple enough question:

"... or do you want me to book two places on the airplane ..."

The answer escaped almost of itself, in a semi-audible whisper. "Yes."

NEXT, I PICKED UP THE RECEIVER TO DIAL MY PARENTS' HOME. I reckoned on the idea that if I persisted in ringing for a long enough time, eventually they would realize that it could be none other than "the kidney," and they would answer it. I rang and rang. No one replied obviously, as it was Shabbos. Next, I tried another number, which very few people knew — but again without success. I then reverted back to the original number — and allowed the phone to ring for about five, perhaps seven minutes. After what seemed like an age, I heard my father's voice, low and very hesitant. He seemed to age tangibly in the thirty seconds I spent in explanation on the phone.

I speedily apprised him of the situation. Next, I picked up some items that stood in the corner of our room, already prepared for just such a contingency[15] I picked up a few other items: tefillin, shtreimel, a small bottle of grape juice, which I had put into the hand luggage for such an emergency, and two *challos*.[16] We fumbled down to the basement to pick up a suitcase. Then we waited for my elderly parents to arrive to take over the children. Ruchi and I gave a few instructions to them, some huge hugs and kisses — all we had time for — we finally ordered a taxi. We clambered into the cab, "Just call, just call!" they shouted after us and we replied, "Don't worry, we'll be back shortly." Thus it came about that within the space of about two-and-one-half hours of my lifting the receiver in our quiet bedroom, we found ourselves in the airport, ready as privileged passengers to be the first to board the plane.

**Ruchi:**

WE TRAVEL TO PARIS WHERE WE DISEMBARK AND WAIT TO BOARD THE Concorde. We are aboard the plane, the airbus bumping through tense clouds and turbulent air. To my right, it is still all thick darkness outside. Strangely suspended as we are between heaven and earth, night and day, I am suspended too — hung in the balance between the known and the unknown, between sickness and possible health, perhaps even between, G-d forbid, life and death or, in another sense, a kind of living death and a new lease of life. So many unknown and unknowable factors. And yet I am able, as if with a special gift, to push

---

15. *According to halachah, we were allowed to travel with whatever could be packed into one case.*

16. *Although I would be flying on Shabbos, I would still not be allowed to eat before kiddush.*

aside the reason for our journey and pretend that we are taking some kind of pleasure trip. I watch my husband unwrap his small bottle of grape juice carefully and place them on the tray in front of him, together with his two *challos*. But I can neither eat nor drink for I am now pre-surgery. Is it possible that his hands are trembling? We continue racing through the clouds, the stratosphere, at the speed of sound. His hands are shaking. As he whispers *kiddush* his voice is uncharacteristically quavery. A steward passes, wearing an oversized mogen dovid. He turns back towards us and mouths the single word, "*Shalom.*" Every little thing seems somehow portentous in this strange situation.

But now my husband is addressing me:

"I must tell you something, now, and it will be better for both of us, I think. It could be that we will travel to New York for this transplant, that you will have the operation and it is not ultimately successful. So you must be prepared for the fact that we could well be making this same return journey, completely empty-handed, in two weeks. We will then have to go back to being just as we were, with nothing at all gained. Nevertheless," he continued as a kind of addendum, and dropping his voice to a whisper, "we have no choice but to go through this experience all the way to the end, to where no one can go any further."

It cost him dearly to look me straight in the eye and voice these seemingly harsh realities, for he was by nature an optimist. If there was ever the tiniest sliver of hope, he would seize on it hungrily. But now he took these hopes and crushed them.

At this, I cried a little again, but with a greater degree of control than the desperate weeping of several hours beforehand.

I saw that Yanky's eyes were glazed too, brimmed with unwept tears.

But I cried not so much for myself — for I was trying so hard to view this experience with some kind of optimism — but more for the children I had had to leave behind in those gut wrenching moments but a few hours ago. A mother's bond to her children transcends everything — time, pain, fear..... But in those brief seconds when I had literally flown out of their bedroom leaving them in the charge of their grandparents, so many thoughts had crowded into my brain.... When would I see them again, would I ever see them again?

I had promised them that the parting would be for a short while only — but then I had said this more with my lips than my mind....

⚜

## Nurse:

WELL, I UNDERSTAND THAT THE BIRDS HAVE FLOWN. I RECEIVED A phone call this morning from a very tense but excited Mr. Guttfreund. Apparently, "their" call had come on the Jewish Sabbath, so there had been no chance to let me know. But strict instructions were left for a message to be got to me as soon as possible. I have a deep instinctive feeling that all will be well — in the end. But these things often take time to settle down. I also think that in this particular case there was little choice in the matter as the "dialysis lifestyle" placed such huge constrictions, such intolerable burdens, on them all. The past three years have been a wearying experience and it is certainly no way for a young family to live in the long run. I always felt sure somehow too, that the transplant would come from abroad for this particular patient, but do not ask me to explain why. On so many occasions I see as I grow older in this profession, that some decisions or actions do not truly bear close or rational scrutiny; they are simply things one feels to be right for a certain patient, at that time... It is akin to a kind of sixth sense, and cannot be learned but is the product of long years of service.

Any patient whose kidneys have permanently stopped working is a potential candidate for a kidney transplant. However, many factors must be considered in choosing between transplantation and chronic dialysis for an individual patient. Among these factors are age, other medical problems and personal considerations of work and lifestyle. Being a mother of young children is also a priority. And what are the general chances of success? Well, this would depend on the closeness of the tissue match between donor complete match had a 95% chance of working. A kidney from a parent, child or half-matched sibling has a 85% chance of working. In this case, in which there is a cadaver donor, the kidney has an 80% chance of working.

At the least, the chances of a younger patient doing well are significantly greater than those of a patient of advanced age, as a rough guide, over the age of sixty. However, with every transplant there is a certain risk of failure. The patient would then have to return to dialysis with nothing gained. I think that Mrs. Guttfreund has well understood these choices set before her and has come to the decision that the only way forward now, both for her and her family, is this transplant which has been offered to them.... My heart goes with them, on this, their most difficult of all journeys...

**Yanky:**

MY FIRST FLIGHT ON A CONCORDE WOULD NORMALLY HAVE BEEN A mildly enjoyable occasion. However, this sense of pleasure was not granted to us now in our present situation. All was a weighty tension in this fraught interim time, as if we were fleeing between enemy lines. This was not sadness, nor was there joy, even if it was such a longed for event. It was something caught quivering in-between. And there was fear. I forgot the fear — fear of leaving behind whatever heavy burdens, now grown light, through their very familiarity. And what were we heading towards? Something which seemed as we were actually approaching it as ephemeral as a shaft of sunlight — only a chance, after all, an off-chance of a new life? I prayed aboard that vast elegant airbird, pronouncing the words *"Atah Yozarta"* for it was *Rosh* Chodesh. I made *kiddush* and washed over *lechem mishneh*. It was hard for me to eat knowing that my wife was at my side unable to wet her lips or let a morsel of food pass her tongue.

The plane flew on swiftly into the next day's dawn, taking us out of and beyond time. It touched the runway. The pilot's voice sounded on the intercom. He announced that we had just touched down at Kennedy airport and also that the flight had been made in record time, coming in to land half an hour early. At this pronouncement, the passengers broke into spontaneous applause. Did any of these well-to-do passengers suspect just why this had been a record flight? I want to tell you all I felt like shouting out loud, that this is no less then a powerful emanation of *siyata diShmaya* for the pale young woman at my side, that all of this was done for her sake, and her sake alone... According to prior notification, we were allowed to disembark first. The crew wished us well, good luck and good health.

Dawn was streaking the skyline. Reaching the arrival hall, we moved swiftly onwards. Suddenly, a voice assailed us from somewhere behind us in that vast vestibule:

"You cheat, fraudster..."

Instinctively we turned around, trying to trace the origins of the voice. A long-haired fellow, guitar in hand, was still waving angrily at us.

"What do you mean?" Ruchi said.

"I am a Jew but a non-observant one, but you... You dress like a *chassid*, yet you desecrate the Sabbath," he spat out the words with real venom.

"Let's go," I said. "We have no time — ignore him."

But my wife apparently wished to stand and offer explanation. She was also obviously stalling for time.

"Let me just say to you sir, never judge any situation by its outward appearance. I am on the way for a kidney transplant at the Westchester Medical Center — we have traveled from abroad today, with full halachic consent. It is a clear case of *pikuach nefesh*." But turning to me, my wife having now expressed the full weight of her feelings, said softly to me: "He reeks of liquor. You are right, let's just ignore him."

With that, we moved onwards, shaken afresh by the real peculiarity of our position.

༄༅

## Ruchi:

WE JUMPED INTO A TAXI AND WERE SOON SPEEDING OUT OF THE CITY towards the Westchester Medical Center. It was a place which neither of us had visited, for we had met Dr. Butt in the last days of his tenure at his downstate clinic. Morning is splattering the sky, washing it in bold streaks of pinks and fluorescent pearly grays. I thought of all those manifold wakings of men and women, all over this continent, to a new day of human strivings. What would this brand new day bring me, I pondered? Now I felt a profound tiredness creeping over me, for I had barely closed my eyes on the plane. I felt weak too from lack of food or drink. We wound our way upstate on dewy, early morning highways, out of the vast sprawling megalopolis which we had scarcely entered. The scenery changed, urban areas gave way to winding long grasses, the trees swaying in the slight breeze. The taxi driver was a little unsure of the way. He made one or two false turns, shouting out for guidance which we were quite unable to give him.

"We've never been here before," we repeated, but this assertion seemingly fell on deaf ears.

Finally, we drew up at the steps of a modern clinic. These tree-lined surroundings were in sharp contrast to the run-down office at which we had had our first glimpse of Dr. Butt. We picked up our suitcase and, even in our exhausted conditions, literally flew up the steps. We entered a brightly lit reception area. The lady at the desk must have been the last remnant of the night shift for she was yawning copiously and pointedly.

"Your name?" she said in a slow drawl.

"Mr. and Mrs. Guttfreund; we have just arrived on an overnight flight from abroad. We received a call last night that there is a kidney waiting for my wife. It is very urgent."

"Just a minute, I'll check," she said, as if time was a matter of little or no significance.

"Have you got any written proof?" she asked.

"No," we both rejoined dismally, not even attempting an explanation. A sudden thought crossed my mind like a dark shadow. Were we both deranged? Had all the years of suffering and uncertainty thrown us both off balance, so that the phone call of the night was nothing more tangible than the fevered imagining of overworked minds?

She looked down a vast register of names, her finger moving slowly downwards. Then she called out in her ponderous way, "Well, there ain't no such name here..."

"That's impossible," we both cried out almost simultaneously. "Look again."

"If you say so," she said a little resentfully.

"Well?"

"Well, I told you before and I tell you again, there ain't no person of that name on this list here..."

We stood rooted to the spot. Throughout all the long, terror-filled night, this one thought had stood between us and total blackness: the team of white-coated staff cheerfully awaiting us in this place, Dr. Butt, with his ready smile of welcome at their head... Now that one all-powerful image was threatening to dissolve like so much tired smoke...

"But its impossible, they called us..." again we spoke almost together. "Please, please lady, my wife has got to have a kidney transplant," my husband interjected. "We've come all this way."

She must have sensed the desperation in our hearts, for it seemed that even she, resolutely unmoving though she had been, now took pity.

"Hey, wait a minute," she cried out in a sudden flash of inspiration. "What did you say you've just come for?"

"A kidney transplant."

"Well, we don't do kidney transplants here. We only do 'head' transplants if you like," and at this she let out a guffaw. And then: "This is the Westchester Psychiatric Clinic, man. What you're looking for is down the road."

So we trudged down the road, where our names were not immediately recognized. We were exhausted, dejected, almost to the brinks of hysteria! I could not believe my ears or eyes. After much confusion with the secretary, and a few phone calls, a nurse appeared at the desk, shock displayed all over her face. It now became apparent that the whole medical team was simply in shock. They had not expected us for another several hours at least, possibly even as late as tonight. Therefore our names were not transferred to the main desk yet.

After the initial shock was over, and our state of mind returned to some sort of normalcy, we silently followed her to the elevator and up to the transplant ward. There we were given a room, told to unpack our things, make ourselves comfortable and wait for a nurse who would take some blood tests as a pre-surgery requirement. We unpacked, I moving numbly, and Yanky gingerly and lovingly placing my belongings in the closet, as if trying to make believe this was some lovely hotel room in which we would be spending our vacation. We then sat down and waited, looking into each others eyes, with unspoken words hanging in the air.

**Yanky:**

UPSTAIRS, THE WELCOME WHICH WE HAD HELD FIXED IN OUR MINDS for so long like beacons of light guiding us safely homewards, was finally enacted.

The entire transplant unit buzzed with the seemingly miraculous news of our arrival by Concorde. We had reached them faster, they asserted, than some local residents would. It was just twelve hours from the moment that I had lifted the receiver in our darkened bedroom and heard the receptionist's friendly voice wishing me a good morning.

Our immediate impressions of the hospital and its staff were that of ease and openness. The doors to all rooms were cheerfully ajar, as if there was nothing here so terrible that it would have to be hidden away behind closed doors. Sunlight was beginning to stream in from floor to ceiling windows, falling on patches of highly polished floor, glinting off a doctor's shining spectacles, a gleaming trolley.

Ruchi was now required to undergo several blood tests. She looked pale, drawn, but for all that, less tense, now that events were moving around her with a momentum of their own. But as for me, sitting in a high-backed chair, watching the interminable blood pricking, it seemed as though all my energies of heart and mind now drained from me in one swift movement. Ceilings, lights, blinds, all tilted alarmingly. I felt at the very howling edge of unconsciousness. And then I began to weep, tears, not of the eyes but of the gut, of the soul. I wept now, not just for the wearying flight by night, the lack of sleep, of food... but for all the soul-wrenching uncertainties, the bone-deep sadness, the slow ponderous, repeated blows to our whole, young lives, for all the unwept tears brimming below the forced brittle cheerfulness... I cried for it all... How does one cry for such prolonged suffering? I cried and could not be comforted...

My wife, alarmed at what was happening to me, stretched out her arms. "Yanky, you've supported and stood by me all these years, you've been strong for both of us. You have been my north, my south, my guiding light in the darkness. Now when I need you most you're deserting me?!"

But I was too far out to hear her, and her pleas echoed ineffectively.

I remember these words echoing on and on soundlessly in my head. "Alone, alone, we are all alone," because it was Shabbos and we could not make contact with the vast network of Ruchi's relatives. Everyone was chattering above me in a strange tongue. This too was a part of it... I could hear Ruchi's voice continuing to exhort me to gather my wits, but I simply did not know the way back.

I got up and left the room. It was one of the only moments that I had ever voluntarily deserted her. We had been in this together all along.

In my exhausted state, I decided that although it was still Shabbos I would avail myself of a '*heter*'. There was only one way I could think of to regain some level of equanimity. And I knew, even in my state of nervous exhaustion, that this was of vital importance. Should I not be able to muster some courage, my wife would surely lose the will to go through with it. In this way, in a short space of time all would be lost.

I asked the nurse to dial my parents' home, and to place the handset on speaker.

I thought to myself at this moment, "*Ribbono shel Olam*, unfortunately in the last twenty-four hours I have had to perform more acts of desecration of the Shabbos (*chillul Shabbos*) than I have ever carried out in my entire life. You, Master of the world, know my heart. Take then, I pray to You, this final act of *chillul Shabbos* and include it in that list of unwitting transgressions."

So the nurse dialed. I spoke to my parents, my brother. I cried again. I wept; I railed against the bitterness of this fate.[17] For the first time I think they plumbed the true depths of despair which I had been concealing all these years. As I replaced the receiver, I felt spent, drained, weary with an untold weariness, but at least

---

17. *It was no longer Shabbos in Europe for we were six hours behind them.*

now somewhat prepared. Is it possible too, that then I remembered those "footprints on the path" which Ruchi was always talking about — it is precisely the way in which the dreamer wakes to the realization that at those times when he feels most alone Hashem is closest to him — for He is actually **carrying** him. With this thought — like a soldier who has watched and waited crouching in rain-soaked trenches through an entire unsleeping night — I knew the moment had come; I was ready to go out there and do battle.

## Dr. Butt:

IT WAS ON A LATE SUMMER'S DAY THAT A YOUNG JEWISH COUPLE HAD walked into my downtown office. For me, it was the worst imaginable moment. Everything was in utter chaos as we were in the throes of a massive operation to move everything, lock, stock and barrel up to Westchester. Boxes, files, forms, agendas lay everywhere — my secretary had already gone ahead to begin the moving-in process. On that cloudy, unsettled day I noticed from my square window that a fine drizzle had begun to fall.

A knock on the door. They enter. I introduce myself. I can see that they are rather taken aback by the disarrayed state of the place. Also, probably by the inexplicable fact that they have managed to reach me with so little ado. This amuses me a little. But I can see that they are both pleased and bewildered by this state of affairs. They begin to tell their story, or rather, the husband speaks. The wife who is the would-be patient looks a little withdrawn, as if it has all passed way beyond her. I listen.

Sometimes in this profession, if I may make so profane a comparison, you feel you are the master of life or death. Sometimes, but not by any means every day, one feels a kind of inversion of this power centered within one's person, within one's expertly moving fingers, one's quick judgement. Now was such a moment of sorts. I knew they were Jewish, obviously religious judging by the man's outward appearance, probably belonging to that selective sect, the *chassidim*. If one lives long enough in New York's famed melting pot, one comes to recognize instantly a vast range of ethnic types.

I do not know in particular what impressed me especially about their case — perhaps it was their youth, their obvious devotion to one another, their quiet desperation. At any rate, I sent them off with a casually worded promise to jot her name down. I could see they were a little let down, but I have a well-tried policy not to raise anyone's hopes prematurely. But, as the last sound of their retreating steps died on the shabby linoleum, I resolved to do everything in my power to help her get a kidney.

THUS, I RE-ENTERED THE ARENA, SEEKING OUT MY WIFE. WE WERE now both placed into the hands of an orderly with whom we entered an elevator. Ruchi was already dressed in her sterile hospital gown. Now it was that we finally met Dr. Butt again, in the tiny pre-operation room after that first meeting in August. He was an extremely tall man, and as his eyes focused on us, his whole face creased into the most genial of smiles.

"Well, well," he cried out in a hearty fashion, and at this he administered a hearty slap on my back. "Caught us all by surprise, my Concorde couple." Within seconds of being greeted by him in this manner my confidence was restored.

"Dr. Butt," I ventured, "when we left your downstate office, I was convinced that you had been having a little joke at our expense!"

"Mr. Guttfreund," he boomed, suddenly serious, "what do you think? I swear to you that not a single day passed since the one on which you left my office, that I did not have you in mind."

This reply left me startled. This, from a man who was obviously not given to wild exaggerations but was a truly genuine and honest human being.

"Now," he continued, "let's get down to real business. We are ready to start. We have a perfect match for your wife, and we feel sure that all will go well. But before I take your wife down to the room shortly as planned, I want you to go away somewhere and get some sleep."

"But, Dr. Butt," I protested, "we Jewish people never allow the patient to be alone, not even for a moment. You must understand that I cannot leave her now at this most critical moment."

"Mr. Guttfreund, I have treated many Jewish patients in my time, and I am thoroughly familiar with your laws regarding these matters. But I well know that at this moment, having traveled a whole night to get here, you are totally emotionally and physically exhausted. Tomorrow, when your wife awakens from the anaesthetic, I need a Mr. Guttfreund who is strong, who is ready and able to support his wife."

Instantly I recognized the inherent wisdom of his words.

"Alright," I said. "I agree, but it is still our Sabbath and I cannot use any transportation until nightfall."

"Very well — you may wait in her room and leave when you are able to."

"Dr. Butt, just one more thing," I insisted. "Promise me that you will let me know how the operation went."

"I give you my word," he said solemnly, "that the moment the operation is finished I will phone you — even in the middle of the night..."

After a few encouraging and parting words to Ruchi, I turned to go.

With these words and with a lightness of heart I had not experienced for months, even years, I entrusted my wife into Dr. Butt's skillful hands, now thoroughly convinced that he was a perfect messenger sent to us at this critical juncture of our lives by our All-Seeing, All-Merciful Father in Heaven. He even wrote down the telephone number where I would be staying in Monsey.

## Ruchi:

I WAS NOW SURROUNDED BY STUDENT NURSES. THEY SEEMED TO WANT TO take endless blood tests. I wished to take a shower even though I knew it was Shabbos and therefore would not be allowed. But somehow I wished to cleanse my body before this intrusion was carried out, so to speak. "No, no," the nurses cried out with one voice. "We cannot allow that. You are weak and pre-surgery. You may catch a cold."

One of the students was quite unable to take blood. His hands were shaking nervously. At this point, I said to him: "Look if you can't do it, just send someone else." However, he insisted.

As I rode down the elevator on the stretcher, Yanky at my side, I felt like an infant in G-d's soothing arms. "This is it, Ruchi," I said to myself. "This is facing mortality head-on." As we rode the numerous floors down to the pre-operating room I muttered in my head the words of the Adon Olam prayer.

"*Adon Olam, asher malach, beterm kol yetzir nivroh,* Master of the Universe, who reigned before any form was created."

"*Beyodo Afkid ruchi, bees ishan veairah, veim ruchi, geviyasi, Hashem li velo irah,* Into His Hand I shall entrust my spirit, when I go to sleep - **and I shall awaken?** With my spirit shall my body remain, Hashem is with me, **I shall not fear.**"

Dr. Butt arrived in a flurry of white coats and lighthearted banter. Suddenly, I realized the moment has finally arrived ... and with this realization, paradoxically, came a deep sense of calm. My husband left on Dr. Butt's strict orders. This was something I had to undergo totally alone, with no comforting shadow at my side. There was simply nothing more for me to do now but to have complete trust first in the beneficence of my Creator and then in Dr. Butt and his transplant team.

Dr. Butt now turned to me and said in an extremely sensitive tone, "Mrs. Guttfreund, I must now ask you to remove your scarf and place a special operation cap on your head. I know how difficult this is for you — but we simply cannot avoid it." As I made the change over from teechel to operation cap he even looked away. I looked up. There was a mass of faces looking down at me. They were all blurred, I was being wheeled...

"Rachel, please place your right hand on at the back of your head," a kind but firm voice instructed me.

I did this. I felt a prick.

I saw no needles.

For in a second all was darkness.

# Yanky:

I RETURNED TO THE ROOM RUCHI AND I HAD FIRST BEEN USHERED INTO — it seemed like a century ago, although in reality it was but a matter of hours ago. Now I stood framed in lone vigil at this very window. I placed the Chassidic work *Noam Elimelech* under her pillow. As I began reciting *Tehilim*, I intermittently raised my eyes upwards. I was searching the entire vast expanse of sky for the three stars which would effectively signal the end of Shabbos and of my isolation. I could then go and phone my wife's family in Monsey. It was not quite nightfall apparently, for I had to wait about ten minutes for their appearance. At this sign, I lifted my hat and took the elevator down to the ground floor. Here in the gleaming lobby, I went to the nurse's desk and asked her to ring my aunt and uncle who lived nearest to the hospital.

"*Gut voch,* Shani," I greeted her as my aunt lifted the phone.

"Oh hello, Yanky, how are you doing? How nice of you to call from...? What's the occasion?"

"No, I am here actually and quite nearby."

"You came on Thursday or Friday?" She seemed confused.

"No, I arrived today."

"Today."

Silence followed by a sudden cry of recognition.

"You're here for the kidney. The kidney — oh-my, oh-my... When? How? Where are you? We'll pick you up..."

In such fashion was the news conveyed to my wife's family.

"Where is she? She's in surgery but Dr. Butt would not allow me to stay."

I waited until my uncle picked me up. On the ride home I was told that Ruchi's parents, grandmother and other aunts and uncles were on their way to Monsey for the sake of supporting each other.

I arrived at my relative's house. They bombarded me with questions. Poor souls, they were in a state of subdued shock and very emotional. Unable to speak. Someone placed some food in front of me. I ate. Someone showed me a bed. I slept. I awoke. Again the phone is ringing. I have been dreaming. We are in mid-flight on the

Concorde. The plane is banking alarmingly. The intercom crackles: "This is your pilot speaking. We are entering an area of strong headwinds..." The steward with the oversized *mogen dovid* lurches towards us — the tray in his hand is tilting. The phone is still ringing. I sit bolt upright. Of course. We have arrived — the phone, the phone — it must be Dr. Butt. I pick up. My throat is parched, bone-dry as if I have been wandering for a long time in a desert under a scorching sun.

I manage to articulate some dry strangled sound.

"This is Dr. Butt speaking..."

"Yes." Again, more like a whisper or a desperate plea for help.

"Mr. Guttfreund, I have just finished operating... The operation took eight hours... I am pleased to tell you that as far as we can see, everything went according to plan. Your wife is now in recovery..."

"When can I come?"

"If you can be here at about nine or ten in the morning — giving her another few hours to regain consciousness fully, I'm sure she would be happy to see you...."

"Dr. Butt," I found my voice, "is she going to be alright?"

"Well, the new kidney has already begun functioning, has actually produced some urine and all the signs are, Mr. Guttfreund, that she's going to be just fine."

"Dr. Butt," I articulated, "one more thing."

"Yes" he said, and I noticed that a slight edge of weariness had crept into his voice.

"Thank you."

Further sleep was impossible. I gave up the attempt and got dressed and went downstairs on tiptoes. The entire house was sleeping. I sat in the small, cozy kitchen and drank a cup of coffee. The refrigerator purred loudly from time to time. At regular intervals something in the central heating system clinked as though it was clearing its throat. Otherwise everything was silent and peaceful. At length, the kitchen became too confining for me. I put on my winter coat, closed the door behind me as quietly as possible and stepped onto the front path. This was a suburban area, some miles outside the city. Here there is grass, more trees, green open spaces, room to breathe. I began to walk. Where I walked to I do not know, but I knew that this way I was walking away some of the time until I could see my wife. I walked slowly, deliberately, as if preserving my energies, measuring the paving stones, the space between the trees, the houses. When I rested for a few moments on a low wall, the sky again seemed a limitless and immeasurable expanse. Was it possible, I wondered, that our torment — that of two tiny specks on the face of this Universe teeming with humanity, but only part of a vast cosmos of endless planets and constellations of interminable worlds and spaces, could be of any real significance? The hugeness and tender impersonality of the early dawn consoled me in a way. It didn't matter so much — it was all nothing, less than nothing. But then I remembered the words of Chazal: "For me was this universe created..." — all of this unbelievable complexity was created just for the sake of that seemingly insignificant individual — me — so that everything, my laughter, my pain, my tears, mattered, were indeed of crucial importance, could change the course of the universe, would rise of its own accord as a song, an offering to the Heavenly Throne itself. Consoled, I rose, for the first time feeling the pinch of the sharpening winter air. I walked with measured steps back, towards the still sleeping house.

## Ruchi:

MY EYES FLUTTER OPEN, CLOSED AND OPEN AGAIN. I COUGH, I GASP, I am aware of tubes, one blocking my throat, my nose, my lips. I try to cry out.

Nurses' faces hovering above me. Tubes from my nose and throat are removed. I gasp for air. I feel little pain but only the so-deep desire to sink back into bottomless oblivion of sleep again. Slept and then slept again. In my dreams, I am in unfamiliar landscapes which I am compelled to enter, climbing dark, shapeless hills or mountains. I wander in and out of rooms of pain, climb hills of pain, am trapped amongst huge rocks of pain. Shadows pass above me and over me — light, slight breezes. Perhaps it is the shadow of death, which seems to me now to be a cool, visited, state — painless, vacant, silent. Every time I reach the top of an incline, there is another slope to climb. I am floating on a vast black sea — seagulls whirl and screech above me. The blackness is vast, incomprehensible, and I cannot distinguish between the darkness of the sea and that of the sky. All boundaries and limits seem to have lost their definition, to have become hopelessly blurred. When will things become clear again? I am floating on a flimsy raft — all alone and so thirsty. The thirst is unbearable but there is no water to drink. Suddenly, a huge wave rises under me — it lifts me higher and higher. I shout to be let down. But the wave carries me relentlessly onwards. There are gaps and crevasses into which I am rolled down, tumbled, abrased. I dissolve into levels of nothingness, pursuing consciousness like an ever-receding mirage and being pursued by it. Finally, I am washed up on some half-deserted shore-line, face downwards. My eyes open of their own accord. The nurse holds my hand and I drop off into another period of deep sleep.

Some time after this, Yanky's face coalesces. I remember thinking how pale and crumpled he looks, as if he has slept all night in his clothes. I try to speak to him, but no voice comes out. He signals me to lie still. I try to lift my arm, but that too is held down with tubes. It seems that there is nothing I can do. I am on the edge of tears, trying to blink them away. But even this is difficult. I incline my head slightly into the pristine white pillow and resign myself again to sleep. This time, it is all whiteness.

I awaken. My lips are parched. I indicate. Someone places an ice-cube on my lips for water is not allowed.

A nurse says soothingly, "There, there, honey!" But I am so thirsty. Then I became aware of something else — a body catheter, for the transplanted kidney has been placed near my stomach. This tube is very uncomfortable.

The nurses lift me a little and sponge me down. I motion to the catheter:

"What's that?"

"A catheter, honey!!"

"Please remove....."

"We can't yet, honey......"

"How long!" I cry out hysterically.

"In a few days, my dear."

I cry out incoherently.

I am wheeled from the recovery room to the elevator, all the while with Yanky at my side. We are in a brightly lit hospital room. The curtains around my bed are of a green, flowery print.

My neighbor is a portly Spanish woman with a string of beads in her hand. She greets me — still holding the big brown beads.

"Oh not, not a busybody!" I pray inwardly, don't bless me with such a neighbor.

"I pray for you," she says in her broken English. "You so young."

But all I wanted was quiet.

After settling me into my room, connecting my bed, tubes and all to the wall, I vaguely notice the nurses' uniforms. They are not the usual whites. They have colorful jackets and matching solid pants, which makes them look so casual and cheerful. The nurses leave Yanky in charge of me, as I am still floating in and out of sleep. I cry. I had been administered steroids on the operating table, so I now felt a deep sense of anticlimax. Yanky is confused: I should be happy, not crying. At this point my parents and relatives begin to drop in. I can't control my emotions, which vary between excitement at seeing them, and crying without control, because of the steroids. I am not in control of my emotions. My relatives seem worried and bewildered at the same time. The pain on my parents' faces was very evident. My grandmother is pained, but as usual has some encouraging words of comfort. I am in a blur – I keep dropping off to sleep. They leave after a while. Yanky continues to sit at my bedside.

Later in the evening, they made me get up to use the bathroom in order to move about after surgery. My blood pressure must have been very low because I collapsed. At this, there was a great commotion as nurses and doctors flurried around me and lifted me back into my hospital bed. They calmed me, gave me some water, took my vital signs, and tucked me in for the night. I was exhausted! My insides were crying out. "I was a *shivrei keli*."

 Yanky:

THEN BEGAN A NEW ERA — AN ERA IN WHICH I WAS BOUND BETWEEN two fixed exigencies: the house where I was staying in Monsey — or more accurately where I ate and slept — and the hospital. Sometimes, after hours of sitting by my wife's bedside, I would feel a deep exhaustion creep over me. Guiltily, I waited for a quiet moment, when she would doze off or say: "I'm alright now, I promise — go home, go home to rest."

Then I would go down into the lobby, get into the car which relatives had loaned to me and start the ignition. But scarcely would I find myself out on the highway, heading homewards, when it would begin — the voices echoing in my head: "Go on, flee from her hospital bed, go as far as you like; even to the end of the earth; but with one twitch of the thread, I will bring you back."

"This is not reasonable; not fair," I would argue, shouting out loud. "I am not fleeing. I have just spent seven or eight hours at her side. I too need something. I need to eat, to sleep, to gather my strength, to speak of other things..."

"Maybe Ruchi is feeling low just now," the voice persisted. "What if she needs you <u>now</u>— imagine her frightened, alone, sick?"

Thus it transpired that in my aunt's house, neither sitting, nor eating, neither conversing nor sleeping, neither by day nor night, did I know real rest. With an almost physical longing, I would at moments long just to leap out of the house back to her bedside. And at her bedside, I would long to be back in my aunt's home, longing for a little rest with which to rejuvenate myself.

But in the deepest recesses of my heart, I now knew that no real rest was possible for me.

It is not as easy as you may think to spent a good number of hours at a sickbed and find something new to say which will amuse, entertain, stimulate, lighten the spirits. After all, my life at this time was not too diverse or interesting, for when I was not at her side I was simply trying to gather the broken bits of my personality together. The nurses' friendly chatter punctuated the long hours we spent together — and also the game of observing the other patients moving in and out of wards. I suppose this is a favorite hospital pastime — looking around, making facile observations about those marooned here with you.

"Do you think he is married?" or "Do you think those two are her children? They are dark unlike her, perhaps nieces or nephews?" we would ask each other. But all this came a little later, when my wife was able to walk up and down corridors, and eventually even to other floors, and thus her horizons broadened a little. But at the beginning, everything was utterly narrowed in, monotone, an unvarying routine of various checks, doctor's rounds, mealtimes. In short, it was a hospital life and as such totally all-consuming.

SOMETIMES, I FEEL SO SORRY FOR YANKY, HE LOOKS SO WORN, SO haggard but in a different way than during the dialysis times. For then, however exhausted he was physically — juggling as he was a multiplicity of responsibilities, home, business, children, me — he derived from these a real sense of achievement. He knew quite well that his efforts were keeping me alive — and this stark black and white knowledge would not allow him ever to concede defeat. I never heard him say: "I cannot do this thing," when to all intents and purposes, he must have been dangerously close to the edge. Now, however, he has been relegated again to the position of a bystander, someone who cheers me on from the wings. Gone is the anticipation for that long awaited phone call. The era of the transplant had arrived. The future was here and now. With it came more plans and trials, which obstacles we would hopefully overcome. Now the real level of his physical and mental exhaustion shows. My anxiety about him sometimes supersedes my own fears. Each day, progress is painfully slow. I am on very heavy drugs. The doctors say: "All is well. You must give yourself time." But oh! How the days, the minutes drag, chained to this hospital bed. Often too, I think of the children — they seem so unreal, like fixed, smiling, brownish images of yesteryear. I cannot remember them in their quick, laughing little faces. I remember only their faces frozen in questioning glances at our bedroom door not long past midnight, saying: "Tatty, *emess*, is it the kidney?"

I TRIED SO HARD NEVER TO ARRIVE EMPTY-HANDED AT RUCHI'S BEDSIDE during these early weeks. Every day, I would seek out some little surprise — a book, a tape, a box of chocolates, to bring her something, anything, which I knew would make her smile a little, a smile which was not yet her old carefree smile, but nevertheless a smile of sorts. My powers of invention grew out of bitter necessity. One day, I went into a Jewish store that allows you to sing and record to any background music you choose. I choose one of her favorite *zemiros* which she loved to hear me sing and spoke a few words by way of introduction: "This song is dedicated to my wife. She is in the Westchester Medical Center, where she has just undergone a kidney transplant and she is still unwell. I would like to send my wife my heartiest *refuah shleimah* wishes..." Hours later I watched her, headphones over her ears as she listened to these words, tears washing down her cheeks onto the small machine she held in her hands... Such small seemingly trivial things, I would guess, touched her more deeply, more nearly, then an array of expensive goods.

Meanwhile, Ruchi's physical condition tends to be a little worrying. Her creatinine level is still high for the kidney is not yet functioning. It would seem, according to all reports, that the operation itself was an unequivocal success. But then came the dreaded rejection. There was always the possibility in the back of our minds that this may occur, but it was still a letdown. Hashem created the human body with its own army against attackers, which may penetrate through cuts and bruises and cause infection. Infections, fevers and headaches are only symptoms of the sickness. Any foreign body would be attacked by an army of antibodies. Being that Ruchi was given immunosuppressive drugs which suppressed her natural immune system, her immunity was very low. She had practically no antibodies. The reason this was necessary was, being that the transplanted organ was a foreign object to her body, there was the danger of it being rejected. Her immunity was suppressed by the drugs, so that it should not fight the new organ.

So here we were, faced with rejection. Ruchi was pumped heavily with more drugs, one of them being ALG, which was meant to specifically target the rejection. Each drug came with its side effects. The medications can cause seizures; therefore, Ruchi was given bedrails as a protective measure.

Also, the ultra-filtration function of the kidney was not yet effective enough, so to our immeasurable disappointment, it transpired that two times during this immediate post-operative period she had to be dialyzed. This dialysis, however, did not include the cleansing process, merely ultra-filtration (releasing excess fluids). On these occasions, we rode the elevator to the eighth floor. Here my wife was dialyzed. At one time we saw two prisoners, still in their prison uniforms and hand-cuffs, on opposite sides of the room. There was a large prison nearby and these inmates needed to be dialyzed. Thus, the specter of the dialysis life rose again to haunt us, like plaintive and uneasy ghosts of some former existence. On each occasion, we watched the sun set over the plains of Westchester — reds, oranges streaking the autumn sky in giant paint strokes.

**Ruchi:**

MY DISAPPOINTMENT AT HAVING TO BE DIALYZED WAS PROFOUND. I FELT as if my whole world had fallen apart. But ultimately I became so full of fluid that I could hardly breathe and I myself begged for dialysis. At dialysis, two psychiatric prisoners are present. They are handcuffed. But I am effectively just as much a **prisoner** as they, although I have committed no crime.

Rejection has entered our lives. It scares me to think that dialysis might become my way of life again. I feel as though my body no longer belongs to me. There is constant pricking and probing by doctors and nurses. I feel as though I'm hanging in the air.

I am growing truly uneasy, the weeks are passing and one by one, the components of our enclosed hospital microcosm are changing. Patients admitted with me have long gone, flown home to some outside life of freedom and readjustment. I became acquainted with all the nurses of the different shifts.

At one time my neighbor was a depressed, suicidal young girl, whom no one visits. It was hard to be positive when surrounded by such traumatic human situations. Later, I was fortunate enough to have a very pleasant neighbor named Marilyn. She seemed to be very much alone in the world but nevertheless she is an extremely positive human being and provided many hours of cheerful company. I was constantly amazed at how differently she reacted to the same medication that I am given. I recall the time I watched her being given a drug that I was given earlier, to which I had severe reactions. I watched from my bed as two nurses administered the drug, while she was doing her nails. The nurse left the room, and a while later Marilyn turned to me, and said, "Hey, Rachel, I'd like to go down to the cafeteria. I'm sitting here, waiting for those nurses to give me the drug. They're wastin' my day." I looked at her incredulously. "Marilyn, you already got your drug," I said. "You can go to the cafeteria."

The severe reactions which I had were mostly severe shaking and shivering, which Dr. Butt would refer to as the "shakes and bakes." Such was the likes of the humor we shared, which helped us pull through.

Only one long-familiar face still remains; as it happens, a Jewish man called Robert Klein, with whom I sometimes conversed a little. I feel like a child who has been passed over in school: "Please, sir, you missed out my turn..." But Dr. Butt insists that he will not allow me to go home until my creatinine level has dropped to a far lower degree. This seems like a magic formula which is becoming increasingly elusive as the days shorten into mid-winter. These numbers would signal the moment of my release from the hospital. So we lived each day in hope, desperate hope!

At one point my grandfather came to see me. He had difficulty walking for he was in the advanced stages of liver cancer. He was frail and pale. His skin was yellow. As I had not been prepared for his changed appearance it was a profound shock to see him in this state. Nevertheless, he insisted on seeing me and doing the *mitzvah* of *bikur cholim*. I was devastated when he left. His appearance kept coming back to haunt me.

Grandmother (on my mother's side) came too. She was in the midst of chemotherapy as well. As I was her eldest granddaughter it was extremely heart-wrenching for her to come. Few words passed between us — we just sat together throughout that afternoon feeling one another's pain, for we had always had a special relationship, Bubby and I.

She had been incarcerated in Auschwitz, yet somehow she remained a shining example of optimism. She would call me up when I was on dialysis and say, "Ruchi, just hold on, there is a light at the end of every tunnel."

Then she would sing to me the words of a Hungarian song that she sang in the cattle wagons rolling towards Auschwitz:

"*Nem lesz mindeg ejszaka la la la.....*

"*Es vet nisht eibig tinkel zein....*, (Yiddish)

"*Es vet noch einmal lichtig zein....la la la*"[18]

It came to be a family song of sorts in times of trial.

---

18. "*It would not be dark forever*
*It will once again be bright.*"
*As a child, Bubby had always told us stories of Auschwitz but somehow these had never been gruesome. They were instead tales of bitachon and*

On another occasion, Chevy, a cousin of my husband's from Antwerp, came to visit me. She was on a business trip and for her to take an entire day off to travel to Westchester was a great sacrifice. So she sat at the side of my bed, doing her figures and every so often she would look up with a comment or a joke. On that particular day I was administered the notorious OKT3 treatment for I was experiencing another rejection. The OKT3 drug is administered to stop rejection — it would not be undertaken lightly for it was an extremely dangerous drug, and was in fact a form of chemotherapy. Therefore, the pros and cons were weighed one hundred if not one hundred and one times. I was strapped to the bed. I had convulsions. Yanky stood by me, whispering soothing words in my ear. And Chevy, the businesswoman, sat witnessing all this, tears rolling down her cheeks.[19]

Very frequently, I would have to undergo a kidney scan. In my daily hospital routine, I still had much to endure in a physical and emotional sense. I was placed on a steel table and a large machine was brought down virtually over my face. I would lie sweating on the bed, claustrophobic, my stomach knotted in anxiety. After this

---

*Hashgachah pratis, always pointing to Hashem's infinite goodness. And when we would question her as children saying "Bubby, how did you survive in Auschwitz?" she would answer that she had always been a firm believer that Mashiach would come tomorrow.*
*So we developed a natural joke. When I grew up:*
*"But Bubby, I live in Europe and you live in America, thousands of miles away, so how will we get together when Mashiach comes," I would ask, a little whimsical.*
*And she would reply: "Don't worry, Ruchi."*
*"Menn vertt zich trefen oif der volkenes, We will meet on the clouds."*
*Before I finally left America, I went to see her and she was in a very weak state. She motioned to me, indicating that she wished to tell me something, but I already knew what it was — "menn vertt zich trefen oif der volkenes."*
*19. At the Bar Mitzvah of my eldest son, when my husband spoke and described my ordeal, she got up and clung to me, thereby giving vent to her emotions. We had shared something.*

test I would be wheeled upstairs to the ward. At the end of my bed were numerous charts but also many medications, all labeled "In case." In an emergency, they would administer these medications to spur the new kidney into action, so to speak. These things were never explained to me clearly, despite the usual policy of openness. And I never asked, but both I and the hospital staff knew that this was the gravity of the situation.

I had to undergo dialysis two times during this period of limbo as there was still no cleansing of the blood since the new kidney was not yet functioning fully.

In conclusion, the hospital was a strange admixture of medications, anxiety, medical tests, visitors, IV tubes, laughter, Shabbosos spent with family, X-rays, porters, orderlies and ups and downs. There were gifts and cards, cards of all types: big ones, small ones, hilarious ones, serious ones. And then there were the prayers. Even my non-Jewish neighbors wished to share the religious feelings exuded by my saying *Tehilim* or simply saying '*Modeh Ani*' each morning as I awoke.

And finally, there were the tears, always the tears of both frustration and joy.

## Yanky:

PERHAPS I HAVE GIVEN THE IMPRESSION THAT DURING THOSE WEEKS SPENT in the hospital, we were totally alone, Ruchi and I. In fact, this was erroneous. There was a steady stream of visitors consisting of relatives, friends and total strangers, and in general an outpouring of kindness of the most overwhelming nature. Gifts literally flowed into the small hospital room. People came bearing spectacular displays of chocolates and candies, flower arrangements, robes, bedjackets, bathsoaps, perfumes, swarms of helium balloons and loads of stuffed animals — more indeed than my wife could ever use herself for a long time.

So, the hospital was not the bleakness you might imagine. For in between the dark hours, there was so much kindness too, that it quite overwhelmed us both. The Bikur Cholim Society not only carried out the obligatory *chesed* but sent cakes and provisions for Shabbos for our visitors too. So much thought went into making the lonely troubled hours less troubling.

❧

## Ruchi:

CLASSMATES WHOM I HAD NOT SEEN FOR YEARS CAME TO SEE ME — spending a whole day coming up to Westchester. On one particular occasion they lost their way, going all the way to Albany. There were jokes and stories to be repeated, there were moments of hilarity so much so that the nurses would say that our room was the "best" one to be in. The walls of my room were covered with cards — there were phone calls from long-forgotten acquaintances. Indeed a whole world of *chesed* opened up before my eyes. One Chassidishe *yungerman* would put his head around the door and say: "Do you need some food? A book perhaps — a Yiddish video to cheer you up?" He would not depart until I had made my requests.

My mother, my aunt Bracha and sometimes a cousin would stay with me for Shabbos (Yanky was too exhausted; we thought it was better this way). They would bring loads of goodies and delicacies, trying to coax me to eat. Most of all they would bring good spirits, *divrei chizuk* and sometimes even dance for me in their sneakers. Visitors would bring flowers, candles for Shabbos, cake not only for me but for our visitors.

My mother received numerous gifts for me from strangers who had heard of my plight. A representative from the local Bikur Cholim of Rockland Country,[20] and groups of women from Mt. Kisco, women would arrive each day, bearing an array of cooked foods, and for every Shabbos, again, full meals consisting of wine, *challos*, soup, a main dish and dessert. All of the above were not only provided for me, but in adequate quantities to nourish any other visitors who happened

---

20. *Reb Shimshon Lauber was the head and driving force of this entire organization.*

to be present. I will never forget their kindness. But even more importantly, there were so many kind inquiries, so many messages of fellow feeling, so many simple, good and healing words that these alone went a long way towards assuaging our pain and bitterness in those long and anxious weeks. (During the course of our prolonged *nisayon*, the years of illness and dialysis, we had longed and waited for just such healing words, borne not of curiosity or a desire to be apprised of the latest news — but of simple enough human-sympathy.)[21]

This spirit of openness and consideration was strangely in evidence too in the general hospital atmosphere. Doctors, nurses, orderlies all exuded a genuine air of friendliness. Nurses would take time from their hectic routines to sit on my bed, ask about my children, to which I would immediately take out large posters (which my husband had made for me) and introduce our family, and also share one of my vast array of chocolates. "Oh Rachel, what beautiful children! Soon you'll get back together again!"

Each patient had a neighbor in her room, with whom one would share thoughts, dreams and hopes, which in normal circumstances would not be shared with total strangers. We were also on first name terms with the nurses. All this conspired to make one feel like a human being. The atmosphere between doctors and nurses, too, was less tense. One day, a nurse dropped some OKT3 medication and Dr. Butt cried out: "Hey Jane, you just dropped a hundred dollars."

All this conspired to make me feel good and not just a patient, an anonymous cog in a machine but a human being, possessed of a name.

21. *This loneliness that we had felt so keenly up to this point, was an important facet of our trial or nisayon. Perhaps, being young and inexperienced, some of our isolation had been self-inflicted. We may have been at times too **embarrassed** to ask for help. But there is a very vital lesson to be learned from our experiences — and it is that the way in which help is offered is of vital importance. It must be carried out in a manner which leaves the one who receives it his integrity and self-respect intact. That is, it must never be offered in a demeaning or paternalistic way, but out of a sense of true fellow feeling and concern.*

**Yanky:**

AS I CONTINUED MY ENDLESS JOURNEYS BETWEEN THE VARIOUS HOUSES where I stayed and the hospital, the trees along the highway began to shed their leaves. When we had first arrived, they had still been swollen, in full leaf. Now, they were almost denuded, their bare branches crisscrossing the leaden winter sky. The desolation of the trees reflected the deepening desolation in our hearts at the passing of time. I would attempt to vary my long familiar journey, trying out a different route to the hospital each day. But soon enough, all possible routes had been traveled, and I had to begin again on the old familiar road. Surely by now, we reasoned, but dared not to voice openly to one another, we should have been beginning to derive the benefits of the enormous, earth-wrenching experience we had so recently undergone.

"If only I could go home," my wife would cry every time the doctors did their rounds.

"Mrs. Guttfreund, we are very sorry, but Dr. Butt ordered that you stay here until your creatinine falls to below two!"

In reality the new kidney had not began to function properly yet. Dr. Butt hoped that the strong medication, which he now began to administer to my wife, would jump-start the kidney into working independently.

❦

**Ruchi:**

STILL NO REAL PROGRESS. THIS IS WHAT I FEEL IN MY BONES, ALTHOUGH no one says this to me openly. I am deeply afraid. My husband's words of warning on the Concorde flight that we might well return empty-handed, now return to haunt me in the long reaches of the night. It is during the nights that I feel desperately alone. During the day, my husband and a variety of visitors keep me company and the interminable hospital routines provide nagging distraction from my thoughts. But, as the winter night deepens with a promise of snow, and my husband finally turns to leave with a sigh, that the endless thoughts return to haunt me. The endless what if's and worries flood my mind. What if this kidney won't work? Will I have to go back to dialysis? Will I ever be the same again?...

Unable to sleep, I toss and turn. A nurse visits me. We talk. She sees I'm unable to sleep. She does a little dance for me. We share some goodies. We talk some more. She leaves the room to check on the other patients.

Thoughts begin to invade my mind again. I feel like I'll burst if I stay in bed. I put on my robe and slippers and walk the long hospital corridors. The hour is very late. All is quiet. Veronica, the night nurse, catches up with me. "Rachel, is that you? Honey, can't you get some sleep?"

"Can't sleep," I murmur, agitated.

"Again?" and then the usual, "Come, I'll get you a sleeping pill."

"No, thanks." This discussion begins and ends. Almost like routine.

"Dear me," Veronica's concerned voice.

She takes me gently by the hands and walks me gently to my bed. She removes my slippers and tucks me in with a gentle pat.

"Good night dear; do try to get some sleep."

**Yanky:**

THEY HAVE BEGUN GIVING MY WIFE SOME POWERFUL DRUGS TO INDUCE the kidney to work. Dr. Butt warned me repeatedly about side-effects: "Do not be shocked, Mr. Guttfreund, for you must bear in mind that these are very potent medications indeed.... However, we feel sure that they will do the job..."

Then began a new era, as the drugs began to insinuate themselves into my wife's nervous system and dictate her moods, her feelings, her state of mind. She would begin to sweat visibly, sometimes she would then have convulsions. At times she could no longer sit on her bed. She would rush to the window shouting: "Let me have some air!"

At other times, she would pace along the corridors. I would rush after her: "Where are you going?"

"I must find a door, an exit, a way out. Please, please... Oh, let me out of this rabbit warren..." and she would turn towards me with huge pleading but unseeing eyes. Her eyes reflected everything — all her twisted pain, her wracked inner turmoil.

⁂

Now, I would arrive every morning, with a new and quite alien sense of fear. What state of health would I find Ruchi in? Sometimes the staff nurse would greet me with maddening cheerfulness: "We had quite a hard night with Rachel..." I would first consult with the nurses: "What kind of night has my wife had?" and next examine the charts. Then I would enter her room, with a slowly sinking heart. Sometimes she was dozing, for all the world like a peaceful child. At other times, she was restless, torn, wrenched apart —pacing, ever pacing. *Ribbono shel Olam*, I would ask at such times, when will it all end? When will the light come — the *yeshuah*? And sometimes, "I cannot go on another day without some real hope." Often, during this period, I would cry all the way home, so that I hardly saw the intermittent headlights of other cars passing, the road signs, the all-pervading darkness outside.

⁂

## Ruchi:

I WOULD WAIT EVERY DAY FOR THE SOUND OF YANKY'S FOOTSTEPS. Being that my room was at the end of the corridor, I would have a few seconds to put myself together till Yanky would stick his head in. Sometimes I could hear his footsteps, but they would stop at the door, without me getting a glimpse of him. He'd be reading the medical charts, hanging over there, to see if progress had been made or there had been any changes from the night before. We would exchange the latest news – such as if he had spoken to the children, how his night had passed, how I had fared, family news and the likes. Yanky had asked the nurses some questions and received the answers. I would choose my robe, and we would make our way to the cafeteria. In the confines of the hospital, this was our daily outing. In the cafeteria, we would make our way to the refrigerators and I would begin to choose a drink. Sometimes I would hold the door open for quite some time; I would be bedazzled by the choice. Yanky would intervene, "Ruchi, can I buy you a drink?" Finally I would choose. We would sit down at one of the tables as if we had an important meeting, and I would savor each sip. Just these seemingly trivial actions gave me some sense of normality.

I AM DISAPPOINTED AND PUZZLED BY THE GUTTFREUND CASE. THE kidney seemed to be such a perfect match, and the operation went smoothly, as well as one can truly hope for. A textbook case almost. Yet inexplicably she does not seem to be picking up as she should be doing. I do not want to alarm them unduly, but I am anxious. There are one or two options open to us. Apart from prescribing high doses of prednisone, I want to order a biopsy on the new kidney to see if we can trace the source of the problem. I can see from their demeanor that they are disappointed, they are longing to be allowed to leave hospital, and also to send for their children, who I understand are still abroad. Usually, I would have expected Mrs. Guttfreund to have left the hospital after two weeks. Sometimes in this profession, when one comes to the limits of one's medical knowledge, there is little else that I can advise more efficacious than prayer. And in this case as it now stands, I think we all need to pray...

**Ruchi:** I UNDERWENT A KIDNEY SCAN. THIS IS A PARTICULARLY UNPLEASANT test, as one has to lie perfectly still on a steel table whilst the function of the kidney is thoroughly checked.

This is done by injecting a dye into my vein, which would then go through to the kidney, and they would then get to see a picture of the kidney. This test was more thorough than an ultrasound, for it enabled them to see the whole function of the kidney. It is a time-consuming process, too. I would be alone in the room with the coldness of the steel on my skin. Shivering, not so much of pain, but of claustrophobia. The huge machine would be placed inches above my face and body, thereby giving me the feeling that I was pinned to the table, although it never actually touched me. I was all alone in the room for half an hour. I felt vulnerable and supine, as I lay there waiting for them to take me off the table.

I would then be taken in a wheelchair up to my room.

Then tests were done three or four times during my hospital stay.

In addition to the scan, I also had to have an occasional kidney biopsy. A speck of cells from the kidney had to be drawn out. It was, however, less painful than the original biopsy on my own kidney in Europe, as that was done on the back. On the transplanted kidney the needle was inserted through the stomach, almost on the surface. There were doctors and nurses dressed in their greens, gathered around the table. Their kind eyes peering out above their masks, sometimes winking, sometimes joking while performing the biopsy. They informed me of every step along the way. The needle which actually was a suction, reminded me of a cookie press, for one didn't feel a needle, rather pressure, and a speck of cells was suctioned in to it. This test, although more painful than a kidney scan, was much easier to endure, for these were "my" very own doctors. They were the ones that bustled around me every day. I was their patient – we were a family of sorts.

At this point I was depressed and physically unwell. I was suffering from extremely high blood pressure, the results of which would be sometimes extreme nosebleeds which would start in middle of nowhere, splatter all over, and we (Yanky, nurses and I) would be changing clothes and squeezing my nose closed in frenzy. And oh! The headaches. Those pounding, searing headaches, till I thought my head would burst. I once commented to Dr. Butt that I feel like someone is sitting on my head. Dr. Butt would humorously answer, "Well, Rachel, tell him to get off."

The general atmosphere in the hospital was one of openness. We were encouraged to examine our charts, and feel a little in control of our bodies. In Europe, charts were kept by the nurses' desk, information was scarcely and stingily given. Even if one would ask, one was under the impression, "this is none of your business. We are the doctors, we take care of life and death."

We have come to a plateau where the kidney seems to be opening up, yet the results of the tests are not exactly the way Dr. Butt would like them to be. So we wait...

Along with the waiting came an escalating anxiety. Side affects from strong dosages of medication, and their physical symptoms, and of course the boredom.

I am bored. The days pass. Most visitors are back in their routine. I crawl the walls and the hallways. New faces come and go. I am still here. I long for ways to pass the endless hours where I do not have to think and think, and worry and worry.

As if reading my thoughts, Dr. Butt, who has been very concerned by my anxious state, walks into my room one day and asks, "Rachel, how would you like to help us with our enormous workload here in the office?" I opened my eyes in surprise. Being treated as a regular person is such a lovely feeling .

"Rachel, we will bring you envelopes from our office to stuff right here on your bed. So you can help us, and make our workload easier."

That is precisely what occurred. His kindness is overwhelming. He makes me feel that I'm helping them. He is a gift from Hashem to us. Dr. Butt is not only a great doctor, but a great human being. He's a *mentch*.

He also went to great extents for me to get more physical exercise, which was very good for me. I would tire easily, and of course crawl into bed. He was also convinced that exercising (or walking the corridor more, and staying out of bed more often) would be good for my emotional well being. And so being the compassionate human being that he is, he even offered to bring his own treadmill into my room! What a doctor!

I had hoped that having undergone this overwhelming transplant so many weeks ago, now I would magically pass into a new realm, where there would be no more dialyses, no more intrusive tests. Now, I know this to be nothing but a mirage. I know that I must never lose hope, because nothing, literally nothing is beyond the ability of Hashem, and I realize too, that this belief must be complete, unlimited, uncompromising. Perhaps, too, since our situation has become so confusing, when the salvation comes at a point beyond what seems to us by natural means, it will be all the more stupendous.

**Yanky:**

MY WIFE'S SITUATION CONTINUES TO BE PUZZLING. HOWEVER SHE IS, stronger, as she now walks freely, as much as she is able to in this constricted space, up and down other corridors and floors. However, her appearance has changed beyond recognition. Where beforehand she was mostly pale and sallow, she is now bloated and swollen, and her skin has a yellowish tinge, an almost suntanned tinge. This lends her facial features a kind of puffy appearance (in medical terms, a moonface) and an impression of this being not quite the same person. It is as if one is looking directly into one of those comically distorting mirrors, seeing oneself, one's own features and coloring, yet at the same time seeing all the proportions altered and therefore, a quite different individual. Two biopsies have now been carried out on Dr. Butt's orders to try and determine what exactly is transpiring. When I arrive, down to the cafeteria we go again. Ruchi dressing up in her robe and slippers for the occasion. It seems to ease her claustrophobia a bit. We choose a drink together. It is this "outing" that recalls something of the hospital-free life for her.

It was a snowy midwinter morning. I arrived a little late at the hospital. I despaired of this hospital imprisonment ever coming to an end. It was as though we had been frozen in time, and somehow the images would not run on and allow the situation to change into the next phase.

A nurse approached me.

"Mr. Guttfreund, Dr. Butt would like to see you in his office. He said to call you as soon as you came in."

I berated my uncustomary tardiness this morning. I raced along corridors, up the elevator. Would he still be waiting for me? There was no time even to feel real fear of what he might wish to tell me.

I knocked.

"Come in. Oh, good morning Mr. Guttfreund, and how are we all this frosty morning?!"

I muttered something to the effect that we were both as well as could be expected. There was a slight edge of bitterness to my tone.

"Now, Mr. Guttfreund, you know very well that I have been keeping your wife here all these weeks, not because I wished to, but because I could not in all conscience send her home with a creatinine as she has been displaying. Before I discharge her, her creatinine must go down."

"Yes, of course Dr. Butt, I understand," I muttered a little apologetically.

"Well, we have been treating her with prednisone. We have also done some biopsies, the results of which should be available shortly, and which should be very revealing. And we have administered OKT3 when the kidney seemed to be rejecting.

"Now, the latest tests show us that your wife's creatinine has been improving. This is not yet as low as we had hoped, but I think it would now be safe for her to leave the hospital."

"When?" I let out in one long breath.

"Well, as soon as you can make the necessary arrangements. Today even, if that is convenient for you."

"It is convenient." I said, and these words bore all the force of a considered statement.

"Now, Mr. Guttfreund, you must make me one promise, and this is very important. Well, really it is not just a promise, but a condition of my allowing you to leave here today. You must promise to attend our outpatient clinic two times a week, in the mornings, for regular tests as is usual. But you must do this absolutely religiously, taking care never to miss an appointment. In this way we will be able to keep a close check on your wife's condition, and hopefully bring down the creatinine level to a far more acceptable level."

"Dr. Butt, I simply do not have the words with which to thank you for all that you have done for us."

"Do not thank me, Mr. Guttfreund, it is all in the hands of the One Above..." he said, pointing upwards and letting out a mischievous chuckle.

"Oh, and one more thing, Mr. Guttfreund. You are still very much in my care and that of my team. Now if at any time, day or night, your wife's condition gives you any cause for alarm, if you notice anything different or strange about her, you must promise to let me know immediately."

"I promise..."

I extended my hand and as I gave him this, my final promise, across the width of the desk, he half-rose and stood for a moment, his fingers on mine, a massive, genial figure, framed against the square windows beyond which lay the entire, pristine expanses of the hospital lawns.

"Goodbye, sir," I brought out finally.

"Goodbye, my friend." he rejoined.

⁂

WERE SPEEDING ALONG A SNOW-BORDERED HIGHWAY, PERHAPS THE VERY route we took on that pre-dawn journey up to Westchester which marked my last moment of free movement for all these weeks. I sit in the car, half dazed, recalling the last few hours. Leaving the hospital was a momentous occasion. There were papers to be processed, papers to be signed, medicines given with last minute instructions, and then came the packing. Packing came with lots of mixed emotions. I had spent the last few weeks in "my room:" it was my bed, my closet, my pillow, my closet, my night table. It was my room. And yet, all I was taking with me was my personal belongings. I felt like a little girl in her first day of school. I was excited to leave the hospital, but my stomach was doing somersaults at the fear of leaving the place I wanted to leave, in order to move on.

As if mechanically, Yanky was busy stuffing my few belongings into a suitcase, as he was very anxious to leave as soon as we could. I got dressed rather awkwardly, for I had been dressed in my hospital garb for quite some time. As I put my *sheitel* on for the first time, some nurses gathered around to complement me, on my wonderful hairstyle. After hugs and kisses from them, we walked down the corridors, saying goodbye to those in whose company I had spent so many months: the nurses, the patients – even the security guard.

I feel as though I am walking on air. After so many weeks of lying in bed, I am finally free. I feel as though I am a living miracle – a modern day medical miracle. A woman with a transplant, ready to blend into normal society. My soul wants to sing, my body wants to shout. Look at the great kindness Hashem has done with me. I ask Yanky to ask a rav if we can make the day I received my transplant into a day where we can give our thanks, and say *Hallel*. With a twinkle in his eye, Yanky responds, "Oh, but it was on Rosh Chodesh." With that we both smile with satisfaction.

It is a strange feeling to be dressed, to walk in the bracing air to the car, to ride as we like or where or when we like. Yes, it is both strange and disconcerting, for it feels a little as though I am a butterfly at the moment of liberation from a long, familiar cocoon. How will I face the real world again? How will I make the necessary adjustments? For the first time, as I speed away from the hospital environs, I see it for what it really is, a self-enclosed microcosm, with its own social divisions, its own exigencies, its own frustrations and disappointments. It operates independently from the healthy world, and bears no real relationship to it. There is a division, as if with a wall of steel, between the healthy and unhealthy. As we exit the hospital main doors, I have a new sense of being apart from this microcosm. I have graduated to the real life. "Have a good life," the nurses called out. "Come back only to visit."

HOME, OR WHATEVER PASSES FOR HOME FOR US AT THIS STAGE IN OUR lives. But a welcoming meal, a warm house, a clean bedroom, even though not our own, all of these things and the ultimate fact that we are here together, now qualify our temporary residence with that most warming of appellations, "home." The days pass in a whirl of unreality. The adjustment period is slow. For my wife, I can see that this is a sorely needed halfway house for her to rest her limbs, as it were, in her long and arduous climb upwards towards that most elusive of summits — normalcy. Despite our early euphoria at being allowed home from the hospital, do not make the mistake of thinking that it all went smoothly from here on. Our days were still bound to the hospital, for my wife was under the closest supervision. Twice a week we made the hour-long pilgrimage towards Westchester. Sometimes it was snowing, raining heavily, but the seemingly endless routine of medical tests continued unabated. We would arrive at the clinic and sign our names.

Next we would place our belongings on two chairs and reserve our seats in the waiting room. We would then go through long corridors through the emergency waiting area, into another building, and finally to the lab. Ruchi would take a urine test and some blood tests. There would always be some light talk with the nurses as we waited for the results. Waiting was not just a wait. There was always the anxiety and fear, and that tiny spark of hope, as to what the results would be. We would receive her computerized results on long sheets of paper, everything clearly printed so that even laymen, could read it. On one side would be the norm, and parallel to it would be her results for the day. This enabled us to compare and assess her medical situation. This was done in order to make the patient feel a bit in control, as part of the healing process. For us personally this would eliminate the fear of what the doctor would say, and did not leave us in the dark.

With these medical reports in our hands, we would then go to the cafeteria, since we still had a long wait in Dr. Butt's waiting area, and unwrap the sandwiches my aunt had so kindly made for us. Every day there would be surprises to lift our spirits. She would sometimes place a sticker, a smiling face or a little note. These were thoughtful gestures and so uplifting.

We would sit for awhile, and then return to the waiting area and to our reserved seats. There we would wait some more, read, say *Tehilim*, converse with the patients, until our names would be called. Finally we were called into the office, and Ruchi would go through the whole medical examination routine. Different medications would be discussed, some replaced with others, and the dosages changed.

As the days wore on and these visits became routine, the longing for our children became more intense. We would speak to our kids more and more on the phone, just to hear their cute little voices, laughs and stories from school. Every time we would put down the phone we would stay with this empty feeling. Both Ruchi and I felt something was missing...

❧❦❧

Ruchi was going through a difficult period of adjustment. She was having bouts of anxiety, usually in the dead of night. I would awake with a deep sense that something was wrong or that I was being watched. Then, I would drag myself from the comforting depths of sleep to see my wife either sitting bolt upright on her bed — or sitting slightly crouched over in the chair by the window.

"What is it, what's the matter?" I would cry out.

But I already knew.

"I can't bear it, I'm scared. Help me. I'm going to be sick..."

She seemed to have broken out in a cold sweat, and all her movements were exaggerated. I could see tears glistening in her blue eyes, the panic jumping out at me.

Then I would say: "Take it easy, calm down. Put on your dressing gown and slippers, wrap this warm blanket around your shoulders and we'll go for a drive." I would quickly dress, grab her pillow and the car keys, and go out through the side entrance into the freezing cold night air. I would put the pillow in the back seat, make sure that she was comfortable, and slide into the driver's seat, always keeping a watchful eye on her in my mirror. I would turn on

**Yanky:**

some soft music, and then just drive in any direction around the deserted streets. The thought that of this whole vast sleeping suburb, perhaps only we two were awake was slightly discomforting, as if we were out of step with normal human modes of living.

I do not know how many miles we would drive in this way, but at a certain point I would look into the mirror and see Ruchi lying curled up on the seat, head on the pillow, now mercifully sunk into a tranquil sleep. Then we would head home...

EACH TIME THEY OCCUR, THEY ARE TOTALLY UNEXPECTED IN THEIR way. I may feel I have attained a level of calm, of growing certainty, and then in the blinking of an eye I am thrown overboard, prostrate with nameless fears, knocked sideways in a toweringly rough sea. I break out in a cold sweat, I shiver but not with cold. I feel wrenched, racked, torn apart inside by a pain beyond physical pain. So began my little bout with anxiety attacks; I was suffering from post-traumatic stress. After all these years of keeping strong, holding on, being "attached" to a machine, there was something inside of me that was afraid to let go. Afraid to start living a normal life, without feeling dependent on the machine for life. In addition, there was the protective environment of the hospital that I had just left, to which I had become dependent on as well. I was finally at a stage where I wanted to be, and yet found myself with a biting fear of having to start to learn how to live on my own.

During the day, I was kept busy, and so it suppressed my fears when they arose. During the night my subconscious would come to taunt me. I would wake up with a start, sweating and gasping for air, all the while feeling the panic rise and my throat tighten. The fear of dying after all I went through overtook me. The panic, the anxiety and the fear caused me to hyperventilate at times. The longing for my children was unbearable and added much to my ongoing stress.

I hear a voice – perhaps it is Yanky's – soft and comforting. He is muttering soothing words. He asks what is the matter. I say I'm scared.

"Scared of what?"

"Scared of living, scared of dying. Scared. Plain scared."

When a mother tries to comfort a child having a nightmare without really understanding his fear, she turns on the light and makes him a drink. Such was Yanky's role of in this phase.

Where does all fear come from? I didn't know a human brain can hold so much fear.

The human voice is persuasive, and also deeply familiar. "Come, come with me for a drive," it persists. So I go.

## Yanky:

CAN YOU BELIEVE IT IS CHANUKAH? AND WE HAD PROMISED THE children blithely that we would be back home within a short while. How the weeks have flown! Neither of us could have predicted how much we have become introverted, sucked into this enormous thing that has happened to us both. We celebrate the first night of Chanukah away from our children. We light the first candle and see the darkness ebbing away. One small light, I think, can extinguish all the darkness, but all the darkness cannot extinguish one small light... In this room, it is all light and warmth as we sing together, eat Chanukah delicacies. But some small sharp edges of darkness remain — our children are not here with us, and as nothing is properly settled yet, we simply do not know how long it will be before we can return home. I look across to my wife; she is laughing at some carefree banter with her cousins, but I see she feels this too. Still, I do not want to spoil this first possible moment of real cheer with depressing thoughts.

As the evening wears on Ruchi starts to feel a little unwell. I think with an inward sigh that tonight will perhaps be broken by another period of anxiety. We decide to retire early; perhaps the excitement has worn her out. It must be nearly midnight when she stands over my bed and shakes me awake. I see immediately that she is in a total panic. She is shivering so violently that her whole body is shaking, her teeth, her every limb, everything about her is a shuddering mass. With some sixth sense, I divine that this is different qualitatively from all her former attacks. For the first time, I get out the small card on which Dr. Butt has written an emergency number (to be used in genuine emergencies only) where he can be reached at any time of the day or night.

"Is this Dr. Butt?" I say urgently into the receiver. "I am sorry to disturb your sleep."

"That's alright. What seems to be the problem, Mr. Guttfreund?"

I describe my wife's condition.

"Just wrap your wife up well and bring her straight to the hospital," he says. "I will meet you there in approximately one hour."

Thus we arrived at this unearthly hour, at the still-lit hospital which we had thought never again to see under such alarming circumstances.

Strangely, almost as soon as Dr. Butt appeared my wife's symptoms began to abate, for his very presence calmed her. He carried out a few routine checks and then said that as far as he could see, whatever her problem had been, it had now passed.

We apologized profusely to Dr. Butt for having disturbed his sleep, but he reassured us that such occurrences were fairly frequent, and he was there to help.

After this episode, Ruchi began to feel desperately unwell for a while — her blood pressure rising and falling continuously. Deep inside I knew that there was something not right but did not like to admit it. My mind closed it out. "No, not another problem, not another setback, it just cannot be."

**Ruchi:**

ON THE FIRST DAY OF CHANUKAH, WE PACKED SOME OF OUR BELONGINGS and decided to spend a few days at my parents' house. We felt the change would be good for me, since I was homesick. We planned our stay till the next clinic visit, and if necessary we would go from Boro Park. Yanky urged me to take walks, strolling up and down the avenue, looking at things, meeting people, even though my face was bloated: in short coming back to society. So we walked, all the while me having this strange feeling that something was not right, all was not well. I was feeling hot, flushed, I felt my blood pressure go up, and down. I was dizzy and out of breath. Yanky, thinking that I was afraid to make a comeback, tried to talk me out of it, but to no avail. I was feeling unwell. So we went back home, all the while feeing guilty for making Yanky feel scared and nervous. I was feeling sick, but upon Yanky's questions as to how do I feel, I couldn't describe it. I was scared to even think it was something to be troubled about. So I tried "behaving."

If one is to understand the state of my health at that point, and the extra burden of "behaving," you need a great imagination. It was torture! But it didn't work. No sooner did I settle down for the night, when at the early morning hours I suddenly sat up with a bolt, gasping for air. The fear began to get a grip on me, again, as I realized, this is for real. Yanky sat up too, and tried to reassure me that it would pass, and I should try to go back to sleep. It didn't work, as I was convinced that I needed oxygen.

Yanky called my uncle who lived nearby and was a volunteer for Hatzalah. He gave me some oxygen, which calmed me down a bit. As I was starting to feel better, and we both wanted to avoid panicking, we decided to stay a while longer in Boro Park, all the while thinking it would pass.

We went for more walks, looked at store windows, bought small surprises for the children and took a short drive in the car. As the day wore on, I was feeling queasy and unwell. I was uncomfortable, flushed and hot, till we finally realized I was running a fever. This was no joke. We quickly gathered our belongings and were on our way, once again, to Westchester.

This was too much. How would I cope? I was shivering. I could feel myself letting go... Letting go with the bumps, into the clouds... Float... as my mother called it. It was a mechanism I had developed so I can cope. It seemed to work, for what I was actually doing was putting myself totally in Hashem's hands. Totally. Release your burdens, your worries, your fear, and Hashem will take care of you. It was such a good feeling when I released the fear after the gut wrenching moments filled with anxiety. I was somewhere else. I greatly appreciated this G-d-given gift, which helped me to pull through my darkest moments, and to never give up.

⚜

Yanky:

ON THE FIRST NIGHT, IT MUST HAVE BEEN NEARLY DAWN WHEN RUCHI woke me again. I could see her gasping for air. After a visit from her uncle, who administered some oxygen, some reassuring words and advice that we should be heading towards the hospital, Ruchi began to feel better again. We decided to wait it out, and whiled away our time in the streets of Boro Park. But with Ruchi running a high temperature, we were again speeding towards Westchester. It was late in the evening when we were admitted through the familiar hospital portals. As soon as we arrived, Ruchi was taken into a room where she was examined by a doctor and asked some questions. She seemed confused and ill. Her blood pressure was high one minute and low the next. Dr. Butt arrived, to our relief, examined her once again, and decided to keep her overnight. The lab was not open at these late hours, and he seemed not quite sure what was ailing her. He had his suspicions, but would need them confirmed with some blood tests. In the meantime, Ruchi was placed in an isolation room.

Later in the morning hours it was confirmed that Ruchi had the dreaded CMV virus (Cito Megalo Virus – it can be prevalent in post-transplant patients, where the virus may be lying dormant in the person's body, or in the transplanted organ. Since they are on large doses of immune-suppressant drugs, it sometimes allows this virus to take hold.) As Ruchi was on the transplant ward, everyone was on immune-suppressant drugs, so she was placed in an isolation room, as for these patients this virus can be fatal.

❧❧❧

Thus, the second night of Chanukah was spent in the all too well-known hospital surroundings. I lit a small child's menorah in the hospital, using colored candles. I allowed them to burn for a half hour and then stepped over and extinguished the flames. It felt somehow demeaning for me to have to resort to lighting children's Chanukah lights when I should have been at home with a silver oil menorah and my wife and children around me. Lighting a naked flame in a hospital room was in direct contravention of hospital regulations.

I left Ruchi, in the isolation room to deal with her fears of the CMV all on her own.

I drove home in a quiet fury of despair. "*Ribbono shel Olam*, how much suffering can You heap on me, how much longer until I crack and split wide open?" and then, "Forgive me, forgive me for these are the cries of a lonely and frightened child crying in the night! Father in Heaven, in our childishness, I thought of the transplant as a golden thread. If only I could reach that ever-receding stage known as transplant, all would be well, transformed instantly as if with a magic wand. Now I know differently. Having a transplant isn't a picnic. It comes with ups and downs. But if I cry out to You at this additional cup of bitterness, it is because I long so intensely to sense Your nearness. Also, to be granted the strength to conquer this test and to reach at long last, some stability ..."

❧❧❧

## Ruchi:

I'M IN THE HOSPITAL AGAIN, THIS TIME IN AN ISOLATION ROOM, FACING out over the slopes to the rear of the hospital, slanting down towards a round small ridge and clusters of trees speckling the green. I am being administered high doses of gammaglobulin. The fever is slow in retreating, but each day I feel a little stronger, a little more myself, if such an expression has any meaning any longer. What is "myself?" Who am I? Where am I? I am marooned within these hospital rooms, seemingly separated forever from my own dear children and my own cozy home. Sometimes in my fevered dreams, I would picture my home, its doors closed, lights switched off, curtains drawn. I imagine myself stepping over my own threshold, switching on a light and then — my children running towards me. I would be about to sweep them in my arms but they turn away from me. I cry out: "Don't you recognize me? It is me — Mommy, and oh how I have missed you."

FORTUNATELY, MY WIFE WAS SLOWLY RECOVERING FROM THIS SERIOUS virus and after two and a half weeks she was allowed home for the second time. Some extra medical assistance was dispatched to us, and the twice weekly checkups continued as Ruchi was being administered gammaglobulin intravenously, continuously, at home. After a couple of weeks, Ruchi was out of the danger zone, but she was still slow in recovering fully. Now, we were anxious to know when we could make the return journey home. But Dr. Butt was still unhappy about my wife's condition, for the creatinine level simply refused to descend. He decided to carry out a third biopsy on the new kidney and, of course, with each biopsy there were the risks.

Attending the clinic one February day, I was summoned to Dr. Butt's office alone. I thought of all the other occasions on which he had asked to see me. I was anxious but not unduly concerned.

The second I entered the room, I saw that Dr. Butt's demeanor was uncharacteristically grave.

"Sit down, sit down, Mr. Guttfreund,"

He coughed a little, again unlike his usual confident manner.

"Mr. Guttfreund," he shifted a little on his chair. "We have the results of the biopsy."

"Yes?"

"Well, I'm afraid we have some bad news for you."

Bad news? I searched my mind for the worst news, the worst that we could now encounter in our present situation. My mind simply refused to work.

"Well," he began again, "it seems that somehow, and this is a rare complication, that your wife's original disease has entered the new kidney. That is why her creatinine level has failed to drop."

I sat silently, making no response.

"Now this disease, as you well know, is a kidney-killer."

"What shall we do?" I cried out in utter and abject despair. "Please, please tell us what we must do."

"Mr. Guttfreund, I promise to you now that it may take time, maybe even months, but I will fight this disease with every means at my disposal. Are you agreeable to this?"

"Yes..."

"I will have to administer higher doses of Cyclosporin (Sandimune) to your wife. You know what this means. She will experience extremely unpleasant side effects. And you cannot rush home, you must be prepared to stay here for as long as it takes to defeat this thing...."

I nodded.

"And Mr. Guttfreund, one more thing — as soon as I tell you the time is right, you must make arrangements to bring your children here...this is most critical, for it will certainly assist Ruchi's recovery to have her children with her..."

**Ruchi:**

MY HUSBAND BROKE THE NEWS SOFTLY TO ME. SOMEHOW, THERE IS relief now that "what is wrong" is not just a vague, nameless thing but an identified enemy, something we can fight against. It has a name. Hashem in His great kindness has sent us a messenger who is prepared to battle this disease. Dr. Butt is prepared to fight it with us, and we are prepared to cooperate with him. With help from Above, we'll succeed. And he has told my husband, one day soon we will be able to bring the children here. All these past weeks we dreamed of little other than this. We took long walks in the snow and talked incessantly:

"How do you think they look? What are they doing? They sound so different, so grown up. Will they recognize us? We must not expect too much," we kept telling each other. "They are so young, and this separation of almost four months must have been very confusing for them." But only I knew how much I suffered from not having the children with me. This is something only a mother's heart can truly comprehend. Only a reunion with them would assure me that I was on the road to normality.

Sometimes we went shopping. Then we would pick up presents for when the time finally came to be reunited.

I would cry, even at this simple action.

"Oh, I hardly remember what each one likes, they must have changed so much. I miss them, oh so deeply. It seems as though we are living on another planet."

It was so heart-breakingly hard — this continuing enforced separation and all the time wanting no more than such a seemingly simple, little thing — to be with my little ones — kiss them, hug them and care for them.

❧

## Yanky:

WITH TREATMENT WELL UNDER WAY WE HAVE TO REPORT TO THE hospital every second day, as Ruchi is being kept under the closest possible supervision. Two or three weeks later, I received a message from Dr. Butt to the effect that in his estimation the time was now right to bring the children.

Accordingly, a week after Tu B'Shevat, I set out for home alone. I carried very little on my person — just a change of clothing and some presents for the children — for I intended to stay just for two nights and then bring them back with me.

How well I recall that feeling when I first saw their little faces at the airport barrier. They came towards me hesitantly, as if not believing I was really here. Tatty?

I embraced them, I wept. It was the sheer cumulative weight of time. It was those almost four months that we had spent apart which would not simply disappear like tired ghosts. Only through time spent together, could we gradually wear away the separation. I now realized that we could not get back to normal life without our children.

The return journey on the airplane passed in a daze. I held onto the children. I spoke to them, played with them as if we had so much lost ground to recover. I was like a man possessed, determined to wear away all the bitterness of our being thrust apart, in the space of a few hours. But of course, in the back of my mind I knew that this would have to be a slow process filled with lots of love and patience.

The plane touched down. The children could hardly contain their excitement — within a matter of minutes they would see their mommy.

EVERYONE THOUGHT IT BEST FOR ME TO GO TO THE AIRPORT ALONE TO meet the children. Oh, how I still remember that ride in the car service. My spine was tingling with excitement and my stomach did flip flops. I was very much aware that my appearance had changed quite drastically, and that for little children that could be shocking or traumatic. Their last memories of me had been of a thin, pale, yellow-looking mommy. I wondered how they would react.

At last we reached the airport. With the huge crowds milling about I could hardly find them. Then Yanky's head appeared, with my three most precious belongings. I bent my knees to be on their level and stretched out my arms wide – wide enough to fit them all in. They came towards me hesitantly, holding hands and carrying the balloon on which was written, Mommy I love you. My heart skipped a beat, and then it almost fell, for they had stopped walking, unsure. Yanky urged them on, but they just stared. My feelings were confirmed, I must have looked so different to them. Then my little girl, who was two and a half years old at the time, walked towards me. With the balloon in one hand, she used the other little hand to feel my cheek and caress it. Only when she felt that she had absolutely confirmed that I was indeed her mother, did she finally put her tiny arms around me. Then she quickly turned to her two older brothers and said while nodding her head, "*Dus iz Mommy.*" They came running into my arms. As tears of joy streamed down my face, they kept touching me gingerly on my bloated cheeks, as if to say, are you real?

Yanky gathered the luggage, all the while watching the scene. I did not have enough hands to hold them all at once, so we took turns holding each other, all the way to the car and home...

My fears that they would find me unbearably changed, had *baruch Hashem* vanished, for my children had taught me a valuable lesson of warmth and love. My outward appearance did not matter to them. It was my being their mommy that mattered to them.

Since the children arrived, the situation feels so much improved. For I now have so much more desire to become healthy, to be a "proper" mother to my children and wife to my husband. We have moved to my parents' home in Boro Park, now embarking on a fairly fixed routine. The two boys have entered *cheder*, and my daughter is attending a preschool. Appointments at the hospital continue on Mondays and Thursdays. On these days we have to leave the house early, before the children leave on their big yellow buses, and rush to be back before they come home from school. But we are still torn between our dual concerns — concern for our children's stability and the still overriding, brooding anxiety over my health. Real progress in this direction remains painfully slow, and Dr. Butt and his team are still trying valiantly to stop the leakage in the kidney. How long this would take, or if it could be achieved at all, we were constantly being told in the words of the tired truism: "Only time will tell."

## Yanky:

PURIM PASSED WITH US STILL IN AMERICA. THE CHILDREN ENJOYED their many cousins, whom they had not seen in a long time.

Then suddenly, the skies began to brighten. Winter was passing here. It seemed that going home was becoming nothing but a dusty mirage. Although we longed for it with an increasingly intense yearning, we hardly remembered of what components an independent life was composed.

Pesach was fast approaching, a Yom Tov now so heavily laden with tense and difficult memories. But with Hashem's help we would pull through. Ruchi was being given higher dosages of the strong medications. Things were improving slowly, imperceptibly almost. The enemies once furiously at work in my wife's system seemed to be gradually wearing down in this slow war of attrition. Thus, seder night became an intense and memorable experience for us all, but one which we directed mainly towards our children. It was towards their childish eager questions that I directed my probings, my textual knowledge, newly and powerfully combined with painfully acquired worldly wisdom. Much of what I said, I can no longer recall, but I well remember how vital it was, how spontaneous, how much a result of all the painful growth which we had both undergone.

## Ruchi:

THE SEASONS HAVE TURNED AROUND AGAIN AND BORNE US OUT OF our long, howling winter of discontent. Then suddenly it was spring. The trees along the highway to Westchester have once more, assumed their green, heavily swollen beauty. Everywhere there is an air of renewal, and within our hearts, a deep feeling that finally, the inner clock of our long ordeal was winding itself down, and we would soon be released on a journey where we now desired most of all to be — homeward.

Lag B'omer

One spring day or other — it hardly matters which — we entered the clinic to be summoned to Dr. Butt's office. He was surveying the familiar long sheets of papers covered closely by hundreds of medical terms.

"Well," he said finally, "I think it is high time now to let you people go home. These medical terms are quite reasonable now, and given proper medical cooperation for which I trust you will make adequate arrangements in your home country, I see no reason to keep you here any longer."

We stood there dumbfounded – all three of us. The air became thick with excitement and emotion.

"Dr. Butt," Yanky and I said. "We have no words with which to thank you. You and your staff have become like family to us. All the weeks and months of dedication, devotion, warmth and encouragement, the likes of which we had never seen, have become a part of our lives."

Dr. Butt responded by calling in his staff. We took turns expressing our gratitude and thanking everyone, with promises to come back and visit. As the staff dispersed and went back to their routine, Dr. Butt proceeded to review all the medication and their possible side effects. He also gave us some valuable information on how to deal with some of them.

"Well," he said, "of one thing I must warn you, Ruchi. You may experience some undesirable side effects of the drug prednisone, such as depression."

I turned to Dr. Butt, looked him straight in the eye and said:

"Dr. Butt, the word depression does not *exist* in my dictionary."

He turned to me, his eyes wide in amazement and responded in half a shout, "I love your attitude, Ruchi. Keep it up!"

His voice softened, and he continued gently.

"I am very glad, you know, that things have finally turned out well for you all. This case has been," and he coughed somewhat shyly, "rather special and unforgettable for me."

"Dr. Butt," both my husband and I said, "again, we have no words with which to thank you."

He grasped Yanky's hand warmly. "Don't thank me," he rejoined, letting out a chuckle, "just do one thing for me. Be well and enjoy your newly found health with your family. After all, that is what we've all worked all these months to achieve. There is a whole marvelous world out there, bursting with vitality. Don't waste a moment of it!"

He walked us to the door.

"Goodbye, family Guttfreund."

At the door we turned and waved, tears threatening to fall, as if still in thrall to this past with all its bittersweetness for just one moment longer, and as if, too, in silent tribute to it.

❧

Leaving after so many months was not as easy as we thought, for my family, friends and even total strangers had been and continued to be tremendously supportive. We left after a quiet family gathering. My grandmother's presence gave us lots of *chizuk*, with her endless stories of *bitachon* and *emunah*. Of course, there were endless phone calls from well-wishers who included former classmates, family friends, aunts, uncles, cousins, my mother's friend. But the silent goodbye was made to my parents and grandmothers. Again there were unspoken feelings of gratitude but also a strong element of anxiety that hung in the air: How would I fare alone in my home surroundings? How would I cope without this network of family and friends to support me?

❧

Yanky:

So WE CAME HOME, FINALLY, SO MANY WEEKS AND MONTHS AFTER WE had expected to and a seeming lifetime away from that quiet autumn Friday night when I had first lifted the receiver in our bedroom. But we were not quite free of doctors and hospitals, for we had to make the necessary arrangements with the doctors at home for Ruchi's continuing care. Surprisingly enough, Professor Bindzwanger was unusually cooperative. He had once met Professor Khalid Butt[22] at a medical symposium and considered it an honor to be sharing the care of the same patient with him.

❧

## Ruchi:

I UNDERWENT A THOROUGH CHECKUP, AND WAS ASKED WHICH SIDE MY new kidney was on, since he had not done the surgery. He then checked through my list of medications, and apparently being very satisfied, his bespectacled face broke out in a smile as he said, "Never change the winning team."

❧

## Yanky:

WHAT CAN I TELL YOU? IT TOOK TIME — WEEKS, MONTHS EVEN, TO readjust to normality. Perhaps it will never truly be the same again — it will be normality in a different way. Certainly, it is true that we have both changed in unimaginable ways. Trivial matters which worried me so much beforehand now seem to have lost their power to frighten me. In truth, there is little now that I am afraid of. I seemed to have climbed a dark and endless mountain and now to have arrived profoundly changed. Sometimes I look up at Ruchi in a quiet moment, and think to myself: "Well, this young woman is nothing short of a walking miracle," and I feel a sudden rush of pride and tenderness engulf me. She has embraced normal living with a passion unknown to the rest of us, so that every seemingly mundane or trivial action, seems to have acquired cosmic propor-

---

22. This "seemingly coincidental" meeting between Professors Butt and Binzwanger represented a huge Siyata diShmaya for it ensured that there would be mutual respect and understanding on both sides, enabling us to work as a team, concerning Ruchi's health.

tions for her. At times, I watch her late at night at work in the kitchen, polishing all the surfaces until they gleam with a relentless light, lovingly filling the children's lunchbags with drinks or snacks for the next day. She is listening to music, a happily intense, self-absorbed look on her face. In truth, from morning till night, her every action or movement — simply walking in a sudden shaft of sunlight in a busy city street, or mounting a bus or accompanying a child to school — all have become in themselves no less than momentous acts of *shirah* — of thanksgiving to our All-Beneficient Father in Heaven, reminding me of the timeless words that now sing soundlessly in our heads, all day, and every day:

"*Va'ani Bechasdecha botachti, yogel libi biyshuosecha, ashira la-Hashem ki gomal alay*, As for me I have trusted in Your lovingkindness. My heart shall sing in Your salvation. I will sing to the L-rd for He has bestowed goodness upon me."

**Ruchi:**

RETURNING TO NORMAL LIFE WAS AT ONCE EASIER AND MORE DIFFICULT than one can ever imagine — it consisted of no less than learning to live again. And deep down, there was always the terrible gnawing fear of anything being amiss, and what all the seemingly minor aches and pains might portend. But in all this, there were the small victories, too — ringing my mother to ask her for this or that recipe, walking alone in the street, meeting a friend — in summary simply, what we call daily living and so often, G-d forgive me, taken for granted. Having undergone a *nisayon* such as ours, one truly understands that we are in the Hands of the One Above at every waking moment. Without His Will the simplest of actions is impossible, and I now understand fully the meaning of that most commonly said prayer, *Asher Yatzar*.

*Baruch atah Hashem Elokeinu melech haolom, asher yatzar es haodom bechochmah uvarah vo, nekavim nekavim, chalulim,*

*chalulim, galui veyadua lifnei kisei kevodecha, sheim yipasei'ach echad meihem oh yisaseim echod mehem, iy efshar lehiskayem velaamod Lefanecha, baruch Atah Hashem, rofei chol bosor umafli laasos!*

"Blessed are You Hashem, our G-d King of the universe, Who fashioned man with wisdom and created within him many openings and many cavities. It is obvious and known before Your throne of glory, that if but one of them were to be ruptured or but one of them were to be blocked it would be impossible to survive and to stand before You. Blessed are You Hashem, Who heals all flesh and does wondrously."

"Who fashioned man with wisdom." This phrase has two meanings: When Hashem created man, He gave him the gift of wisdom and secondly Hashem used wisdom when He created man, as is demonstrated in the exact balance of his organs and functions, openings and cavities: The mouth, the nostrils and other orifices are the openings that lead in and out of the body. The cavities are the inner hollows that contain such organs as the lungs, heart, stomach and brain. And acts wondrously — the delicate balance of the organs is a wonder of wonders; alternatively it is wondrous that the spiritual soul fuses with the physical body to create a human being."

I feel that the greatest *hakaras hatov* that I can possibly show the *Ribbono Shel Olam* for his goodness, is to take care of my body, which is imbued with new life, and my soul, which shall be singing His songs of praise forever. To see every day, despite its difficulties, as a beautiful day infused with life, of which I want to be a part.

And of course, also the *Modeh Ani* prayer which we say on waking:

"*Modeh ani lefanecha Melech Chai Vekayam, shechechzartah bi nishmasi bechemlah, rabba emunosecho.*"

"I gratefully thank You, O living and eternal king, for You have returned my soul within me with compassion — abundant is your faithfulness."

This prayer I now said not only with my heart but with my soul. "A Jew opens his eyes and thanks Hashem for restoring his faculties to him in the morning. Then, he acknowledges that Hashem did so in the expectation that he will serve Him, and that He is abundantly faithful to reward those who do."[23]

---

23. *The Complete Artscroll Siddur*

All those nights I had lain awake saying over and over again: "*Ribbono Shel Olom*, don't leave me!"

I repeated the passuk from Tehillim "*Leiv tahor bera li Elokim … Al tashlichaini milfanecha Veruach Kodshecha al tikach mimeni* — A new heart create for me, O G-d,… Do not cast me away from your Presence, and do not take Your Holy Spirit from me." When I would be feeling really afraid, I'd repeat the closing words of *Adon Olam* to myself, "*Hashem li velo ira* — Hashem is with me, I shall not fear."

Another interesting point too — during dialysis whenever I would go shopping I would buy only a garment in the gray color. I suppose this was how I saw life at that point. So to counteract this feeling, I took up gardening like never before. I filled up those empty flower boxes that had been waiting for so long with colorful flowers and vegetables. I suppose I wanted to see things living and sprouting forth. So I continue this custom to this very day — but with a very different intent and feeling. For life is no longer gray — but multicolored and fascinating. And always I talk to myself: Ruchi you are so fortunate. Some people live to be eighty and are never granted the knowledge of their purpose on this earth, and here I have had the privilege to have been shown a purpose in black and white. Hashem gave me this great *nisayon* which I had to pass, learn from it, grow from it, strengthening my *emunah* and *bitachon*. To begin never to take things for granted, and learn to live every day with joy and purpose. So I never asked, "Why me?" for I considered myself a soldier in Hashem's army — and I had to do as I was instructed. And do it with joy — even though this was excruciatingly hard at times. It would have constituted a breech of honor not to receive this *nisayon* with *ahavah*.

While on dialysis, I had been granted a special gift. It was almost as if then I was beyond myself, floating high above — literally cushioned in Hashem's loving arms. Now that that special time has passed, I sometimes miss that intensity of feeling. But in return, we have been given what we always wanted so hard to create — the gifts of being a normal, loving family.

# Nurse:

WELL, IT IS NOW QUITE SOME TIME SINCE MRS. GUTTFREUND'S TRANS-
plant, and things, thank G-d, are going well for them. Today I
received a phone call from her. She has a request to make. She would
like to show a visitor around the dialysis unit. I am a little intrigued.
They arrive. The visitor does not speak the local language. She looks
around silently, observing the proportions of the room, the
machines, the people sitting attached to machines, the shabby, graying linoleum, the high grasses and crimson flowers beyond the glass
door. Occasionally, she jots down something in a small notebook.

Mrs. Guttfreund is showing her everything in detail.

"This chair here is where I sat when I was first dialyzed. Those
were the gardens beyond, where I ran, Nurse Julia running after
me," and here she turned to smile at me, "to escape the machine."

Today, old Henry is sitting at his machine. I introduce the two
women.

"This young woman," I say, "is one of you. She was on dialysis
for three years but she has been transplanted."

"Transplanted, she?" The shock is visible. "But she is so young
and healthy-looking."

"Yes, two years ago," I add cheerfully, enjoying the minor frisson
of shock I have just administered to him. I have the feeling now that
the companion is recording all this. Perhaps she is a writer about to
write the true and engrossing story of these two extraordinary
young people.

Once I have decided on this solution to the puzzle, it seems to fall
in place like the final recalcitrant piece in a jigsaw puzzle, and I smile
knowingly at Mrs. Guttfreund.

They turn to leave. Apparently, they have seen all that they came for.

"Goodbye," I stretch out my hand.

Somehow, I feel this to be a goodbye which has a greater aspect
of finality in it than all the others which have passed between us,
during the long years of our friendship. I feel it inexplicably too, to
mark a great turning point in this personal chronicle. So closely and
intricately interwoven with conflicting feelings, despair and hope,
darkness and light.

So, under my breath I mutter inaudibly, "Goodbye, my dear and may the G-d of Israel be with you...."

# Our Story:

MAYBE WE SHOULD CONCLUDE OUR JOINT STORY WITH A MESSAGE OF thankfulness to Hashem — for all the beneficence He has shown us. For we were given what is granted to so few, "a second chance" to live — so that along with this gift too, we live every second more profoundly, and with greater intensity.

The sky is bluer, the sun shines brighter — and if we may leave you, dear readers, with one thought it is that even in your darkest moments, or perhaps especially in your bleakest moments, the Almighty is watching over you. He stands, as if it were, with a satisfied smile and states: "My son and daughter, you have learned, you have grown. Continue to use the many gifts which I have bestowed upon you, to fulfill the purpose for which I have created you, and to be *Mekadesh Shem Shamayim* wherever you go.

How to tell,
The way we feel?
This *seudah* at *shalom,*
Was almost unreal.

For a fraction of time,
You lifted us out,
Of our daily routine,
Of our going about.

The depths of your feelings,
We were privileged to see;
Your expression of thanks,
So rare, so full of beauty.

Much have you taught us,
But that Wednesday night,
We saw how friendship,
Is an enduring light.

*B'ruchnius u'vgashmius,*
We were in a world apart,
And for this we thank you,
With all our heart.

*"The Tuesday Club" and friends*

# MEDICAL AFTERWORD

IN WRITING AN AFTERWORD TO THIS BOOK I FEEL IT A SPECIAL PRIVILEGE to be associated with Mrs. Dansky in this venture. Perhaps my best qualification for this task is not my medical degree, but the many hours I have spent listening, encouraging, comforting and generally providing support to patients with all types of problems: medical, emotional, social and even financial.

The lack of adequate counselling for the couple portrayed in this book is symptomatic of an era now fast disappearing from Western society as a whole. Gone is the doctors' attitude of imparting as little information as he feels the patient requires. Ushered in is an atmosphere of information — as much as the patient can bear — as much as the patient demands. Gone are the secretive words whispered out of the patient's earshot. Newly arrived on the scene are specialist nurses, specialist counsellors, leaflets to explain every aspect of any treatment, in easy language — and in the patient's own language.

These changes have gathered pace over the last ten years and are now making even the most awful scenarios touched with humanity, sweetened with sympathy and lightened with understanding, hope and encouragement.

Hashem in his wisdom has endowed the human body with an apparent surplus in many areas. It is perfectly compatible with a healthy existence to have only one lung or one kidney or only one third of one's liver, no stomach and of course no appendix. That we have the "spare" capacity is one of the wonders of creation, and makes us capable of withstanding extremes of weather, of exertion and of deprivation. This is especially true of the kidneys. Many a parent, brother or sister has donated one kidney to their ill relative — and both live healthy lives thereafter. The other side of this, however, is that when kidney failure sets in it must mean that more than half the capacity of the kidneys is not functioning.

**Nephrotic syndrome** is an exception. This is a condition in which large quantities of protein "leak" out of the kidneys into the urine. The result is dramatic swelling of the person's body due to water seeping into the tissues, with not enough protein in the blood to draw the water and retain it in the circulation. Fortunately this condition is frequently completely reversible.

Sometimes the cause of nephrotic syndrome may be a progressive destruction of the kidneys. This is called **nephritis,** meaning "inflammation of kidney" or **glomerulonephritis,** which specifies that it is the filtration parts of the kidneys called "glomeruli" which are inflamed and not functioning.

Glomerulonephritis is one of the common causes of deteriorating kidney function. One of the ways of assessing kidney function is by measuring the amounts of certain substances in the blood which are supposed to be removed by the kidneys. The most commonly measured of these substances is **creatinine.** The usual level of creatinine in the blood is up to 100. Figures of between 100 and 300 indicate problems with kidney function, but are often reversible. Creatinine of 800 or more heralds the onset of "end stage renal failure," in which the kidneys almost stop functioning altogether.

It is often only possible to reach a clear diagnosis of the nature of kidney disease by performing a **biopsy,** which means taking a small piece out of the kidney to examine under the microscope. Other diagnostic methods include X-rays; X-rays taken in sequence after injection of a dye into the patient's vein; **CT scans** which use X-rays to produce an image which portrays a "slice" through the body; and **MRI scanning** which uses powerful magnets to produce very clear images of the internal organs. The function of the kidneys can also be assessed by injecting a radioactive substance and then measuring how quickly the kidneys eliminate it from the system.

If harmful substances build up in the system when the kidneys fail, the condition is called **uremia. Dialysis** is the name of the artificial process used to replace the function of the kidneys.

In the early days of "artificial kidneys" in the 1960's, dialysis took place in a bowl, perhaps 50cm across and 15cm deep. Modern dialysis machines use dialyzers which are 30cm long and only 5 to 7cm in diameter, and are disposed of after only one use. Blood is pumped through the dialyzer at a rate of 220 to 300ml every minute, and dialysis fluid is also pumped through the dialyzer at a rate of 500ml (a bit more than one pint) every minute. The dialysis fluid (**dialyzate**) and the blood are separated by a thin membrane which allows water and some dissolved substances through, but keeps the blood cells and large-size substances, such as proteins, from leaking into the dialyzate.

Thirty liters of dialyzate are used for every hour of dialysis, and most patients require between 9-12 hours of dialysis per week. Domestic tap water is run through filters and de-ionisers to remove almost all the dissolved substances in the water. Specific quantities of specially prepared solutions are then mixed with the purified water to make the final mix of dialyzate.

The use of computers and microprocessors has made the modern dialysis machine much smaller than the one used in this story, and much more readily adjustable to the individual patient's requirements. However, modern machines are so expensive that dialysis at home, as in this story, is discouraged. This is also in order to allow each machine to benefit more people. Hospital dialysis wards commonly have twenty machines, and are run for twenty-four hours a day, six days a week. Most patients are "on the machine" for three sessions a week on say, Sunday, Tuesday and Thursday or Monday, Wednesday and Friday, leaving one day a week when the unit can close.

Originally, membranes in dialyzers were made of cellophane, just like what florists use to cover bouquets. Now a variety of more than ten different types of material are used to produce much more efficient membranes.

Dialysis consists of three processes which take place simultaneously. Firstly, the dissolved substances in the blood cross the membrane until the concentration in the dialyzate rises to the same level as in the blood (**equilibration**). Secondly, harmful substances which accumulate in the body when the kidneys fail also cross the membrane into the dialyzate (**detoxification**). Finally, water is removed from the blood by a process called **ultrafiltration**, which forces water across the membrane both by having higher pressure in the blood than in the dialyzate, and by adding glucose to the dialyzate, which draws the water out of the blood, rather like salt draws blood out of raw meat.

Ideally, dialysis should remove all harmful substances; preserve all essential substances and nutrients in the correct proportions; and establish the correct amount of water in the blood. The machine should do this using the smallest possible volume of blood, almost all of which should be washed back into the patient at the end of dialysis, and without causing clotting within the machine. All this needs to be done reliably and at low cost.

To get the blood in and out of the machine in the early days of dialysis, one tube (cannula) was inserted into an artery, and another tube into a vein. They were removed at the end of a dialysis session and the artery and vein were tied off. The blood vessels would be so damaged by the necessity to tie them off that different vessels would have to be used until there would be no more usable vessels left and the patient would be left to die of kidney failure. In 1966 the technique of making an **arteriovenous fistula** was developed, and is the most widely used method nowadays. An artery is connected directly to a vein in the arm (or leg). Over a period of two weeks (approximately), the vein enlarges and develops a thick muscle wall as it adapts to the increased flow. This newly enlarged vessel can be easily entered and does not leak when the needles are removed. Artificial vessels have been developed which can be inserted into the forearm and these perform almost as well as the fistula described above.

There is an alternative method of dialysis, which does not need to pump blood through a machine (**hemo-dialysis**). This is called **peritoneal dialysis**, or CAPD (Continuous Outpatient Peritoneal Dialysis). Instead of using an artificial membrane, this process uses the lining of the abdominal cavity as the dialyzing membrane. This is in many ways a better membrane than any synthetic one. A tube (catheter) is inserted through the abdominal wall. Four times a day, dialysis fluid is run into the abdominal cavity, where it lies for 6 hours before being run out again. Each change of fluids must be done with strict attention to hygiene and sterility to prevent infection of the abdominal cavity (peritonitis). CAPD is frequently used nowadays.

However, it is not possible to maintain a patient on CAPD for as many years as on hemodialysis, because a certain amount of functioning kidney is required for CAPD to be effective. When the kidneys have failed completely, hemodialysis is the only option.

Transplant of a kidney is, however, the only hope for a patient to ever be really healthy again. Even the best machines cannot take over all the functions of the kidneys. The best success rates with **transplantation** are achieved when the new kidney most closely matches the make-up of the patient's own body (**tissue type**). An identical twin makes an ideal kidney donor to the affected twin. Sometimes parents, or non-identical brothers or sisters, can donate a kidney. Most kidneys however, come from non-related donors who have died from some cause which did not include kidney damage. If the patient's body rejects the kidney, it will fail to function and eventually shut down. The drugs **Cyclosporin** (Sandimmun) and **Prednisolone** are commonly used to prevent rejection.

**Erythropoietin** (Eprex) is a synthetic substitute for the substance produced by the kidneys, which stimulates the bone marrow to produce red blood cells. Without this substance, most patients with kidney failure become very anemic.

Finally, I would like to refer back to my earlier statement. Hashem has provided each person with two lungs, two kidneys, a huge liver, a stomach, ten meters of intestines and many other exam-

---

*CAPD (Continuous Outpatient [Ambulatory] Peritoneal Dialysis).*

ples of the bountiful provision of much more than we may ever require for healthy living. That is in the physical realm. It is my firm belief, borne out by this book, that Hashem has provided each and every person with a spiritual capacity; not just sufficient to match the trials and tribulations that will be experienced in life. On the contrary, Hashem provides bountifully; He gives us capacities much greater than our minimum requirements. In fact, we should realize that we are spiritually much greater than our *nisyonos*.

May *Hakadosh Baruch Hu* bless the people whose story is told here, the author who has so eloquently recorded their *nisayon* and all the readers with a great capacity to understand and bear their own *nisyonos* in such a way that they will draw near to Hashem Who is *Bochen lev v'choker keloyos*, Who examines hearts and fathoms kidneys.

May we all merit the fulfillment of the words of Kind David: "*Leiv tahor bera li Elokim, veru'ach nachon chadeish bekirbi*, G-d create for me a pure heart, and renew within me a righteous spirit."

Dr. S. M. Rutenberg
Gateshead

This volume is part of
THE ARTSCROLL SERIES®
an ongoing project of
translations, commentaries and expositions
on Scripture, Mishnah, Talmud, Halachah,
liturgy, history, the classic Rabbinic writings,
biographies and thought.

For a brochure of current publications
visit your local Hebrew bookseller
or contact the publisher:

*Mesorah Publications, ltd.*

4401 Second Avenue
Brooklyn, New York 11232
(718) 921-9000
www.artscroll.com